FIGHTING CHANCE

THE GREGOR DEMARKIAN BOOKS
BY JANE HADDAM

FIGHTING CHANCE

A Gregor Demarkian Novel

JANE HADDAM

MINOTAUR BOOKS

NEW YORK

FIGHTING CHANCE.
Copyright © 2014 by Orania Papazoglou.
All rights reserved.
Printed in the United States of America.
For information, address St. Martin's Press, 175 Fifth Avenue,
New York, N.Y. 10010.

www.minotaurbooks.com

The Library of Congress Cataloging-in-Publication Data is available upon request

ISBN 978-1-250-01235-7 (hardcover)
ISBN 978-1-4668-4871-9 (e-book)

Minotaur books may be purchased for educational, business, or promotional use.
For information on bulk purchases, please contact Macmillan Corporate and
Premium Sales Department at 1-800-221-7945, extension 5442, or write special-
markets@macmillan.com.

First Edition: September 2014

10 9 8 7 6 5 4 3 2 1

FIGHTING CHANCE

October 30

It was almost Halloween, and out there in the world of normal, people were putting jack-o'-lanterns on their front steps and stuffed suits of clothes on their mailboxes. Bennis Hannaford Demarkian found herself wondering if what she was seeing was even allowed. She'd grown up in Bryn Mawr. They got fussy in Bryn Mawr about lawn signs and unraked leaves and whatever you wanted to call "blight."

It was early in the day, and bright. The houses sat back behind broad lawns. The light was the kind that made everything seem to have hard edges, including the leaves. Bennis couldn't stop herself from wondering how she must look. She was driving a tangerine orange car that was not only highly visible, but also the wrong *kind* of car. A lot of trouble had been taken to make this part of town look rural, but it wasn't really. There were no sidewalks, but there were people.

Her mother used to warn her that it was a bad idea to run

away from your background. No matter how hard you tried, you always made a mess of it. That was a long time ago, and Bennis hadn't listened. She'd been too busy running away from her background.

The GPS was winking at her, but she didn't need to consult it. She'd been out this way twenty times in the last four days. She slowed down as she saw the very low, very small, very discreet sign that told her the driveway to the Glenwydd House was right up ahead. She wondered who'd decided that it was the ultimate in Upper Classness to pretend to be Welsh.

The driveway was there, and the gate. Bennis pulled up next to it and rolled down her window. "Bennis Hannaford Demarkian," she said to the guard.

The guard consulted first a computer screen and then a written list. Then the gate went up. Glenwydd House was very, very discreet. It never asked you the name of the patient you'd come to see. It only checked to make sure you were one of the people Allowed to Come In.

She was thinking in capitals today.

The drive curved around and then around again. It was a silly drive, bad for ambulances, and they got a lot of ambulances at Glenwydd House. Bennis remembered the place from ages ago. It belonged first to a Cadwallader, and then, when something had happened that nobody spoke about, to a family named Finchley. God only knew what had happened to the Finchleys. They weren't "real Main Line," as people said in the old days. Nobody Bennis might know would have any news of them.

She was also thinking in anachronisms. If she kept this up, she would start in complaining about the way nothing was the same and nothing ever would be. She would sound like she was eighty years old.

She was, in fact, forty-six. The house came up out of the trees in front of her. It had been a castle once, in England. One of the Cadwalladers had it taken apart stone by stone and reassembled here. People complained that the rich of today were ostentatious and vulgar. The rich of today had nothing on the rich of the era of the robber barons.

A wide parking lot with abnormally broad spaces had been carved out of what used to be a topiary front lawn. There wasn't a single car in the spaces. There was a staff parking lot somewhere in the back. The kind of people who put their loved ones in Glenwydd House didn't want to visit them.

Loved ones. Bennis made a face.

She pulled into the space closest to the narrow stone walk that led to the front door. She cut the engine and stared straight ahead, not ready to go on yet. If it was hard to understand how they got an ambulance up the drive, it was impossible to understand how they got a stretcher up that walk.

Maybe they didn't get stretchers up that walk. Maybe, when somebody died, they took him out the back, out the servants' entrance, like—

There was no "like." *Died* kept reverberating in her head.

She took off her seat belt and grabbed the tote bag in the seat next to her.

Then she got out of the car and headed up the walk.

Halfway to where she was going, she stopped. She put the tote bag on the ground. She bent over and pulled out the only thing in it: a big package of books and audiotapes, fastened together with thick rubber bands and carefully labeled in thick black marker ink: TIBOR KASPARIAN.

It was cold. October was always cold in Pennsylvania. Wind went through her wild black hair. Cold made her neck muscles clench. She stood looking at the parcel for a long time. Agatha Christie. Boris Pasternak. Lawrence Ferlinghetti. Dead.

Dead.

You didn't take audiobooks to someone who was dead.

Bennis dropped the parcel back into the tote bag and hefted the whole damned thing up again.

PROLOGUE

1

Once, long ago, Father Tibor Kasparian had come to Cavanaugh Street on a temporary assignment, a sacrificial lamb meant to placate all sides in an impossible situation. Father Tibor himself was one side of that situation. He had appeared suddenly and out of nowhere from the never-never land of religious persecution, eyes sunk into the back of his head, weight barely enough to keep him standing upright. Priests used to come out of the old Soviet Union like that, and then the Church had done what it could for them. It had no other choice.

By the time Tibor arrived, the situation was different. Persecution was still going on, but there were rules to the game. There were procedures. The Church was not expecting a ghost on its doorstep, one who needed not only help but affirmation.

The other side of the situation was Cavanaugh Street itself, one of the oldest Armenian churches in America and, by then, one nobody wanted. In those days, all Armenian priests were trained in Armenia, and all of them had grown to adulthood in Armenia. They had expectations about the relationship between a priest and his parishioners. The priest should be the most educated person in the parish. He should be the intermediary between his parishioners and the outside world. His parishioners should defer to him on all things, even the naming of their children.

When the bishops and the patriarchs asked their priests why they wouldn't go to Cavanaugh Street, the priests had very good answers. The parish was "too worldly," most of them said, or "the people are falling away from God." One inventive priest claimed that he had visited there and found the place impossible. It was full of people with "Roman tendencies." If there was one thing no Armenian priest was going to put up with, it was a parish full of people with "Roman tendencies," the kind of people who would be Catholic if they could, but didn't know how.

The bishops listened to all this talk and said nothing to contradict it, even though they knew it wasn't exactly true. The real problem with Cavanaugh Street was both simple and unfixable. The people of Cavanaugh Street were, indeed, "worldly," in the sense that they had a lot of money. What had once been a small immigrant Armenian enclave of tenement houses had changed over the years into a street of elegant town houses and co-ops as expensive to buy as a Harvard education and almost as expensive to rent.

And it wasn't the money alone. The first generation of immigrants had given way to a generation of American-born overachievers. That generation had given way to one where every last child was pushed at colleges and universities with famous names and serious social pretensions. By the time Father Tibor arrived, the street was full of people who not only thought they knew better than any immigrant priest from Armenia, but probably did.

Tibor Kasparian took up residence in the cramped little apartment next to the old church, and a very odd thing happened. The people of Cavanaugh Street, who had driven away six priests in less than seventeen months, decided that they liked this one. The bishops waited patiently for the complaints to start rolling in, but it never happened. They sent observers, just in case Father Tibor was preaching the prosperity gospel or maybe Marxism instead of good solid orthodoxy. They could find nothing objectionable in his celebrations of the liturgy.

Eventually, the hierarchy had decided it was best to leave well enough alone. The impossible parish had a priest it could live with. The office of the Eastern Diocese was not being flooded with reports about how the man had to be shipped back to Yerevan or angry Monday-morning phone calls about how the man was impossible. The Armenian Church in America was growing. There was a lot to do. The Church even had Web sites, and Armenian American experts to run them.

Tibor Kasparian never asked why things worked out so well. He'd heard all about Cavanaugh Street before he got there. He'd heard how terribly they treated priests, and how little they had of piety and charity, and how they had become "Americanized" in the worst possible way. Then he showed up at the church door, and a small woman in an enormous chinchilla coat had taken his books out of his right hand, shaken the hand vigorously, and said, "*Valley of the Dolls*? I love *Valley of the Dolls*. Wherever did you find a copy at this late date?"

Tibor would have told her where he'd found the copy if she'd stopped talking long enough to listen. She hadn't, and she'd made no comment on the rest of the books, which included both Aristotle's *Nichomachean Ethics* in Greek and Saint Thomas's *Summa* in Latin.

On the morning of September 9, Tibor got dressed in the oversized bedroom of the new rectory apartment that the parish had built him when they rebuilt the old church. There were too many mirrors in the room, which he did not like to look into. He hadn't been all that attractive when he was a young and healthy man. These days, he was neither young nor particularly healthy, and he thought he looked like the less colorful kind of garden gnome. Still, the mirrors were a fact of life, along with the Jacuzzi built for eight and the refrigerator the size of a railway transport vehicle. He wasn't going to complain about them.

Somewhere out in the foyer, his bells were chiming. He asked himself if he looked "professional" this morning. He decided that he did not look like a homeless person, which was better than he did three out of seven days a week. Then he made his way out through the stacks of books and into the hall.

The hall was also full of stacks of books. So was the living room and the dining room, and the kitchen beyond that. So was the foyer. The books were of every possible kind and in almost every possible language. There were the works of the Church fathers in Greek. There was that old copy of the *Summa* in Latin that he'd brought with him. There were books on history in English, German, and French. There was Dostoyevsky in Russian and a complete set of the Harry Potter novels in the original English. There were books on art and books on music and books of literary criticism. There were even cookbooks, although Lida Arkmanian—she of the

8

chinchilla coat—always said that giving Father Tibor a cookbook was like giving a mad bomber a guide to explosives.

In the foyer were the books he hadn't read yet, and a small stack of books he'd tried to read but couldn't make himself finish. On the top of that pile was something called *Fifty Shades of Grey*. It embarrassed him just to look at it.

The bells chimed again, and as they did, Tibor could hear giggling just beyond the door. He opened up to let in Donna Moradanyan Donahue and her small son. Her older one, Tommy, must already be out at the Ararat. If Donna didn't hurry, one of the Melajian girls would stuff Tommy full of pastry and he'd be wired all day at school.

Donna wasn't hurrying. She was decidedly young and decidedly healthy, and the small boy she had with her was positively ecstatic. Tibor tried to pick him up, but he raced away into the living room and could be heard squealing from there.

"He's happy this morning," Tibor said.

"He's always happy," Donna said.

She went into the living room and corralled the child, who let loose with another stream of giggles. Then she came back into the foyer and looked Tibor over from head to foot.

"There's something wrong," she said.

Tibor took his sweater off the brass coatrack that had been a gift from Bennis Hannaford Demarkian four Christmases ago. It was still warm this early in September, but he got cold easily. He got cold for the same reason he looked like a garden gnome.

"Are you sure you're all right?" Donna asked him. "You're not getting sick or something?"

"I'm not getting sick or something," Tibor said. "If we don't hurry up, Tommy will be full of sugar."

9

"Tommy's with Russ," she said absently, meaning her husband, but not Tommy's father. She was still staring him up and down.

Then she opened the door to the hall and ushered the small boy out.

"I still say there's something wrong," she said.

Tibor didn't waste his time arguing the point.

2

Judge Martha Handling didn't like going into court early, and she didn't like staying late. In fact, for the last five years, she hadn't liked going into court at all. Actually, it was much worse than that. For the last five years, Martha hadn't liked going much of anywhere.

This morning, she pulled her little Ford Focus into the parking space with her name on it behind the court building, cut the engine, and made herself take a deep breath. She knew it was ridiculous to get this upset about what everybody else took for granted, but she couldn't help herself. She couldn't even believe that everybody else took it for granted, no matter how often they said so. Back when she was in college—Bryn Mawr, class of 1976—she'd taken a sociology course on the history of law enforcement, and in that course she was introduced to a thing called the Panopticon.

The Panopticon was either a prison or a plan for a prison where the guards could keep constant and uninterrupted surveillance of everything the prisoners did. Martha couldn't remember whether the prison had ever actually been built, but she did know that its principle had surely come to pass, and not just in prisons.

These days, the cameras were everywhere. They were in restaurants. They were in grocery stores. They were even pointed at the street here and there. Most of all, they were in the courthouse. They would have been in the dressing room she used to enrobe if she hadn't had a complete nutcase fit and put a stop to it.

The problem, of course, was that she wasn't sure she *had* put a stop to it. She didn't like the people who worked for the City of Philadelphia these days. She didn't like the people who worked for the Commonwealth of Pennsylvania, either. She wouldn't put it past any of them to lie straight to her face and go on filming anyway.

She had her cell phone out on the front passenger seat, where she could grab it in an emergency, and she had the other cell phone out, too—the one she bought at the kiosk in the King of Prussia Mall. That was not entirely satisfactory. Martha was sure there were security cameras all over the mall, including some trained on that kiosk. There could be a tape somewhere with a picture of her on it, buying that very cell phone.

Then there was the whole GPS tracking thing, or whatever it was. They could tell where a call had been made and where the person who received it had been. It didn't matter how "untraceable" the phone was if it could in fact be traced to someplace you were known to be. That meant she couldn't use it to call someone from home, and she could use it in the car only if she was moving. She could not use it while she was parked right here behind the courthouse, no matter how much she wanted to.

She stared at the prepaid phone for a bit and then reached over to put it into her bag. She would have used nothing but prepaid phones if she thought she could get away with it, but in the end, she'd decided that wouldn't be a good idea. A woman in her position was expected to have a cell phone. She was expected to have an expensive one. That was how Martha had ended up with the iPhone 5, which she honestly felt was more annoying than functional.

Martha stuffed that phone into her bag, too, then picked up the bag and grabbed her briefcase. There were five security cameras in this lot. One was trained on the front gate. The rest were installed to make sure all parts of the lot could be seen at all times. She'd heard once that there was no such thing as a perfect surveillance system. Every system of security cameras had a blind spot.

If that was true, Martha had never been able to find one.

She got out of the car and locked it up behind her. She sent up a little fume of annoyance on the subject of John Henry Newman Jackman, the city's mayor. In New York, Bloomberg and Giuliani had made the city nearly as safe as an upscale suburb, but Jackman was a first-class ass. He didn't care if the city burned to the ground, so long as his base was happy.

And Martha knew exactly whom his base consisted of.

She went up the small flight of concrete steps to the courthouse's back door. There was a security camera there, and she got out her little can of black spray paint. She aimed it at the camera lens far over her head. Then she double-checked it to make sure she'd gotten it all.

She put the can back in her bag and punched in her access code on the pad at the side of the door. Martha's watch read 8:35. It was early for the courthouse, but it was not exactly early. Court wouldn't get into gear until ten o'clock, but that was because the court system was also run by asses.

The security guard was already on duty, a uniformed police-woman with a gun on her hip and a strained expression. Martha saw her look of surprise and pretended she hadn't.

"Is Celia in already?" she asked.

Martha had no idea if this was something the guard would know. Celia was her personal assistant, and came to work every morning by bus.

The policewoman started to say something. Martha sailed right past her. She didn't really care if Celia was in or not.

She went down the back corridor that was painted such an awful shade of beige—vomit beige, she always thought of it. They brought the kids through that corridor when it was time for court. The idea was not to expose them to ridicule or public-ity by bringing them up the sidewalk. Martha thought that was asinine.

Martha passed the door to the corridor that went to the court-rooms themselves and opened the thicker one that went to the offices. There were security cameras in these corridors, too, but she had spray-painted them last night, and she was pretty sure that security hadn't managed to "fix" them yet. She took the can out and did the one closest to her door, just to be safe. Then she went on through.

Most of the offices were dark. One, her own, all the way at the end of the hall, was lit up like the proverbial Christmas tree.

"Celia?" Martha said.

Celia Markhall put her head out the door and made a little wave. "Good morning, Your Honor. I wasn't expecting you for at least another hour. I'm afraid I've got things in a mess in here."

Celia Markhall was the fifth assistant Martha had had in the past nine years, and she wasn't any better than the rest of them.

She was blond in the only way people can be blond when they've reached the age of fifty-six, and she was much too peppy.

Martha pushed past her into the outer office. There were paper files on the desks there, placed about in little stacks. She went past them without bothering to think about what they were for and into the inner office with its big mahogany desk and its antique wall clock. The antique wall clock was Martha's own, brought from her home in Wayne.

There was nothing at all on her desk except the felt blotter. The blotter was there because she thought desks ought to have blotters. She could not have said why.

She put her briefcase and her bag on the desk and sat down. She looked at the dark screen of her computer. It sat on a little "work-station" shelf to her left. She suddenly felt enormously stupid about having come in this early at all.

"Your Honor?" Celia said. She looked like she was hovering. She was like a hummingbird.

"The first thing this morning is the Maldovanian case?"

Celia looked immediately uncomfortable. "It's actually the second thing," she said. "The docket says eleven o'clock, but you know how that goes. The scheduler did try to give you the greatest possible leeway, but the first thing up is that She'bor Washington girl, and you know—"

"Oh, Lord," Martha said.

"Yes, well, the scheduler tried to give you enough time."

"It's not going to take time," Martha said. "It's going to take keeping my temper. We should all thank God on our knees that Cathy Laste is finally retired and off this court. God only knows what she thought she was doing. You can't go easy on these kids. Half of them are sociopaths and half of them will end up that way if you don't lock them up the first time. The Maldovanian kid is coming in at eleven, you said?"

"From lockup, yes. The way they do that, he'll probably be in early."

"I know the way they do that," Martha said. "Is that priest going to come in?"

"Father Tibor Kasparian, yes," Celia said. "I think—"

"I had a check run on his immigration status," Martha said. "The kid's illegal, there's no reason why the priest shouldn't be illegal. He isn't, though. Came here years ago as a political refugee. Whatever that means. I notified Immigration about the kid, but you can bet your ass they won't do a thing about it. They never do."

"Yes," Celia said. "Of course, he is only fifteen, and—"

"And he's got friends in the city government," Martha said. "I know. Our esteemed mayor. Our esteemed governor. And they're not even on the same side. People don't understand reality anymore. They don't face up to it. You can't just let these things go."

"Yes," Celia said again.

The woman looked stressed. Martha could tell. Martha wanted to throw something.

"Listen," she said. "Get me all the stuff about She'bor Washington. I want to get through that as fast as I can. Maybe if I get through that, I can bring the Maldovanian kid in early and Father Tibor Kasparian won't even be at the courthouse yet. God, how I want to get through with that before he ever gets here."

"Yes," Celia said again. "There is one other thing. The funeral service. For Stella Kolchak. It starts at eleven, and all the assistants will be off the floor. I think the best estimate for return is going to be about twelve thirty, because most of us will be going out to the cemetery. Of course, I won't be going to the luncheon, you did say you need me here—"

"I do need you here," Martha said. "I can't believe I'm still dealing with Stella Kolchak. The woman was such a twit. And about as useful an assistant as a cheese Danish. That's Cathy Laste for you. Nothing done right."

"I do promise to be back as soon as I can," Celia said. She looked like she was going to say something else, make some protest, but Martha knew she wouldn't do it. She knew better by now.

Martha swung her chair until it faced the computer station and started to boot up.

3

Petrak Maldovanian was not having the worst day of his life. Not even close. He wasn't even having the worst day of his life in America, which had occurred exactly a week ago. He was only having a kind of day he had never had before, and it was setting him off balance.

The day had actually started in a way he liked, with his American Government: Histories and Processes class at Philadelphia Community College. There were a lot of things wrong with Philadelphia Community College that people would tell you about if you gave them half a chance. It was situated in one of the worst parts of the city. That did not make the campus unsafe—the campus was well patrolled. It did make *getting* to the campus, or leaving it, something of an adventure. Petrak didn't have a car, and he learned his first semester never to schedule a class or an appointment too late in the day. His American Government class started at eight in the morning and ended twenty minutes after nine.

Petrak didn't mind the forced early-morning scheduling, because he loved the entire idea of the Philadelphia Community College and everything that went with it. If anybody had asked him what he thought the most important difference was between Armenia and the United States, he would have said the Philadelphia Community College and said it without hesitation. All the other things were either trivial or ambiguous. The level of government corruption was a lot lower, but there was still government corruption. The money was much more abundant, but Petrak didn't have access to much of the money.

No, it was the Philadelphia Community College that was the shock—a place that offered a university education to anybody who walked through the door who had graduated from high school, and offered it at practically no money. In Armenia, you went to university if you passed the entrance exams, and practically nobody did.

Just after coming to America, Petrak had seen a clip of a speech President Obama made somewhere or other, saying that the country should make it a goal for every student to go to college. That was long before Petrak had even started at PCC. He knew nothing about American politics. After that, though, he'd always thought President Obama was okay.

He mostly thought that his American Government class was okay, too, but this morning he hadn't been able to attend to it. He hadn't heard half the lecture. His mind was on his brother, Stefan, and what was going to happen to Stefan today. And he was worried that the trouble Stefan was having was entirely his fault.

All right. Maybe not *entirely* his fault. Stefan had behaved like a jackass. Even so. Stefan was in the country illegally, and he was in the country illegally because Petrak had told him to come. This had seemed like a good idea at the time. Stefan was in Canada, and it took nothing at all to get across the Canadian border into the United States. Stefan didn't even bother to tell their aunt and uncle that he was going until he had already gone.

Of course, that had been Petrak's idea, too. He was the older one. He was the one who was supposed to have the intelligence and the experience and the maturity to—

Petrak recognized the patter of footsteps behind him, the particular shotgun click of the heels, the odd almost-limping sound of a slight shuffle. Dr. Loftus spent a fair amount of time chasing him in hallways.

He stopped and turned around to wait for her. She was a small woman, barely five foot two, compact and neat looking. She was also indescribably old. Petrak was sure she was at least sixty.

"Petrak," she said as she reached him, breathing just a little too hard.

"I'm sorry," Petrak said, "I would stay to talk, but—"

"But you have that court date for your brother," Dr. Loftus said. "Yes, I remembered. I could tell you were having a hard time paying attention today. And I don't blame you. I know you're very conscientious, but you could have taken today off. I would have understood."

There were two kinds of professors at Philadelphia Community College: One kind was like Dr. Loftus, who always understood. The other kind behaved as if every student were an incipient criminal and had to be kept in line in any way possible. After his first semester, Petrak discovered RateMyProfessors.com, and after that, he'd never had to bother with the second kind again, except in mathematics, where there was no alternative.

Dr. Loftus was still out of breath. She stood still for a moment to catch up with herself.

Petrak didn't want to be rude, but he did want to be going. "I'm supposed to meet the lawyer—"

"Yes, yes," Dr. Loftus said, "and I really won't keep you. I only wanted to know, did you get in touch with Kasey Holbrook at Pennsylvania Justice? Because she really can be of help to you and to your brother. And it's very important. This woman, this Martha Handling—it's more than just that she's harsh. Kasey is sure there's something going on, something worse, and if you don't fix the something worse, it gets even worse, and—"

"Yes, Professor," Petrak said, "I understand. But I am supposed to meet the lawyer, and I have to take the bus, so—"

"The bus?" Dr. Loftus looked startled. "Oh, don't be silly. I've got a car. I'll run you down to the courthouse. This is my only class today anyway, and it's not as if anybody ever comes to office hours. I've got my car right outside. I'll get you there in no time."

"Thank you," Petrak said awkwardly. He felt very, very awkward. He felt, suddenly, very panicked. He didn't know why, but he couldn't stop feeling that letting Dr. Loftus drive him was exactly the wrong thing to do.

This, Petrak was sure, made absolutely no sense.

Dr. Loftus was fussing around with her tote bag. She came up with an enormous set of keys and jangled them triumphantly.

"There we go," she said. "Now, come on out with me, and I'll get you there in no time flat. You don't want to be late for Martha Handling. The way that woman works, you want to be early.

She'd have no compunction at all at starting things before she said she would just so she wouldn't have to listen to you. It's the privatization, you understand. It's like what we talked about in class."

Petrak did remember something about "privatization," but it was vague, and things were moving very fast. Dr. Loftus was marching into the large open space that led to the front doors. She was moving fast, much faster than Petrak would have expected somebody that old to move.

The alarm bells were going off in his head, and so was a little voice telling him he was being irrational.

Dr. Loftus pushed open the door to the outside. Petrak raced after her. He got to the door to the outside just before it would have snicked closed.

"Dr. Loftus," he said.

She was marching on resolutely. He was having trouble keeping up.

"Dr. Loftus," he tried a second time.

She pressed her key ring, and the lights on a car a half block away blinked.

"Listen," she said. "This is important. Never say 'illegal immigrant.'"

They reached the car whose lights had been blinking. It was a new car, shiny and silver. Dr. Loftus unlocked it with the remote.

"Of course," she said, "I'm sure Martha Handling says 'illegal immigrant.' It's the kind of person she is. She's the kind of person who's ruining this country and everything it ought to stand for."

"Please," Petrak said.

Most of the time these days, he could think in English, but he wasn't thinking in English now. The little woman was just marching into the distance at warp speed, and he couldn't stop her; he couldn't even explain himself.

She popped open the passenger-side door and told him to get in.

He got in. He tried desperately to think of what to do next. He imagined Stefan sitting in that jail in the jumpsuit thing he'd had on for visiting hours yesterday. Petrak had no idea why, but he still felt absolutely certain that if Dr. Loftus came along, she would ruin everything.

She locked the doors around them, and Petrak realized that the car was a Prius.

4

Mark Granby owed his job to two unshakable realities.

The first was the fact that he was willing to do whatever it took to get the job done, and if "whatever it took" meant something illegal more often than not, he was willing to live with it. That was a decision he had made when he first left Drexel University at the height of the 2008 recession. Everybody you talked to gave the same stupid spiel about striving for excellence and commitment to purpose and blah blah blah crap crap crap. Mark had never understood what any of it meant, and he was pretty sure the recruiters didn't understand it either. They gave the rap because they wanted to look good if anybody asked about your interview, but what they were really thinking was that this was Drexel, not Penn, and all the real talent was across town.

Mark Granby was a realist. He knew he would never have been able to get into an Ivy League school, even a tenth-rate Ivy

League school like Penn. He wasn't some kind of supergenius, and he really didn't come from money.

"I don't come from money. I come from New Jersey," was what he'd said to the recruiter from Administrative Solutions of America when he went in to talk to him, and as soon as he'd said it, he realized he was going to get the job.

The other reality was something Mark only guessed during his interview, but he'd confirmed it later. Administrative Solutions liked to pretend it was an enormous company, a corporate giant with operations spanning the globe, but it wasn't really that big, and it wasn't at all "well regarded."

As far as Mark could tell, nobody who knew what Administrative Solutions really did wanted to have any part of it. It had taken him only a couple of months on the job to stop telling people the truth about what he did. Then he asked his wife, Bethany, to do the same, and found out she'd been doing it all along.

"I think it just sounds wrong," she'd told him at the time. "I mean, private prisons. How can there be private prisons?"

Mark hadn't bothered to give her the spiel he learned in orientation: The prisons weren't really private. They were Pennsylvania prisons. It was only the administration of the prisons that was private. It was a private sector solution to a public sector problem. Administrative Solutions could run a prison much more cheaply than the Commonwealth of Pennsylvania could. For one thing, it didn't have to pay public sector benefits to guards and administrators.

Mark had thought it sounded like a pile of shit then, and he definitely thought it sounded like that now. His job was not to provide a "more cost-effective" administration of Pennsylvania's prisons. His job was to keep bodies in the beds.

"Think of them like hotels," Carter Bandwood had said. "The principle is essentially the same. Every empty bed represents a net loss of revenue. Optimal return on investment requires operating at full capacity."

Mark had never been able to pin down Carter Bandwood's exact position in the company. He could have been a lowish-level flunky just lucky enough to get a New York office. He could have been one of the owners of the whole shebang. It was hard to get accurate information about who ran Administrative Solutions, or who owned it.

Mark did have one piece of accurate information this morning, though. He knew that Carter Bandwood was panicking.

"She didn't tell you why she'd suddenly changed her mind about our arrangement?" he asked. "She didn't give you a clue?"

"She didn't even tell me she'd changed her mind about the arrangement," Mark said. "She called this morning, from her car, for God's sake, because she won't call from a stable location—oh, no, that would make the calls all too clear—"

"If she didn't tell you that she wanted to change the arrangement, what did she tell you? What the hell is going on?"

"She told me she had to consider the possibility that, in the event of a criminal investigation, she'd be likely to come out more cleanly if she were the one who walked the information in the door."

"She meant if she was the one who went to the police and told them about the arrangement."

"That's what it sounded like to me."

"Christ on a crutch. She doesn't even care that she'd go to jail herself? She doesn't even care?"

"Carter, honestly, I couldn't tell you. We were doing that thing again where I could only pick up one word out of three."

"She would go to jail herself," Carter said. "If she thinks she wouldn't, she's insane. It's a juvenile court she's dealing with. The press will go insane."

"Probably."

"She didn't tell you when she was going to do this? Today? Next week? At a press conference? What?"

"She didn't even tell me that she was going to do this. It's like I told you. The reception was all crapped up. She refuses to talk anywhere but in her car."

"Well," Carter said, "you're going to have to call her. Or go to see her. You're going to have to go do something. If she's going to do this, it's going to be bad no matter what, but I can tell you it's going to be a lot worse if we're not ready for it."

"Ready for it or not, Carter, I don't think it's going to make any difference. We paid a juvenile court judge a lot of money to make sure she sent kids to juvie for as long as possible to make sure the places were, uh, operating at full capacity."

There was a long, drawn-out silence at the other end of the phone. When Carter Bandwood's voice came back, it was flat and metallic. It didn't sound panicked at all. "I don't know what you're talking about," he said. "And if you're taping this, I'll find a way to make you dead."

After that, there was nothing. Mark shut off his phone and then disassembled the recorder device he'd bought at the advice of a private detective he knew. The private detective was the only person Mark had ever known who was more cynical than he was himself.

Somewhere upstairs, somebody flushed a toilet. Mark put the device into his inside jacket pocket and called up. "Bethany? Or is that Kaitlyn? Everybody's late today."

Bethany came down the stairs with a towel around her head. "Kaitlyn's not running late," she said. "She's not home."

"She left early?"

"No," Bethany said.

Mark looked at his wife. She'd been a pretty girl at school, and she wasn't bad now. But that wasn't the point. Her sister was the point.

"We're going to have to do something about this," he said.

"We've got a judge and a lawyer," Bethany said. "We are doing something about this. She just needs a little time to grow up."

"She may not have any more time," Mark said, tapping his chest.

But then it just seemed wrong, somehow, to bother Bethany with all this, especially when he wasn't sure how it was going to work out. The only thing he had decided was that he wasn't going to jail alone, and that didn't begin to cover the situation.

5

When Russ Donahue first agreed to take a case in juvenile court, he had been more than half convinced that he would fail at it. Lose your temper, lose the argument, his father had always said. The very idea of a "juvenile justice" system made Russ lose his temper. Surely there was something wrong with a country that could think of nothing else to do with its troubled children but lock them up and parade them around in leg irons anytime they went outside.

Russ had seen the leg irons once when he was late for a court session and went around the back way as a shortcut. The kids brought in from juvie had had a delay of their own, or the door they were supposed to use had had something wrong with it, or something. Russ didn't really know. Still, there they were, lined up along one wall, their hands in cuffs behind their backs, their ankles in irons—as if every one of them were a precocious Jeffrey Dahmer, ready to commit murder and mayhem if given half the opportunity.

That night he'd gone home to Donna and Tommy and the baby and stared at them all through dinner, as if the fact of them could make sense of the fact of what he had seen at court. Tommy was close to the age of many of the kids he had seen. Russ tried and tried to think of something Tommy could do that would make leg irons a necessity. He even tried to think of something Tommy could *want* to do. He'd come up blank. Eight-year-olds didn't rob banks and gun down all the tellers. They didn't carjack little old ladies in grocery store parking lots and shoot them in the woods to get their wallets full of one-dollar bills.

Some of the kids against the wall had been older, teenagers at least. That had made a little more sense. Teenagers were at least capable of doing real harm. A seventeen-year-old was more or less an adult—in size and strength, if not in maturity.

Then he found out that there were almost no seventeen-year-olds in that line against the wall, or sixteen-year-olds either. Sixteen- and seventeen-year-olds who had done truly bad things were almost always charged as adults.

"That's why you should do it," Donna had told him when he was thinking about accepting that first case. "There aren't enough people to take these cases, and not enough of them don't think we should be putting children in jail."

"Wouldn't there be less of the kind of thing you were talking about if lawyers who didn't like it got involved with it?" Bennis Hannaford asked him.

Russ was helpless enough when Donna went after him on her own. When Bennis joined the party, he had no idea how to get himself out of the mess he'd gotten himself into.

That first case had been one of Father Tibor's, a case like the one he was working on now—a kid newly in from Armenia, not a case of criminality as much as of culture shock.

Well, there was more criminality in the case today but it was still something small. If Russ had left well enough alone after that first time, all the juvenile cases he handled would have been small, and he wouldn't have ended up where he was now.

Instead, he'd let the word get out that he was willing to take juvenile cases, and the excrement had hit the fan.

The second case he'd taken involved a twelve-year-old boy who had first raped and then murdered a three-year-old in his neighborhood. The case was sensational, an international news circus of truly epic proportions. There were still Web sites devoted to vilifying the kid, three years after he'd been sent away. Hell, there were still Web sites devoted to vilifying Russ himself.

The kid, of course, had been tried as an adult—sort of. He'd been tried in an adult court, but there was no possibility that someone that young could actually be incarcerated in an adult jail. The other inmates would eat him alive.

The compromise had been to remand him to the juvenile justice system until he was eighteen, then to transfer him to an adult prison for the rest of his natural life. Russ had rehearsed all the arguments he had ever made against locking up juveniles forever: Their brains weren't fully formed. They didn't have the impulse control. They would mature out of violence if only you treated them right.

The arguments all came to a crashing halt against the reality of John-Ray Croydon.

The first time Russ met with him, the kid had sat tilted back in his hard wooden chair and said, "They told me in there you couldn't tell anybody anything I said to you. Is that right?"

"That's right," Russ had said.

Even in those few seconds, Russ was able to feel something going wrong in the room. John-Ray's eyes were hard little pits, all the more disconcerting because they were such a clear, bright blue. The kid looked like he'd been called up out of central casting to play the Carefree Barefoot Boy in some retro version of *The Waltons*.

Except for the eyes. The eyes had been—absolutely literally—unbelievable.

John-Ray broke out into a huge grin. "I did it before," he said, almost *hooting*. "I did it twice before, and I can prove it."

I did it twice before, and I can prove it.

They'd found the girl's body in an abandoned building in North Philadelphia, torn up by the feral cats that roamed that part of the city the way coyotes once roamed the frontier towns of the Old West. She was only barely recognizable. To be absolutely sure, they had had to rely on DNA.

Half the country was calling for Russ to be jailed along with the kid, just for agreeing to defend him. The other half—well, he didn't remember what the other half had been doing. Donna and Bennis had both insisted that even the worst criminals deserved a defense. He had told them so himself.

And he still believed that. He really did. The system worked only if everybody got representation, if the government was required to prove its case beyond a reasonable doubt, if you dotted all the *i*s and crossed all the *t*s.

What he didn't believe, anymore, was that there was no such thing as a bad boy, or that no one who was under the age of eighteen should be tried as an adult or put away for life. He knew now that there were "children" out there who weren't really children. They were on a ramp up to becoming truly horrible, and the only way you could stop them was to lock them up early and lock them up irrevocably.

A lot of people railed against Martha Handling's sentencing practices, but Russ Donahue did not. He knew what she was up to. He even admired her for it. He thought she was a woman of principle.

This morning, he thought even women of principle could run late, and he found it very annoying.

The court was a big, bland room with the judge's bench set up very high. There was the United States flag and the flag of the Commonwealth of Pennsylvania. There was Stefan Maldovanian sitting next to him at the defense table and Stefan's aunt Sophie and brother, Petrak, in the seats just behind.

Petrak Maldovanian leaned forward and said into Russ's ear, "Where is Father Tibor? Father Tibor is supposed to be here."

This was true. And, Russ reminded himself, Stefan Maldovanian was not a John-Ray Croydon. He hadn't raped or murdered anyone. He'd just gotten himself caught trying to shoplift DVDs out of a Good Times Movies store at the King of Prussia Mall.

"I think maybe he's had an accident," Stefan said. "He promised he would be here. Father always does what he promises."

This was absolutely true. Russ thought it was too bad that Stefan Maldovanian didn't always do what *he* promised, since the last thing he'd promised was to stay away from the Good Times Movies store at the King of Prussia Mall. That was after the first time he'd been caught shoplifting, when the store decided not to prosecute.

"Let me go look," Russ said, getting up. "Maybe he got lost in the maze."

"Where is the judge?" Petrak asked. "Isn't she supposed to be here?"

"She's here somewhere," Russ said. "Her first case ran. She must have heard it."

"It's after eleven o'clock," Petrak said.

Russ gave no answer to that, and made his way out of the courtroom and into the hall.

He felt enormously relieved, as if there had been rocks sitting on his chest, and now they were gone.

6

Dr. Janice Loftus was lost, and not only lost, but agitated. She was so agitated, she was finding it hard to think straight. If there was one thing Janice had always taken pride in, it was her ability to outthink anybody in any room anywhere, including men and the kind of university administrator who liked to rule by bullying.

At the moment, she was in some back corridor somewhere, and the clock on the wall and the watch on her wrist both said it was after eleven o'clock. Somewhere in the building, the hearing on Petrak Maldovanian's brother must have started. Janice wasn't sure where. When she'd first decided to drive Petrak to the court-house, she had a vague idea of serving as a Moral Witness. She'd thought of herself as sitting at the very back of the courtroom, looking up at Martha Handling, staring in a way that Martha could not ignore. Janice remembered Martha from Bryn Mawr. She'd been a fascist in those days, too.

What bothered her most about finding out that the hearing was closed was that the possibility hadn't occurred to her first. The Authorities were always closing hearings and meetings and everything else they had a hand in. They would close trials themselves if they thought they could get away with it. They usually couldn't, because the right to a public trial was right there in the Constitution. Janice didn't think much of the United States Constitution. She did think it sometimes had its uses.

In this case, the hearing might have been closed because there was something peculiar about it, or because Martha Handling wanted her hearings closed so that nobody would know what she was doing, or because all juvenile hearings were closed. Janice didn't know.

She was very well versed on the ways of adult courts and hearings, but until now, she had never taken much interest in juveniles. There was something about juvenile law that always seemed to her to be squishy and unsatisfying, even when she knew it was a prime example of oppression. It was really incredible how many prime examples of oppression there were in the world.

The corridor was empty. All the corridors leading into it or out of it also seemed to be empty. Janice could not hear anything she thought she should—like footsteps or talking. She had no idea how she had managed to get to where she was, or what she was supposed to do now that she was here.

First she was at the little desk in the front. That's where they had taken her cell phone and searched her bag and sent her through a metal detector. Then she had gone to the second desk right outside the hearing room. Then she was arguing with the guard about coming in. Then another guard was called, who was probably somebody of higher rank. Janice couldn't tell. The other guard had been adamant. Janice had stalked off to pace.

That was it. That was all Janice could remember.

"Idiot," she said out loud, just to hear noise in the corridor.

She felt as if she were deep underground, although she didn't think she was. There were no windows anywhere, and no doors to offices or closets. It was a strange place, made even stranger by the complete lack of sound.

Superstition was a tool of oppression; she knew that. So was the belief in ghosts and goblins and God and all the rest of the supernatural universe. When people believed in those things, they also believed in their own powerlessness. They believed that their lives were controlled by a ghost in the sky and that they could do nothing to help themselves.

That was why you had to be so careful all the time. Those ideas had been instilled into all of us as children. They could come back to haunt us even when we thought we had purged them completely.

Up above her head there was a security camera, and there was something wrong with it. She couldn't put her finger on what it was. The best she could come up with was that the thing looked *flat*. She was sure it wasn't supposed to look *flat*.

She kept moving along the corridor, looking from one side to the other so that she could spot all the cameras. There were millions of the things. They were everywhere. Welcome to the surveillance state.

All of them looked just as flat as all the others. She kept squinting at them. They just sat where they were. They didn't move. They didn't tilt and follow her when she moved.

She got to a bend in the corridor and began to wonder if this was the way the cameras were supposed to be. But just as she turned the corner, she saw something else.

One of the camera lenses seemed to have something hanging from it.

She stopped and stared. The camera was all the way up on the wall at the ceiling. There was nothing she could climb on. The corridor was completely, absolutely, and irrevocably empty.

What was hanging from the camera lens was a little drop of something that looked like coagulated plastic, or maybe paint.

There were a lot of reasons why someone might put black paint over a security camera's lens. They could want to keep the camera from recording anything definite, without shutting it off completely, which might be noticed. But the act of painting might be noticed, because there were so many other cameras. Even if you were painting the lenses of every one, the others you hadn't gotten to yet would record your progress.

She made herself pick up speed. She was wearing tie shoes with soft soles, but she could still hear her own steps—*slap slap slap, pound pound pound.*

She forced herself along, looking at the lens of each security camera she found. They all had that *flat* look, but now Janice knew that somebody had deliberately put black paint over the lenses of every single camera.

Janice reminded herself that most things that looked like they had been done by the deep forces of conspiracy hadn't been. That was another way the oppressors kept the oppressed in line. All you had to do was to start thinking you were crazy. If you were crazy, then everything you saw was an illusion. It wouldn't be just the paint on the camera lenses that was a delusion. It would be everything everywhere.

This leg of the corridor was short. There was another turn, and Janice found herself right at the edge of a long row of doors. She couldn't remember when she'd felt so relieved.

She strode up to the closest one as quickly as she could. She knocked on the door. There was no answer. She tried the knob and found it turned without trouble. She looked at the nameplate by the door. It said MARILYN ALLEGETTI, but gave no other identification.

Janice opened the door and looked inside. It was an ordinary office. There was a desk with a little L to the side, where the computer sat. There were some bookshelves. There were some chairs. It could have belonged to anybody, doing anything.

Janice closed the door and stood very still. This corridor was not uninhabited. She could feel it. She could *hear* it.

She could hear breathing.

She went down the hall a little farther, stopping at each door and listening. Mostly what she heard was nothing. The names on the doors meant nothing.

The name on the door in the middle of the line was finally one she recognized: JUDGE HANDLING, just like that. No first name. The other women in the corridor must be some kind of assistants. At any rate, they wouldn't be judges.

Janice stopped in front of Martha Handling's door and listened some more. There was definitely breathing. It sounded labored and quick, unhealthy. Maybe Martha was in there having a heart attack. Maybe Martha was in there drinking.

The breathing came on and on, heavy and shallow and rapid all at once. Janice rapped against the door as loudly as she could.

For a moment, the breathing stopped.

Only seconds later, it started up again.

Maybe Martha *was* having a heart attack.

Janice gripped the doorknob and twisted. The door swung open soundlessly, the hinges so well oiled, the door felt as if it had no weight.

The two people in the room were both on the floor, and in the first few seconds, Janice recognized neither of them.

Then the blood on the floor and the wall and the desk came into focus and the bloody gash in the side of the head came next.

Janice would have screamed, but she was wondering if the white stuff all over the edge of the wound was brains.

7

Father Tibor Kasparian had not screamed, and was not screaming. He was sitting where he had been for the last four minutes, one hand holding Judge Handling's heavy custom gavel, the other lying in the blood that covered both his knees.

The room smelled of blood. Father Tibor knew the smell of blood. It had a hard metallic edge.

It laughed at you.

He wondered who the woman was who had come through the door. He wondered why she wasn't screaming.

Then he told himself that there was only one thing he really had to remember, and that was that he had the right to remain silent.

PART ONE

ONE

1

Somewhere back in the mists of time, Gregor Demarkian had trained to be an accountant. First he had taken a degree in economics from the University of Pennsylvania. That had sounded very practical to his parents, who were immigrants from Armenia and heavily invested in making sure their children had careers that could carry them in America. Gregor never had the heart to tell them that academic economics was not the same thing as a business degree. To this day, he wasn't sure what it was most of his professors had been getting at. Whether they were socialist or capitalist, mercantilist or Marxist, they all seemed to be living in cloud-cuckoo-land, where "rational actors" and "historical forces" bumped about the landscape doing things no actual existing human being would ever do, "inevitably" coming to conclusions that contradicted everybody else's inevitability.

After college, Gregor went on to the Harvard Business School, where he'd been given an MBA that should have been spectacularly practical. He'd been enabled to go by the Armenian American Professional Fund, which was set up by an earlier generation of immigrants than that of his parents, dedicated to turning Armenian Americans into doctors and lawyers and that kind of thing.

"We can't go on and on with the rugs," the secretary of the fund explained to him when he'd gone by to pick up an application. "It's embarrassing. It's a stereotype. Nobody wants to be a stereotype."

Gregor had been a contrarian even then, and something in the back of his mind observed that not only did everybody rely on stereotypes to get by in everyday life, but that it could sometimes be to your own advantage to be taken as one. Fortunately, he'd had too much sense actually to say that. He'd just taken the papers home, filled them out, and sent them in. Two months later, his tuition at Harvard was covered.

His father thought he'd been in school long enough already, but his mother was very pleased. "They take you very seriously," she'd said. "You want to be taken seriously."

Gregor supposed he did want to be taken seriously, but at the moment, it was mostly a side issue. He'd done well at Wharton, and while he was doing very well, he had assumed that he would spend his life after graduating working for some enormous corporation, or for one of the Big Eight accounting firms. He'd had his sights set on Arthur Andersen when the man from the FBI showed up at a recruitment day.

From the moment he met the man from the FBI, he'd been hooked.

The problem as things now stood was that, although the FBI had hired him because he was an accountant—in those days, the FBI preferred its recruits to be either lawyers or accountants—it hadn't ever really used his expertise in accountancy.

Part of that was his own damned fault. He'd graduated. He'd been sent off to get enough experience to be certified. He'd trained at Quantico. In no time at all, he was able to see that the really interesting work in the Bureau had to do with bodies.

For a while after that, Gregor kept up his certification and made some effort to keep up with accounting. But it was only for a while. Kidnapping detail had given way to murder investigations on Indian reservations and then to the early days of the Behavioral Sciences Unit. And after that, Elizabeth got sick with breast cancer.

Gregor could not remember a time when he had been sorry that his career went the way it had gone. Until now. Now he was sitting at the Federal Reserve, waiting for an appointment and sifting through computer files. He had been sifting through these files for several weeks, and they still didn't make even a modicum of sense.

He was rapidly reaching the conclusion that they were not making sense, because they could not be made sense of.

He heard a discreet little cough near the top of his head and looked up to find a middle-aged woman standing over him, looking faintly disapproving. Gregor did not take that seriously. This was a confidential secretary of the old school—not a woman who typed and took dictation, but a woman who manged five or six other secretaries underneath her and knew more about what her boss did than her boss himself. She knew because she was convinced that bosses knew next to nothing, and she was probably right.

"Mr. Carpenter is ready for you now," she said. "If you'll just follow me this way."

Gregor said thank you and got up and followed. It had been many years since he was last inside the Federal Reserve, and he was both surprised and a little depressed to see that it had changed almost not at all.

It wasn't very far to Mr. Carpenter's office. It was just off the reception area to the right and barely down the corridor. Whoever Mr. Carpenter was, he was not a force to be reckoned with.

That made Gregor Demarkian decidedly relieved.

The middle-aged woman stopped at a blank wooden door, knocked twice, and opened it.

A young man stood up from behind a solid wood desk and held out his hand. "Mr. Demarkian? I'm Terry Carpenter. The Director has told me a lot about you."

Gregor could not imagine what the Director of the Federal Bureau of Investigation had had to tell Terry Carpenter about him. This was not a Director under which Gregor had ever worked. He wasn't even the second Director after one under which Gregor had worked.

Gregor shook Terry Carpenter's hand and sat down in one of the seats the man was gesturing to. The office was only big-ish. Gregor wondered what Carpenter spent most of his time doing.

Terry Carpenter sat down behind his desk again. Gregor put his briefcase on the floor.

"I'm not sure I'm actually the person you need to talk to," Carpenter said. "We looked through the material you sent the Bureau, and we tried to work it out, but you have to understand that these things are very complicated. Worse than complicated."

"'Bat shit crazy' is what Mike Engstrom told me."

Carpenter flushed slightly. "Yeah," he said. "I know. And I hate to admit it, but I think it's actually getting worse."

"It's been years," Gregor pointed out. "The mortgage meltdown was in 2008. And you don't know anything?"

"Oh, no," Carpenter said. "We know a lot. We're just not sure what we know is right, and we're not sure what else is out there, and as to the problem of titles—well."

"Well?"

"When you take a mortgage and slice it into a dozen pieces and sell the pieces to a dozen different funds that sell securities based on the pieces to hundreds of different clients, it begins to get to be a problem figuring out who actually owns the property."

"That's what your e-mail said," Gregor poined out.

Carpenter flushed again. "I know. It's going to be years yet before we get this all straightened out, and we may *never* get this straightened out. There may be hundreds of properties out there without any clear title at all—"

"You mean people are going to be living in houses and nobody's going to know who owns them."

"That's the thing," Carpenter said. "Yes."

"I'm only interested in one property," Gregor said. "Apartment Four, 1207 Markham Street, Philadelphia, Pennsylvania. It's right around the corner from my house. The man who lives there is named Mikel Dekanian. He immigrated from Armenia fifteen years ago. He's got a wife named Asha and two children, both boys. The boys are both under ten."

"Yes," Carpenter said. "But you must realize that as affecting as these personal stories are—"

"It's not just that their house is in foreclosure. It's that their house is in foreclosure due to the legal action of a bank that, as far as I can figure out, never had a mortgage on the house. Never. You can do things about a foreclosure if you know how to go about it right. But I can't do anything about a foreclosure when the bank that's foreclosing doesn't actually hold the mortgage on the house. And I really can't do anything about it when everybody admits that the bank doesn't seem to have the right to foreclose, but nobody will stop them from foreclosing. This ought not even to be an issue. We should have been able to go into court, show the judge that the bank did not have the lien, and walked out with the foreclosure stopped."

"Yes," Carpenter said miserably. "I know."

"Instead," Gregor said, "the court is acting as if Mikel Dekanian is pulling some kind of scam, and as if I'm aiding and abetting it. And the priest from our local church. And my wife. And before you say yes again, let me point out that this isn't the only case like this we've had. There have, in fact, been four of these cases over the last three years in our own parish alone, and we lost one of them."

"I'm feeling a little stuck on yes," Terry Carpenter said.

"And does yes mean there's nothing you can do about it?"

"Not exactly," Terry Carpenter said. "Give me a minute and let me show you what I've managed to put together."

2

What Terry Carpenter had managed to put together was an even bigger mess than what Gregor Demarkian had managed to put together for himself, and it was far more surreal.

"I just have to do a little setup here," he promised while Gregor sat in his uncomfortable visitor's chair and watched the razzle-dazzle roll out in the hands of two assistants who looked far more nervous than they ought to be.

Gregor was willing to bet that these were not Terry Carpenter's own personal assistants, and the ferociously competent woman who had brought him to Carpenter's door wasn't either. The ferociously competent woman would belong to a higher-up who wanted to make sure Carpenter made a good impression. Carpenter wasn't making a good impression.

He was barely making a bad impression.

Computers rolled into the office, mostly laptops with very big screens. These were lined up on the edge of Carpenter's desk facing Gregor. The screens of the laptops all had very colorful graphs on them—bar graphs and pie graphs, overlapping circle graphs that reminded Gregor of elementary school forays into set theory. The whole thing gave off a distinct odor of panic.

"There," Carpenter said. "There we are. I think that if we refer to these graphs, I might be able to explain what's going on with your Mr., uh, Mr.—"

"Mikel Dekanian," Gregor said.

"Yes," Carpenter said.

Gregor gave the computer screens a sweep. "You know," he said, "I don't really need to understand what's going on here. What I need is to find out what I have to do to fix it. I have a young man who's done that thing we're always talking about, and played by all the rules. He's never been late on a mortgage paper in his life. He hasn't dealt with any of the big banks exactly because he's heard too much about the way they operate. And in spite of all that, he's got letters threatening to send officers to his door. And—"

"It really would help if you understood it," Terry Carpenter said. "It will only take a minute."

"We'd let it go and laugh it off if it wasn't for the case we had last year," Gregor said. "I mean, for God's sake, if something like this had come up twenty years ago, it would have been resolved in a week and the bank would have been falling all over Mikel, try-ing to pay him enough not to sue—"

"But that's just it!" Terry Carpenter said frantically. "That's just it! Twenty years ago, the lien would have been filed on paper in your local property tax jurisdiction, somebody would have taken a paper copy of the lien down to the wherever it is, wher-ever you file deeds and liens on the deeds—it would be the town hall in most places, but with a city the size of Philadelphia, I'm just not sure, so you see—"

"Are you trying to say that Mikel's deed isn't on file with the real estate office? Because I can tell you're wrong. It's there. I've seen it. What's more, what isn't there is any lien whatsoever besides the mortgage from the American Amity Savings Bank. I know. I went down there and looked myself."

Terry Carpenter seemed to be trying to get control of himself. Gregor thought he'd head him off at the pass.

"Don't try to tell me that American Amity sold the mortgage," Gregor said, "because I know it didn't. American Amity never sold any of its mortgages. I checked it out."

"Yes," Terry Carpenter said, "but the thing is—"

"And if you're going to try to tell me that Mikel took out a sec-ond mortgage with J.P. CitiWells, you're going to have to show me the paperwork. Mikel said he didn't, and I believe him. I believe him because I know him. I believe him because there is no record of such a lien in the city records. And I believe him because less than a year ago, we had a case where this same bank tried to fore-close on a house that hadn't had a mortgage on it for nearly thirty years. No mortgage at all. Free and clear."

Terry Carpenter had been standing up, leaning toward the

open laptops, as if he needed only a break in the conversation to jump in and get going. Now he sat down again with a thud.

"Oh, God," he said. "You got one of those."

"*One* of those?" Gregor asked.

Carpenter looked defensive. "There weren't many of them," he said. "I mean, hardly a thousand all told throughout the entire system—"

"You had a *thousand* cases where banks tried to foreclose on houses without any mortgages on them at all? None? A thousand cases—"

"I keep trying to tell you," Carpenter said. "Everybody used to register their deeds and their mortgages at town hall, but back around 2000, people began to feel that was a really old-fashioned and time-consuming way of going about things. You had to hire people to go running all over the country. It could take weeks to get mortgage liens filed. So a group of the bigger banks got together to found an electronic filing database, one big database for the entire country. Which was not entirely stupid, you have to see that—"

"Was it legal?" Gregor asked. "Is it legal?"

Terry Carpenter looked miserable. "We don't know."

"You don't know," Gregor said. "I've got a man with a wife and two small children about to lose his house over a mortgage he never took out, and you don't know if the way it was filed was legal—"

"There are a lot of different jurisdictions involved," Terry Carpenter said. "What's legal in California isn't necessarily legal in Nevada. What's legal in Atlanta isn't necessarily legal in Savannah."

"I know about jurisdictions," Gregor said.

"It's easy to say that the banks should have stuck to the old system," Terry Carpenter said, "but you've got to see that that isn't going to be sustainable. We live in a digital age. You don't type on a manual typewriter anymore, and you don't vote by paper ballot. We really are going to have to do something about updating the recordkeeping—"

"Mikel Dekanian's house is in jeopardy because you hired a bunch of cut-rate data entry people, didn't hire enough of them, made them work like crazy, and they made mistakes. Lots of mistakes. Some of which—"

"After all," Terry Carpenter said. "They really were just mistakes. The banks aren't deliberately trying to steal people's houses out from under them—"

"How do you know?"

"You've got to expect that there are going to be some glitches when a new system goes into place," Terry Carpenter said, sailing right past anything Gregor was saying. "The thing to do, right this minute, is to get your proof together—"

"We don't have proof," Gregor said, "and we shouldn't be the ones trying to prove anything. J.P. CitiWells should be producing the loan documents, which they are not, and—"

"—and then it's just a matter of time," Terry Carpenter said. "It's just a matter of time—"

"We don't *have* any time," Gregor said. "The court has refused to issue an injunction. We can't get the process stopped. By the time your matter of time has run its course, Mikel Dekanian is going to be out on the street. And then what happens?"

"You have to see it from the banks' point of view. They have billions of dollars at stake. They're trying to recover from enormous financial losses. They have to protect themselves if they're not going to go down in flames, and—"

"And then I've got to ask what I'm doing at the Federal Reserve anyway," Gregor said. "Why is the Federal Reserve—?"

"Oh, I'm not part of the Federal Reserve proper," Carpenter said. "I mean, we're in the building, but that's just because they were able to find space for us here. We're really, I mean we're actually—"

There were two sharp raps on the door. Gregor and Terry Carpenter looked up at the same time. Then the door popped open, and the formidable middle-aged woman stuck her head in.

"I'm sorry to disturb you," she said, "but Mr. Demarkian's wife is on the phone, and she's very insistent. She says it's urgent."

TWO

1

Afterwards, Gregor could never remember the order in which things had happened. He did remember wondering what the phone call was about, but mostly because Bennis was not, as she put it, "a crisis kind of person."

If he'd been asked what he thought the crisis could possibly be, he would have said the very mortgage he was working on. Mikel Dekanian's mortgage had been a crisis on Cavanaugh Street for weeks. There had even been images out of a silent movie serial: Mikel's wife, Asha, had come to the Ararat with a head scarf over her head, trailing two young children and weeping uncontrollably because she'd had a letter that sounded as if she would be out on the street before nightfall. Mikel himself had stood on the steps of the church and ranted on and on in a frantic mix of Armenian and English about what he was going to do to the next idiot who called his wife and threatened her on the phone.

It was just one of those things it was impossible to get any-body to take sanely. And although Gregor didn't blame them, they also made him tired.

The things he did not remember included just who had said what when, and just how long it had taken him to understand what Bennis was trying to tell him.

He wasn't entirely sure he'd understood it even when he got to Penn Station, and then he was stuck in what felt like an endless round of phone calls and dropped phone calls and areas of no service and the whole insanity that made him hate cell phones.

At the same time, he felt guilty. He knew it was ridiculous, but part of him felt that nothing would have happened if he hadn't shut his own cell phone off while he was talking to Terry Carpenter. He'd had perfectly good reasons. He didn't want calls to interrupt the conversation. Interrupted conversations never quite worked out the way you were planning them to. But then the call had come in on the landline, and it had just seemed to be all his fault.

It had taken everything he had not to force the conversation out into the open right there in Terry Carpenter's office.

"Father Tibor has been arrested," Bennis said. Gregor could hear the heavy breathing, and everything in him went on high alert. Bennis kept her head almost always, but now she sounded as if there weren't enough air in the universe to fill her lungs.

"Father Tibor's been arrested," Bennis said, "and I can't—there was blood everywhere. Russ came in and Tibor was on the floor with the body and Russ tried to pull him out and then other people came and tried to pull him out or something, I'm not sure, but everybody had blood on them. Tibor was covered with it and Russ had it all over and other people and then the police came and I wasn't there, but he's not talking to me anyway, and—"

"What do you mean he's not talking to you?"

"It's on CNN already," Bennis said. "If you could just get to a television, or bring it up on your phone, I showed you how to bring things up on your phone—"

"Bennis, for God's sake. I'm in Mr. Carpenter's office, I can't talk and I can't figure out—"

"I don't want you to talk," Bennis said. "I want you to get out of there right this minute and get home. Get home as fast as you can. Take an Amtrak Express if you have to. Hire a bloody limousine if you have to. Just get here."

That was the point at which things got a little hazy. He half thought he'd made a lot of excuses before he slammed out the door and down the hallway and out onto the street to find a cab. Then he was sitting in a plastic molded chair in Penn Station, trying to get his phone to work.

He bought a ticket on an Acela Express. He got it out of a self-service kiosk after checking the board a dozen times, just to make sure the train was running on time. You could never tell with Amtrak.

It took him only five minutes to get CNN to load on his phone, but it felt like an hour, and he had to stop himself from smashing the thing on the ground to punish it for being so slow.

Then he was staring at CNN's home page and reading the little blurb under the picture of a building. He thought the building might be the court where the incident had happened. He clicked on the link that said FULL STORY.

He read the story three times. It was like reading gibberish.

He looked at the board again. His Acela Express was still slated to be on time. He had half an hour to kill. He tried phoning Bennis.

Bennis didn't pick up.

He texted her: PICK UP. In capitals. It needed capitals.

He tried phoning her again. This time she picked up.

"I'm sorry," she said. "I had the phone off. I'm very, very sorry. I should have realized you were going to call. But you don't understand how crazy it's already been, and it hasn't been more than a couple of hours. I can't understand—"

"Stop there. A couple of hours."

"Just after eleven thirty or eleven forty-five, I think," Bennis said. "The police were called just after eleven forty-five, and they were all there—Tibor and Russ and Petrak Maldovanian because his brother was arrested for shoplifting or something—"

"Bennis."

"It doesn't make any sense. The news says they found him in this judge's office and he had the murder weapon in his hand and there was blood everywhere. And there was this woman there, not the judge. I'm not sure who she was, but she started screaming her head off and Russ was in the corridor because he was looking for the judge, and I don't know. Gregor, I wasn't there."

Gregor tried to think of what could calm her down, but he had never had to calm Bennis down. "All right," he said. "You weren't there. But Russ was there. That's right, isn't it? You said Russ was there. Is Russ with you now? Can you put him on the phone?"

There was a long, strained silence. "He isn't here," Bennis said finally. "He's still at the jail, where they took Tibor, and—"

"And he's working on it," Gregor said. "That's what I'd expect. There's nothing wrong with that. There's going to have to be a bail hearing. And whatever went on, Tibor shouldn't be talking to anybody without a lawyer present."

"I don't think that's anything you have to worry about." Bennis sounded as if she were strangling. "He's— Tibor isn't talking. To anybody. According to Russ, all he'll say is 'I have the right to remain silent.' That's it."

"But that's good." Gregor was trying his best to sound reassuring. "That's just what he ought to say. Don't start acting like a ninny and thinking he ought to be talking his head off so that he doesn't seem to be guilty, because—"

"No, you don't understand," Bennis said. "That's all he would say. Not just to the police, but to anyone. It's all he would say to Russ."

"What?"

"And Russ says he presented himself as Tibor's attorney and Tibor said Russ wasn't his attorney and then the police pretty well threw him out of the station, and now he doesn't know what to do and I don't either. I mean, if Tibor wants another lawyer, I can pay for one. There's enough money, but Russ says they wouldn't let me in to see him anyway and it doesn't sound like he's made a phone call to another lawyer and does this make any sense to you? Isn't Russ his lawyer? I mean, isn't Russ his lawyer to the extent that he ever has a lawyer?"

"I never really thought of it," Gregor said. "I never expected anything to come up."

"Tibor can't have killed anyone," Bennis said. "He wouldn't kill anyone. You know that."

"I do know that."

"I know you can't work miracles, but Tibor will talk to you. Maybe you can get him to tell you what happened. Maybe you can get him to stop being an idiot and listen to Russ or somebody, get him to let me pay for another lawyer if he wants to, something, because the way things are now—"

"They're calling my train."

"Good," Bennis said. "Go."

"I'm moving as fast as I can," Gregor said.

That was true, but it wasn't much help to anybody.

2

The Acela Express was an hour and a half late getting into Thirtieth Street Station, and by then Bennis had texted him four times with a link. The problem with riding on a train was that service went in and out with no rhyme or reason Gregor could tell.

It didn't help that the few seconds of film he was able to see as the connection went in and out was all disturbing.

He was sure it could not be accurate. It *seemed* to show Tibor kneeling on the floor in a large room, next to a large desk, holding an outsized gavel in his hands. That was all right. It was much like the still picture Gregor had already had a chance to see. Then the film would move a little and it would look as if Tibor was raising the gavel in the air, far over his head. Then the gavel would start to come down, and Gregor would lose service again.

Gregor knew that his best bet would be to calm down and wait until they came to somewhere where he would both have service and where the train was going to be at a full stop for fifteen minutes or more. God only knew that there were plenty of places where the train felt it had to stop for fifteen minutes or more. If the Acela WiFi worked anything like reliably, we could use that. But right this minute, it wasn't working at all.

When the train arrived, Bennis was not waiting for him on the platform. Gregor got out with his single airline bag and his briefcase and headed straight for the waiting room.

He got to the waiting room and looked around. It was full of people. None of the people looked like Bennis. He tried peering at all the places she'd waited for him before and got nowhere. Then all of a sudden she was there, right next to him.

"Let's go," she said, grabbing him by the arm. "I just paid a cab a hundred dollars and promised to pay him a hundred more if he waited for us around the corner. I made him put his off-duty light on."

"Why do you have a cab?" Gregor asked. "Is something wrong with your car? Did you have an accident? What the hell—?"

"My car is bright orange," Bennis said, tugging at him without mercy. "It's the easiest thing to spot in three states. Cavanaugh Street is full of reporters, and I do mean full of them. They're jamming the street solid, and they're waiting for you. I called John Jackman, and he sent out some cops to disperse them, but when I left, it wasn't going very well."

"They're waiting for me," Gregor said.

"Of course they are," Bennis said. "Who else would they be waiting for? I left by bus. It was the only way I could get out of the neighborhood without being seen. And there isn't a hope in hell that we're going to be able to get you back into our house without being bombarded."

"I couldn't watch that video you sent me," Gregor said. "The service problems were ridiculous."

They were outside. They were around the corner. They were moving so fast, Gregor was losing any spatial organization that he ever had, and he had never had much. Then Gregor saw a cab parked at the curb with its off-duty light on.

"In," Bennis told him, opening the cab's door.

She crawled in behind him and handed a thick stack of twenties to the cabdriver.

"Thank you," she said.

"We going somewhere in particular?" the cabdriver asked.

"1207 Markham Street," Bennis said.

The driver was an older black man who looked like he'd heard it all by the time he was seven. He pulled away from the curb.

"Markham Street?" Gregor said.

"It's practically right behind us. Think about it for a minute." Bennis handed over her phone. "I've got it downloaded. All you have to do is hit Play."

Gregor hit Play.

For what seemed like forever, the video—it looked handheld, and not very well. The picture kept bouncing all over the place—the video went on and on and on. Tibor was holding the outsized gavel. He was raising it over his head. He was bringing it down. He was raising it over his head. He was bringing it down.

"For God's sake," Gregor said.

"It was the most watched video of the day on YouTube before somebody complained about the violence and they took it down," Bennis said.

"What's YouTube?"

"Oh, for God's sake," Bennis said. "You know what YouTube is. It's the Web site where Tommy Moradanyan put up that video he made of the cats getting into the cabinets in Donna's kitchen. And I keep telling myself that the way these things work, they'll never let that in as evidence in a trial, but you know what? I don't really know that. And it looks like—it looks like."

"You can't see the body," Gregor said. He had started the video playing again. "Where's the body?"

"Presumably it's on the floor under where Tibor's arm is going—where it's—oh, for God's sake, Gregor, this can't be right. There has to be some other explanation. He can't have done that."

Gregor had gone very, very cold. "Who took the video? Where did the video come from?"

"Nobody knows at the moment," Bennis said, and now she was crying. "The first thing I thought of was that it must be a security tape, but I've been talking to John's office all day, and according to them, there's not really any security tape, because something was wrong with the security tape. I don't know."

"If this isn't a security tape," Gregor said, "then somebody must have been standing there with a camera filming this on purpose. A phone camera, something like that. And if what was going on was that Tibor was bludgeoning someone to death, then the person taking the video was either part of the project or a bystander who decided to film it instead of running off to get help."

"If you're asking me if I think it's possible that some bystander came along and filmed a murder instead of calling 911, then yes, I think that's possible. I don't think it's possible that Tibor ever bludgeoned anybody to death. Ever. Tibor is not a violent person. He's never been a violent person."

"You can't see a body," Gregor said. "There's blood on the gavel in the first frame. It doesn't start out clean and get bloody."

"Does any of this make any difference?" Bennis asked. "Because it doesn't make any difference to me. And Tibor's in jail somewhere, and he won't talk to Russ. And he won't talk to me or Donna. And he sent word that he wouldn't see you, either. And I'm going completely and absolutely crazy, Gregor, I really am."

Out on the street, everything had begun to look familiar. The cab slowed and began to pull to the right. The houses looked down-at-heel and pinched. The one belonging to Mikel Dekanian had a foreclosure notice plastered over its front windows, as if the dispute about the mortgage were already settled.

Bennis leaned forward and threw another pile of bills into the front seat next to the cabbie. The front door of 1207 opened and a small, dark head peered out. Then the door swung wide.

"Let's go," Bennis said. "We don't want to give anybody any ideas."

They went. They went quickly. Asha Dekanian grabbed Bennis by the arm as soon as she reached the top of the steps and pulled her inside. Gregor was inside a moment later, and the door was shut.

"I watched the whole time," Asha said. "I watched the whole street. There wasn't anybody there. Nobody knew you were coming here. It will be all right."

"We go through to the back and out the back door and there's an alley. Where they keep the garbage cans. Then we go down that three houses and that's the back door to our place. With any luck, nobody will know you're home," Bennis said.

"It is a complete impossibility," Asha said. "Father Tibor is a very good man."

Bennis looked away. Gregor took note of the fact that, even under the thick accent, it was impossible not to hear the faint wobble of doubt. Asha Dekanian must have seen that video, too.

Bennis was already chugging down the long center hall toward the back. The house was very shabby but meticulously clean. It reminded Gregor of the way houses and tenements had been on Cavanaugh Street before everybody started making serious money.

What was at the very back was the kitchen, and it was not only very clean but also newly remodeled. There was something in a cast-iron pot on the stove that smelled familiar. Gregor was too distracted to recognize it.

Asha rushed ahead of Bennis and got the back door open. She held it wide and stuck her head out to look up and down the alley.

"It's all right," she said. "There's nothing here. There's nobody. You should move fast, just in case."

Gregor wondered what circumstances in Asha Dekanian's life in a Soviet country had taught her how to do this, and then he was out the door himself. The garbage cans were set up against the back walls, all of them decently closed.

"I noticed it when the kitchen guys were here," Bennis said, moving them both along. "They brought a lot of their equipment in from the alley, and I stood out here one morning and got myself oriented. It's a good thing I did, too, because I never would have guessed. This is us. The steps suck. We should have them fixed."

The steps did suck. One of them was nearly off. Gregor marched up them and into his own kitchen—that fully remodeled kitchen that always made him think of *House Beautiful* magazine.

Bennis closed the door behind them. "Give me a minute and I'll make some coffee. Or get you a shot of something serious if you want it. I've been forcing myself not to all day. I've also been forcing myself not to scream."

Gregor put his bags down on the kitchen table and then sat. Bennis moved away to fuss with the coffee things. Gregor got his phone again and watched the video one more time.

Bennis came and sat down across from him. "Listen," she said, and she was crying again. "I know this can't be true. I know it.

Tibor can't have done this thing. But the more I hear, the worse this gets. Worse and worse. And that woman who died. She was that judge, you know, that Martha Handling he was so upset about. He was on the local news talking about her not a week and a half ago. And this other woman, this Janet somebody, who says she came in and found him—found him killing—Gregor, I don't know what to do. Russ is losing his mind," Bennis said. "Donna called me up a couple of hours ago, scared to death that he's suicidal."

"And he left word that he wouldn't talk to me? And all he'll say is—?"

"Is that he has the right to remain silent," Bennis said. "Yes. According to what the people in John Jackman's office have been able to find out, anytime anybody tries to talk to him, all he'll do is take the Fifth. But Gregor, it's not just that he won't talk to any of us—he won't talk to anybody. They had a guy come down from the Public Defender's Office, and Tibor wouldn't talk to him either. He just keeps saying he has the right to remain silent."

"You're right," Gregor said. "Whatever's going on here, it's not that Tibor murdered somebody."

Bennis brightened. "Do you mean that? Are you sure?"

"I'm absolutely sure," Gregor said. "Unfortunately, I don't know why I'm sure."

Bennis's face fell again. She got up from her chair to tend to the coffee. Gregor could see that she had also started crying again.

THREE

1

By the time Janice Loftus was released from the courthouse, she had been hanging around for *four hours,* and she was fighting mad. Even the more than slightly relieving fact that she had not been required to go down to a police station somewhere didn't help. Rights were much more than being left alone, no matter what those idiots in the Teabaggers Party said, but being left alone was certainly a right. Janice had not been left alone. She had been harrassed and intimidated. She had been accused of a dozen things she couldn't possibly have done. She had been asked questions nobody had a right to ask and been told—all right, not outright—that if she didn't give the answers, it would be very suspicious.

Very suspicious.

They really thought she was going to fall for that kind of thing. No wonder so many people of color were in jail. It would be hard to stay out of jail if your schools absolutely sucked and you barely had a fourth-grade education and you were subjected to tactics like *that*.

In a free society, your thoughts were you own. It didn't matter what you thought. It only mattered what you did. Or sometimes it did matter what you thought, and America wasn't a free society, and—

Janice couldn't think straight. Every muscle in her body was twitching, going off like a string of firecrackers. It took everything she had not to run down the street. It took more than everything she had not to say something nasty to the reporters who ringed the building and crowded the halls. *There* was something that would be all over the place in a minute. The police had had no business accusing her of taking that video, and no business confiscating her cell phone as evidence.

She was around the corner and down the street and—well, she didn't know where she was, exactly. She'd been walking without looking where she was going. Now that she looked around, she thought she might have landed in a very bad neighborhood. It was wrong to categorize people by what they looked like but even so, the people around her right now made her very nervous. She was the only white person she could see.

The important thing was not to be afraid. Predators against women were always male, and they were always on the lookout for fear. You couldn't look intimidated. You couldn't give out vibes that said you were intimidated.

The taxi emerged out of nowhere. It could have been sent by God in a poof of smoke but Janice didn't believe in God. God was not just the opium of the people. God was the Big Lie that kept everybody else in line.

Janice ran out into the street and raised her hand. The cab pulled over immediately.

Janice grabbed the door and hopped in. She shut the door behind her with a slam. She gave the address of the offices of Pennsylvania Justice. Then she buried her head in her bag so that she couldn't see what was going on outside.

As an example of white skin privilege, getting that cab had been pretty spectacular. Janice was willing to bet the cab wouldn't have stopped for anybody else on the street.

The offices of Pennsylvania Justice were apparently not very far away. At least, the cab didn't take a long time, and the meter didn't go up much. Janice tried to think, but she really couldn't remember where anything was in relation to anything else.

She carefully counted out too much money and put it into the cabdriver's hand. She got out of the cab and shut the door carefully and slowly behind her. The worst of the evidence of shock and angry was draining away. She was able to walk slowly toward the door in front of her without giving the impression that she was afraid of the cabdriver and wanted to get away from him quickly.

Pennsylvania Justice had a storefront office with a plate glass window, with private cubicles in the back for anything that shouldn't be seen by the general public. They wanted to encourage walk-ins, people with problems who might be intimidated by the stiff formality of an ordinary office.

Janice went through the plate glass door and looked around. There was a waiting area with cheap plastic chairs and no one in them. There were three even cheaper desks where one man and two women were working away at computers. The computers were anchored to the desks with thick chains.

One of the women looked up from whatever she was working on and said, "Oh! Janice. Are you all right? We've all been so worried about you. And Kasey wants to talk to you. We've been calling you and calling you, and you never answered your phone."

"I don't *have* my phone," Janice said, the indignation rising up in her throat like bad shellfish. "I had to leave it at the door. And then I ran out of there and I forgot it. And now I don't know if I'm ever going to get it back."

"Oh, my God," the other woman said. "Are you all right? Did they get rough with you?"

There was a rumble and a bump and another woman came out from the back, where the private cubicles were. She was extremely tall, and extremely slender, extremely electric. Her hair was a cascade of red that ended at her waist.

"Oh, *Kasey*," Janice said. "Oh, thank God."

"They took Janice's cell phone," one of the women said. "Just look at her. She's *shaking*."

Kasey looked her up and down, and Janice felt immediately better. There were people who said it was a bad idea to have Kasey as head of Pennsylvania Justice, because she fed into all the stereotypes that said no organization could succeed without playing into the sexual demands of men, but Janice wasn't having it.

"I'm glad to see you," Kasey said. Her voice had an odd flat tone Janice was never able to define. "We've been watching the news back here all afternoon. *Did* they rough you up? Physically?"

"Oh, no," Janice said. "There wasn't anything physical. But there wouldn't have been, would there? There were security cameras everywhere."

"Probably," Kasey agreed. "Come on back here and talk. We'll get you a cup of coffee or chamomile tea or whatever it is you're drinking these days."

"Chamomile tea," Janice said. She was very grateful that Kasey had remembered. Most people in her position wouldn't have. "Except maybe there weren't security cameras everywhere, because some of them looked like they had paint on the lenses. Does that sound crazy?"

Kasey turned back toward the cubicles, and Janice followed her.

"It really was incredible," Janice said as they wound their way to the very back. Kasey's cubicle was no bigger than any of the others. That was the kind of person she was.

"They kept us all round forever, and they questioned us over and over and over again, and that man, the one in the video, the one who did it, all he'd do was take the Fifth. And then there was my student—"

"Your student?"

"Oh, yes," Janice said. "That was why I was there. I drove my student. Petrak. Petrak Maldo—Maldonian? I'm sorry. It's one of those incredibly long East European names and I can never get it right. His brother was having a hearing about something, I don't know what. Stefan. That's the brother. He was undocumented and it was Martha Handling he was appearing before. Petrak doesn't have a car so I offered to drive him. And, all right, I'll admit it. I wanted to get a look at how she operated."

"Did you?" Kasey asked.

Janice shook her head. "It turns out that juvenile hearings are closed. Or this one was. They wouldn't let me in."

"So you went down to see Martha in her chambers?"

"Oh, no," Janice said.

The cubicle was invaded by another woman, this one very small and intense. She had cup of tea. "That'll make you feel better!" she said chirpily.

Then she went out. Janice wondered if she was an intern. Interns were often chirpy.

"Janice?" Kasey said. "How did you end up in Martha Handling's chambers?"

"It was just an accident, really. There's this guard at a table near the door, and he told me I couldn't go in, and there were a lot of other people trying to get in, so he went and talked to them. And there were two halls on either side of the front door without any guards on them, so I just started wandering."

"Just like that."

"Yes, of course, just like that. They've got to know that themselves, don't you see, because there really were security cameras everywhere. I could see them the whole time. Except there was something strange some of them. They had paint over the lenses. Little blobs of paint. Can you understand that?"

"It would explain why they don't have enough security tape footage to know what actually happened," Kasey said.

"Honestly, it was just so odd. I mean, all the cameras, and the paint, and then I got to the door and her name was on it and I thought I'd just go in and see. And there he was, sitting in all that blood and with that gavel in his hand."

"And you screamed your head off," Kasey said.

"Not at the beginning," Janice said. "At the beginning I just stared at it. I was trying to remember it. It's like you always told us. Keep as much of the evidence as you can secure. So I did. Except there really wasn't much evidence that I could get my hands on, but I took some notes. And it was a good thing I did, too, because, well, look at this."

Janice hiked up her poncho just a little and flipped at the base of her skirt. It was encrusted with something dark and hard, and the dark and hard stuff went up the skirt proper almost to her waist.

"Blood," Kasey said.

"Her blood," Janice said. "I have no idea how it happened. It got very crazy and there were tons of people wandering around even before the police got there and there was blood everywhere and the next thing I knew, there was blood on my skirt. And then, well, you know how things get. They just got worse."

"Did you also post a video to YouTube?"

"Oh! The video! I heard about that, but I didn't get a chance to see it. A video of that man murdering Martha Handling. They were all talking about it after a while. It's supposed to be absolutely gruesome. But I thought that was a security tape."

"No," Kasey said. "I've seen it. The one thing it is almost certainly not is a security tape."

"Well, I can't tell you," Janice said. "I've got no idea. But there's something else. And I can't help feeling a little guilty. Except not guilty, if you know what I mean."

Kasey looked unmistakably puzzled.

Janice plowed on: "It's better this way, don't you see? Murder is a terrible thing, and that man is a priest on top of everything, but Martha Handling is dead and that means that almost every juvenile defendant in the system is going to be better off. There isn't another judge in the system that's as harsh as Martha Handling was, at least not in Philadelphia. So maybe it was a pretty fair trade."

"A pretty fair trade," Kasey said.

Janice tossed her head. It didn't work so well as when she was younger. It had no effect on Kasey Holbrook at all.

"Sometimes," Janice said, "I think we're just too polite. We want to act like ladies. Sometimes I think that ending injustice directly is the only thing that will ever work."

2

When Mark Granby left the courthouse, he started walking in a straight line. He was lucky. He was out and on the street when the first cop cars pulled up, their sirens screaming and their tires squealing and the whole world stopping to watch what they did next. It was one of those moments that no one in their lives is supposed to have. He felt like he was in an action movie. There he was, the villain, right there, standing on the edge of the crowd and watching the chaos unfold.

Mark liked action movies, as far as that went, but he'd never thought they bore much resemblance to reality. Real villains wouldn't stand around and watch. He was sure of it. Real villains would get their business done and get the hell out of Dodge as soon as possible.

Mark had been standing on the curb when the police cars pulled up because he hadn't been able to figure out what he was supposed to do next. He did not consider himself a victim. He had done absolutely nothing but find the body and not report it to anybody. That might be against the law, but it wasn't some kind of big moral deal.

If he ever got stuck having to answer questions about it, that was what he would tell them—that and nothing else. They would never be able to prove anything else, no matter how hard they tried. He was pretty sure they would never be able to prove he was in the room in the first place, unless they were already looking for him. He had left fingerprints. He had left fingerprints everywhere. He hadn't been able to help himself.

He walked and walked, always going in a straight line, never paying attention to anything he didn't have to. He had no idea how long he had been walking. He had no idea where he was. The only thing he was sure of was that he hadn't found it, and if he hadn't found it, somebody else would.

He had reached the point where he wasn't really breathing anymore. His chest hurt. He felt as if it were about to crack open. He had never been in really good shape. These days he was in really bad shape, except that he wasn't all that overweight, at least as overweight as people he worked with.

He came to an abrupt stop near a mailbox and looked around. Given how long he'd been walking, he was sure he was far enough away that nothing about his being *here* could be taken as indication that he had ever been *there*.

"Here" was one of those "mixed" neighborhoods the magazines always talked about when they talked about Philadelphia. There was a McDonald's on one side of the street and a Starbucks on the other. There was a Panera. There were small shops selling art supplies and other small shops selling drug accessories. In the window of the store with the drug accessories was a big pile of books with the title *Best Bongs*. The bong on the cover had been made out of an eggplant.

Mark had lived in Philadelphia long enough to know that the neighborhoods were only superficially mixed. The great Philadelphia racial divide didn't ease up for anybody. Standing where he was, Mark could see the patrons going in and out of McDonald's and the patrons going in and out of Starbucks. All the people going into McDonald's or coming out of it were black. All the patrons going in and out of Starbucks were white. It was like the entire city of Philadelphia had signed up to be in some kind of racial stereotype enforcement project.

Mark didn't actually like Starbucks. On the other hand, he was trying very hard not to call attention to himself. He headed into the Starbucks.

All Starbucks looked alike, just as all McDonald's looked alike. That was the first rule of chain store restaurants. Mark bought some kind of coffee he didn't understand and headed for a little round table at the back. He took a swig of it right before he sat down. It tasted, as the man said, like goblin piss.

The store was mostly empty except for a few people who had converged at the counter. That was exactly what he needed. He got out his cell phone and called Beth. Beth picked up immediately, she must have seen the caller ID before she'd heard the ring.

"Where are you?" Mark asked her.

"I'm at work," Beth said. "But it's all right, really, there's nobody much here at the moment. Where are you? I've been looking at the news, I've been looking—they say—"

"Shut up," Mark said. "I know you say there isn't anybody around, but there may be somebody you can't see. Just listen to me."

"I am listening," Beth said. "I'm just scared to death. Wasn't that the woman—?"

"Shut up," Mark said again.

Beth made a strangled little noise, but after that, there was nothing.

"Listen," Mark said again. "I'm not exactly in a position to talk, either. I'm in a Starbucks. I don't know where exactly, but nowhere near the courthouse. The bad news was that I was near the courthouse. In fact, I was in it—"

"Oh, my God," Beth said. "Oh, my God. I knew it. I just knew it. I kept looking at the Web sites and there she was and there was that talk we had this morning and I just knew—"

"*Shut up.* The bad news is there are security cameras all over that damned place and they have to have some pictures of me somewhere. The good news is that there's no reason at all for these people to know who I am or to think I'm anything but a regular person in the courthouse to do some business. Got it?"

"Yes, Mark, I know, but—"

"Forget the buts. There's no reason for anybody to know. Even if everything else we were worried about were true, even if she talked to somebody already, even if there's some kind of federal investigation going on—any of that—it doesn't matter. I'm not a high-profile figure. I'm not recognizable on sight. If we just shut up and stay shut up, they should never figure out I was ever there."

"The news sites say they have a suspect in custody," Beth said. "They say it's that man, the one who you said was messing with everything. The priest person. He's going to know who you are, isn't he? He's going to be able to tell them about you."

"At the moment, as far as I know, he'd have nothing to tell them even if he wanted to. I didn't see him in the courthouse. I don't see how he could possibly have seen me."

"Did you get the—the thing? The thing you were talking about?"

"No," Mark said. "That's the bad news. I looked for it, but I couldn't find it."

"You looked for it? But Mark, how could you have looked for it? Was she there, where you were looking? For God's sake, was the body there? And that man? What did you do—?"

"I looked around while I had the chance and I got out as soon as I heard someone coming. Try to focus. Did Kaitlyn ever come home?"

"What? Oh, yes. Yes, she did. Right after you left this morning. She got herself a tattoo, can you believe that? A little rose thing, it's not too bad, but it's right on her ankle, and I can just see where this is going—"

"Is she still home?"

"As far as I know. I told you, I'm at work. But she was just exhausted. And she said she wasn't going in to school. And I didn't know what to do about that, because I had to leave to come here, so—"

"I'm not worried about her being out of school. You can write her a note. But I want her home and in and not on the rampage anytime soon. If you don't read her the riot act, I will. She's got to keep a low profile. A very low profile. And not just because our personal pet judge is dead."

"Oh, Mark. But you can't think—"

"Of course I can't think," Mark said. "Kaitlyn has a motive on the surface. I have a big one. It'll come out in no time that we were fixing things for Kaitlyn—that I was using Admin Services to fix things."

"Oh, Mark, for God's sake. If you did something, you could tell me. I wouldn't tell anybody and isn't there some thing where wives can't testify against husbands? But I need to know, Mark, please, I need to know—"

"If there's somebody out there listening to this, you've just hanged me for real. Because you know and I know that nobody is going to want to see that priest convicted of anything, and a whole hell of a lot of people are going to want me dead as soon as any of this gets out. And it will get out. Because I didn't find it. And that means somebody else will."

Mark hung up. His coffee was sitting on the table in front of him. He took off the top and looked into what should have been plain black, but instead seemed to be something white that was congealing. He put the top back on and gave up. After he got his other phone call through, he'd go find a liquor store and set himself up for something lethal to drink.

He punched in the code for the office in New York and got himself ready to tell Carter Bandwood that the shit was about to hit the fan.

3

There was almost nothing Father Tibor Kasparian remembered about this day, except the one important thing, the thing that would change everything forever. It was lodged in his brain more firmly than any memory he had ever had. It was stronger than his memory of Anna dying.

It seemed so long ago, Anna dying. Long ago and far away. That phrase kept running through his head, "The past is a foreign country: they do things differently there." But he couldn't remember who had said or written it. He wasn't sure why it mattered anyway.

One of the reasons today's memory was so strong was that it was, in every way, tactile. He could feel the squish of the blood and muscle under his knees as he knelt on the floor. He could feel the wet stickiness on his hands. It had surprised him to realize that he had never been that close to a violent death before. He had witnessed them, but he hadn't touched them. The touching made all the difference.

After that, there were things he had to do, careful things that had to be done right. He hadn't finished all of them when that woman had come in, knocking only as a formality. There was something he didn't know and couldn't begin to guess. Why did people knock when they weren't going to wait for an invitation to come in? He did it himself, but he'd never understood it.

The woman had come in and then she was screaming her head off, screaming and screaming. There was something fake and forced about the screaming. She had stood there for what felt to Tibor like a long time. Then she'd started screaming. Tibor hadn't believed it.

She screamed, and then she ran out into the hall, still screaming.

A moment later, Russ came in, staggering and breathless, and Tibor heard him make the worst sound in the history of the world.

After that, it had all been messiness and blur, and there was no point in listening to it.

There was only one thing Tibor Kasparian could do, and he set about doing it.

They would ask him questions.

He would say, "I have the right to remain silent."

Then he would remain silent.

He did that over and over again, as if it proved something.

The only time he changed anything was when they asked him if he wanted Russ to act as his lawyer, or if he wanted another lawyer, or if he would talk to Bennis or Donna or Krekor or anybody at all.

When those things came up, he just said no.

Someone had told him what jail he was being taken to, where he was going, what would happen to him next. Everybody was very polite and very careful to let him know everything he needed to know. If this was the way police behaved in America, he didn't know what people were complaining about.

It was odd to think that in all these years, and all the years of knowing Krekor Demarkian, he had never been on the business end of a police investigation.

The cell they put him in at first was very small and very isolated. He was the only one in it, and instead of bars, it had a thick metal door with a little window three-quarters of the way up and a little swinging slot at about waist height. The little swinging slot was where they pushed in trays with food on them. After Tibor had been in the cell for he couldn't tell how long, they pushed in a tray with a cheese sandwich and an apple and a carton of apple juice on it. He had no idea why it was apple juice rather than a hundred other things.

He had expected people to come and talk to him again, and to ask him questions, but they didn't. He lay for what seemed like hours just where he was. They had taken his watch and his belt and his cell phone and his clothes. He wished someone would bring him a book, even though he was sure he wouldn't be able to read.

He reminded himself that even though he had been in prison before, it had not been in America. It had not been a jail like this one. He had no idea what to expect.

He knew that the Commonwealth of Pennsylvania had the death penalty. He thought that if it came to that, he would be all right. He had never been one of those people who had doubts about his God or doubts about his fellow human beings. God would accept him for what he was, and for what he had done, and for what he hadn't done. His fellow human beings would behave like human beings.

He ate the sandwich and the apple and drank the apple juice. He didn't like the toilet stuck into the wall at the back of the cell. It felt insulting. He didn't like the sandwich. There was no window except the one in the door looking out into the corridor. He had no idea what time it was or what was happening in the world outside this place.

He told himself over and over that it would work out the way it should if he would only do what he had promised himself to do.

He had drifted into an odd little daydream about his first week on Cavanaugh Street when the guard came to the door for what would turn out to be the very last time that day.

"You're wanted downstairs," he said, and Tibor stood up and cooperated as calmly as possible with that ridiculous ritual, where you had to put your hands through the slot so that you could be handcuffed before they opened the door to the cell.

When the door swung wide, it didn't feel as if it were really open.

There were two guards in the corridor, not one.

They applied leg irons, as if he were a ravening beast who would jump out at them at any moment.

The guards gave instructions, which Tibor didn't listen to. He followed along silently. That was what they seemed to want him to do. They went down the corridor the cell was on and then through a set of doors that had to be locked and unlocked and locked again in a bewildering sequence. It reminded Tibor of the tumbrel sequences on very expensive combination locks.

They went down some stairs and around some halls and down some stairs again. They came to a door that was completely blank and without any windows or slots in it at all.

One of the guards opened the door and stepped back. There was a largish conference room with a big square table and many chairs.

A man sitting in one of those chairs stood up. "Set him loose," the man said. "And when you've done that, get out of here."

"But," one of the guards said.

"Don't start," the man said. "I know what the rules are. But right now, you're going to set him loose and get out of here. I'll buzz when you're needed."

"If you get a chance to buzz," the other guard said.

The man said nothing. His face was a perfect blank. His suit was impeccable.

The guards got the work done faster than Tibor would have thought possible. In no time at all, his handcuffs and leg irons were gone, and the guards were gone, too, with the door closed behind them.

The man looked Tibor up, down, and around. Then he gestured to a chair and said, "Good afternoon, Father Kasparian. My name is George Edelson. I'm with the office of the mayor. Please sit down."

Tibor took a chair and sat down. He didn't like the sound of this at all.

George Edelson sat down. He had a briefcase he had left on the table. He didn't touch it.

"I want to make this clear before we start, Father Kasparian.

I am not only from the office of the mayor—I am also one of John Jackman's personal aides. I'm breaking about five hundred regulations in order to have this meeting. I not only don't like the situation I'm in at the moment, I positively hate it. That notwithstanding, if we were to have a meeting like the one we're having now, this would be the place to have it. This is a secure room. One of only two in the building. I'm a lawyer. That means that when I leave this room, I'll be able to claim attorney–client privilege and refuse to answer any questions about anything you have told me. I will be able to claim that even if you claim that I am not your lawyer, because the record will show that when I walked into this room I was your lawyer, and you had requested me to be."

Tibor started. "But that—"

"Isn't true?" George Edelson said. "Of course it isn't true, but the record will be there all the same, and you can shout your head off about how you never asked for me. I'll have a paper trail that says you did. So if you think you're going to make another histrionic stand about your refusal of all legal help, don't bother. You can't win that fight, no matter what you do."

"It is my right not to have a lawyer," Tibor said. "I can fire you even if I never hired you."

"That, I don't care about. All I care about, all anybody cares about, is finding out what is going on around here. John Jackman has made it a priority. Do you understand that?"

"I don't have to talk to you," Tibor said. "I have the right to remain silent."

"Would you prefer to talk to John directly? That would break another hundred and fifty regulations, but we can get it done."

Tibor started to feel panicked and claustrophobic. He hadn't felt claustrophobic in his cell. He felt claustrophobic here. "I don't have to talk to you," he said again. "I will not talk to John Jackman."

"Would you rather talk to Gregor Demarkian? The office of the mayor has been in touch with Mr. Demarkian. He has returned to Philadelphia and is presently at his home. We could have him here in less than half an hour."

Tibor nearly choked on that one. Krekor, for God's sake. Krekor was the last person he wanted to see. Krekor was the last person he could talk to. If they ever got him into a room with Krekor, the whole thing would be over in a second.

George Edelson was one of those people who could go forever without talking. He sat in his seat and stared. He stared and stared. Tibor thought he was about to faint.

It would have been the perfect thing if he had been able to faint, but of course he couldn't.

"Is this room soundproofed?" he asked.

George Edelson looked surprised. "What do you mean by soundproofed? I can tell you with assurance that it is not in any way bugged."

"I didn't ask about bugged," Tibor said. "Could somebody standing outside the door listen to us?"

"Well, Father, I suppose he could. As far as I know, this room is not constructed to eliminate all levels of sound. But there is really nothing like that for you to worry about. It's a very thick door. There are bookshelves filled with books on both the walls this room shares with other rooms. The best anybody could hear from inside this place is incohate noises."

"It doesn't matter," Tibor said. "If you don't go away and leave me alone right this minute, I will start screaming at the top of my

lungs until somebody hears the noises and has to come investigate. Someone will come to investigate. They will have to."

George Edelson looked impressed. "You're out of your mind,"
he said. "You're stark, raving bugshit. Don't you know that people
are only trying to help you? Don't you realize that as things look
at this moment, you've got a one-way ticket to the electric chair?"

Tibor folded his arms across his chest.

"I have the right to remain silent," he said.

And he didn't say anything else.

FOUR

1

Terry Carpenter's business card was lying in the middle of Gregor's place at the breakfast table when he finally got down to breakfast that morning. For a few minutes, he couldn't remember what it was.

TERRENCE CARPENTER

Interagency Task Force on
Mortgage Institutions and Practices

Gregor picked the thing up and put it down again and picked it up again. It was one of those government agency names that seemed to have been invented by gerbils.

It was early enough for them to go to the Ararat, but Bennis obviously wasn't intending to go. There were place mats set out on the kitchen table and place settings as well, the heavy pewter ones that Bennis used for "everyday." It was one of the things about Bennis that Gregor couldn't help but wonder at. His family's idea of "everyday" had been a cheap set of tin, and even his late wife's had run to nothing fancier than stainless steel. This was the kind of thing people did when they'd grown up to be debutantes on the Philadelphia Main Line.

Gregor sat down and put Terry Carpenter's card away from him, toward the middle of the table. There was orange juice already out in a tall crystal glass. There was coffee percolating in the machine on the counter. There were napkins folded under the forks. Bennis had once explained to him that it was never right or proper to put napkins in napkin rings. Gregor couldn't remember why.

Bennis came in dressed in jeans and an enormous cotton sweater that must have been one of the ones she'd bought him.

"I thought we'd avoid going out in public as long as we could," she said, taking their coffee cups to the coffee machine to fill them. "I looked outside when I got up, and there doesn't seem to be much of anything out there, but it's hard to tell."

"We can't hide in the house indefinitely," Gregor said.

Bennis brought the coffee over and went to the stove for whatever else she had made, which seemed to be some kind of omelet. Gregor told himself he was cautiously optimistic. You could never quite tell with Bennis and food.

Bennis sat down across from him. "I wasn't thinking that you'd hide out indefinitely," she said. "Or that any of us would. I was thinking that it might be a good idea to get some things settled before you have to talk to reporters. And I don't see how you're not going to have to talk to reporters. It would have been bad enough if it was just that some friend of yours committed a murder, or was arrested for committing a murder—"

She stopped, embarrassed.

"I'm sorry," she said after a moment. "There's the major part of my brain that says Tibor could not possibly have done a thing like this, and then there's that little part that can't get off that damned video."

"Don't worry about it too much," Gregor said. "You're not going to be the only one."

"I know I'm not," Bennis said, "but that isn't saying much, is it? If his best friends can't see past the video, what's going to happen with everybody else? I've been staying away from the news channels as much as I can, but other people are going to be watching them. Everybody in the country is going to be watching them. And I don't see what we can do about it."

"We can find out what really happened," Gregor said.

"What if what really happened was that Tibor bludgeoned this woman to death?"

"Then we'll deal with that when we get there."

"Do you think we're going to get there?"

"No," Gregor said. "I told you that forty times yesterday, Bennis. I'm dead certain that whatever happened in that room, Tibor didn't bludgeon Martha Handling to death. And don't go on about how I can't say why I'm so certain of that, and how it's probably my intuition and nothing else. It's not my intuition. I've noticed something very wrong. And you can't see the body in the video."

Bennis cut her omelet into very small, very precisely square pieces.

"That fell out of your jacket pocket when I hung it up this morning," she said, pointing at Terry Carpenter's card in the middle of the table. "Is that who you went to see yesterday after you testified? Is that the person who's going to help Mikel Dekanian save his house?"

"That's who I went to see yesterday," Gregor said. "I don't know how much help he's going to be. It seems the bottom line is that the entire mortgage situation is a mess beyond all understanding and nobody actually knows what's going on. I was in the middle of tearing him a new one when your phone call came through. I was just thinking we were going to have to try another tack."

"Is there another tack?"

"I can only hope so. Apparently, this isn't the first time this has happened. Well, we knew that. It's happened before just to members of the church. But from what Carpenter was saying, it's happening quite a lot, and I got the impression that at least some of the time, the banks were prevailing and people were being forced out of their homes in spite of the fact that the banks forcing them out didn't actually own their mortgages. My guess is that there's something to be done after that, some court procedure, and then people are compensated."

"I hope they're compensated out the wazoo," Bennis said. "How do you compensate people for being put out on the street when you had no claim on them at all?"

"My guess is that 'out the wazoo' is nothing at all what we're looking at. But I did think that we probably ought not to wait to let it get that far. And we should be working on it now. I'll call Russ later. And I'll call Chelsea Kevinmeyer's office and see if I can get anywhere with that."

"Chelsea Kevinmeyer's office? Chelsea Kevinmeyer the congresswoman?"

"Your congresswoman," Gregor said. "Also Mikel Dekanian's. Assuming they'll talk to me at all with all this other thing going on, they ought to be happy to jump in and make a fuss in public. She's put a lot of work into trying to get something done on the mortgage situation. The least she could do is to use Mikel Dekanian's problem as the basis for a speech in Congress and a couple of press releases. Sometimes if things go too public, the banks will back off. Sometimes."

"By which I suppose you mean not all that often," Bennis said.

"There are bureaucracies," Gregor said. "There are also computers."

Bennis had arranged the little squares of omelet into a circle around the edge of her plate. "You might want to rethink talking to Russ," she said. "Donna called right before we went to bed last night. He really isn't in good shape."

"It's not surprising," Gregor said, "but the world won't stop for anybody, and the notices are already up at the Dekanian house. You must have seen them yesterday."

"I did."

"So we'll all have to get to work today, whether we want to or not," Gregor said.

"Donna says he feels responsible for it all," Bennis said. "And I get that in a way, but I don't in a way, and it's one of those things. I look at it and look at it and I don't know what to do."

"Today," Gregor promised, "we'll think of things to do."

The phone on the wall went off with a ring so loud, it made Gregor jump in his chair. His fork hit the floor. His plate tipped sideways and then righted itself, the untouched wedge of omelet never budging.

"Okay," Gregor said. "I may be a little on edge."

Bennis got up and got the phone. It was a faux-antique black and gold one, made to look like the kind of thing that had been fashionable in the early days of telephones, but mounted on the wall.

"Hello," Bennis said. And then, "John? What time is it? And you're in your office? Now? I mean—okay, yes, I understand. You didn't have anything to worry about, we weren't going out anyway. I was a little too worried—okay, yes, just a minute. He's right here."

Bennis held out the phone. "It's John Jackman. He's in his office. He wants to talk to you right away."

"What time is it?" Gregor asked.

"Six ten."

Gregor got up. "For God's sake," he said.

2

The place John Jackman had decided would be a good one to meet Gregor Demarkian was not the office of the mayor, but it might as well have been. Gregor thought it was close to certain that there was no place in the City of Philadelphia where he could meet with the mayor without the news getting out. He thought it was almost as close to certain that there was no place in the country where he could do it.

It was hard to tell which stories would "go viral," as Tommy Moradanyan liked to put it, but Gregor was very familiar with stories that did just that, and he knew there was no stopping them. The best anybody could do in cases like this was to let them run their course. If you were lucky, they ran it fast. If you weren't, you would find yourself staring at headlines months down the line, with everybody stoked and ready to roll at the first hint of a development. There were no cases in which these circuses were of any benefit at all to legitimate law enforcement. Reporters liked to imagine that all the publicity helped to mobilize the public to catch perpetrators. It certainly mobilized the public. It didn't help to catch anything but innocent bystanders, and not even those very often.

The place John Jackman wanted to meet was in City Hall. Bennis called Gregor a cab. Gregor left the house only when it was waiting at the door. He looked up and down the street and saw nobody he wouldn't expect to see. He knew that didn't mean there were no reporters there. He got into the back of the car and tried to force himself to stop worrying about it. There was a reporter in the street or there wasn't. If there was, the reporter would follow him. If there wasn't, somebody in City Hall would leak the meeting. One way or the other, it would get out.

It was too early in the morning for City Hall, but the city was pumping into rush hour. The streets were full of traffic. It moved with reasonable fluidity. It was just about light out.

When the cab got to where it was going, Gregor got out, thinking there was no one around and that he'd have to search for whatever door he was supposed to enter by himself. Then, just as the cab pulled away, a woman emerged from the darkness near the side of the steps.

"Mr. Demarkian?" she said. "If you'll come with me."

The woman was African American, and very young, and almost

blindingly pretty. Gregor supposed she was one of the horde of young women who always seemed to overrun John Jackman's offices. They were always supervised by John's longtime confidential secretary, Ophelia. Ophelia was also African American, and she could have held off a Russian invasion with a good stare and the tapping of her foot.

Ophelia was waiting for him when he got in the back door and up the back stairs to the second floor. She was neither glaring nor stamping her foot, but she was not happy.

"Good morning, Mr. Demarkian," she said. "If you'll come this way. They're waiting for you."

"They?"

Ophelia had turned her back to him and was walking away down the hall. "You and I have always been on good terms," she said, "but you have to understand where I'm coming from. It's him I care about. This is not going to be good for him."

"If you're talking about this meeting, I agree with you," Gregor said. "But I'm not the one who asked for the meeting."

Ophelia stopped outside a door, opened it a bit, and said, "I know you didn't. But I think maybe you should have turned it down."

Then she swung the door wide open, and Gregor went in.

Inside the room there were chairs and low occasional tables. It seemed to be a waiting room of some kind. John Jackman was on his feet and pacing. The other two men were sitting down. One of them, in defiance of decades of city regulations, was smoking a cigarette.

Ophelia closed the door behind her as she went. The two sitting men stood up. John Jackman stopped pacing.

"Well," he said. "Here you are."

"Here I am," Gregor said. "But Ophelia's right, John. I shouldn't have come. It's one thing you talking to Bennis on the phone. But having me here—"

"I'm going to get into trouble for worse things than having you here," John said. "This is George Edelson, and, the one with the cigarette, Dickson Greer. They're both my aides. They both have official titles that would make your ears bleed. They're both getting into trouble with me."

Dickson Greer put his cigarette out in a little cup made of tin foil he'd produced from his pocket.

"Look at the idiot," John said. "African American men have some astronomically high chance of getting early heart attacks, and he thinks he's the Marlboro Man."

"Just feeling a little tension," Dickson Greer said mildly.

John gestured Gregor to a chair, but he didn't wait to see if Gregor sat, and he didn't sit himself. He went back to pacing.

"The first thing you should know," John said, "is that George here went to see Tibor yesterday afternoon."

"And Tibor agreed to see him?" Gregor asked.

"Not exactly," George Edelson said. "I threw my weight around. There was no way he could refuse to be in a room with me. I got a secure room. I thought I could—we thought I might be able to—"

"I thought that if I could get Tibor into a room with some-body who was good at talking sense to people, we could talk sense to him," John said. "He'd already refused to see you or Bennis or Russ Donahue, or any of the other usual people, so I sent George. George is a lawyer. Hell, everybody here is a lawyer except you. We did a little voodoo, and George went in as Tibor's attorney of record."

"I thought he'd refused to talk to an attorney," Gregor said. "Bennis said something about Tibor being offered a public defender and turning it down."

"Yeah," John said. "There was that."

Gregor shook his head. "Did Mr. Edelson here manage to talk any sense into him?"

"No," George Edelson said. "Not even close. I don't know this man, Mr. Demarkian. I only know he's a friend of John's, and of course yours. But after that session we had yesterday, I can't say I agree with the idea that he isn't capable of murder. I'd think he was capable of anything."

"I wouldn't go so far as to say anything," Gregor said.

John Jackman grunted. "Is that some roundabout way of saying you think he did commit this murder? Because I have to tell you, Gregor, the only reason I don't believe it is because it's Tibor. If this were anybody else on the face of the planet, I'd think this was open-and-shut."

"I know," Gregor said.

"Well?" John Jackman said.

Gregor decided that sitting down was the better part of something or other. He sat.

"I don't know," he said finally. "I presume the motive is supposed to be Tibor's anger with this person for giving harsh and unwarranted sentences to juveniles—"

"It's worse than that," Dickson Greer said. "You know we have private contractors running the prisons here in Pennsylvania?"

"Don't look at me," John Jackman said. "That's Harrisburg is what you've got there. It's almost made me ready to run for governor. I mean, what the hell did they think was going to happen?"

"There have been rumors for months now that Martha Handling was taking bribes for giving unusually long sentences to juveniles. The contractors get paid a certain amount per inmate. The more inmates there are, the more money they get."

"Yes," Gregor said. "That, I'd heard about."

"And?" John said.

Gregor sighed. "It's the right kind of motive," he said. "It's better if Tibor knew that the woman was taking bribes. If she was taking bribes—"

"We've got someone for you to talk to about that," Dickson Greer said.

Gregor shook his head again. "But the setup is wrong, somehow. It's just sort of off. That probably sounds very fuzzy."

"It isn't much to go forward with when that video is all over the Internet *and* there's that woman talking to every media outlet she can find *and* he won't talk to anybody."

"I know," Gregor said. "But think about it. What's supposed to have happened, exactly? He had some kind of meeting with her before the court hearing on Stefan Maldovanian, or he ran out to her office to see her before court was supposed to start? That doesn't make any sense, because there's no reason why he would have expected to find her in her chambers instead of in the courtroom. She was hearing another case before the Maldovanian case. And he wasn't there then. Was there any indication that he had a meeting arranged with her—?"

"Not a thing," George Edelson said.

"Well, then," Gregor said, "I can't even see a reason why he'd be there in the first place. And then there's the crime itself. I supposed bludgeoned to death is the correct diagnosis?"

"We won't have the preliminary autopsy reports until later

this morning," Dickson Greer said, "but that looks like the way it's going."

"Okay," Gregor said. "Mr. Edelson says he thinks Tibor is capable of just about anything, but I've got a problem with the bludgeoning thing. It's one of the hardest kinds of murder to commit. It's virtually never a deliberate choice. People recoil from it instinctively. That's why, most of the time, when it happens, it happens in a state of rage. Blind rage. It's the rage I don't find believable."

"You don't think that man could work himself into a state of rage?" George Edelson said.

"I think he could work himself into a state of rage," Gregor said, "but I don't think it would be blind rage. If Tibor is subject to rage, it isn't the hot, blind, go-berserk kind of thing. It's the cold kind. And when you are enraged but cold, you're still thinking. And if you're still thinking, if you're still fully conscious, you're going to have a very hard time standing next to someone and battering her brains out."

"It's a thought, Gregor," John said. "But it isn't much help. I don't think a defense attorney could get it past a jury."

"No," Gregor said. "I agree with you. But it's true, just the same."

"And is that it?" John said. "Is that the reason you don't think Tibor did it?"

"Partly," Gregor said.

"What's the other part?" John asked.

"I don't know," Gregor said. "I just can't put my finger on it. But it hit me the very first time Bennis told me about this—hit me that something was absolutely wrong. That some part of this is not what it would be if Tibor were actually guilty. And on top of that, there's that video. Someone must have taken that video.

But when? Bennis tells me the first person on the scene was that woman who ended up screaming. But if that's the case, where's the person who took the video? Or did she take it?"

"I don't think so," George Edelson said. "They didn't find a phone on her, and it's a phone video. I suppose she could have ditched the phone somewhere."

"And where was everybody else?" Gregor asked. "There should have been other people. There should at least have been secretaries."

"That one, we've got an answer to," Dickson Greer said. "The secretaries were at a funeral of a secretary for a judge who retired a while ago. The judge retired, the secretary died of breast cancer. The whole support staff was out at the funeral and the judges who were in at all were in court."

"And this doesn't feel wrong to you?" Gregor asked. "This doesn't feel out of whack?"

"Gregor, I hate to tell you this," John said, "but that's no help at all."

"I know it isn't," Gregor said. "But at the moment, that's the best I can do."

John Jackman looked at the ceiling for a moment and then seemed to come to a decision. "All right," he said. "We've got some problems, and I think the three of us have figured out at least some ways around them. You know and we know that this meeting is going to leak, and when it does it's going to be crap from here to eternity. But we knew that going in, and we all took the risk anyway. So let's let that go. The big issue, first of all, is that there is no way the City of Philadelphia is going to be able to hire you as a consultant on this case."

"Ah," Gregor said. "I really didn't expect you to. I hadn't even considered it."

"Good," John Jackman said, "because it's not just the political problems that are insurmountable in this case—it's the legal ones, too. There are so many conflicts of interest running around here at the moment, it makes my head spin."

"I've got a conflict of interest myself," Gregor said. "He's probably my closest friend after Bennis. I'm not an objective investigator."

"You may not be an objective investigator, but you are an investigator," John said, "and I'd think you'd be investigating no matter what the circumstances were. So what we've done is figured out a way to get the information to you, and also to lay off any charges of impeding a police investigation or that sort of thing."

"Would I be impeding a police investigation?" Gregor asked.

"It would depend on what you were doing," John Jackman said. "What I want to say here is that I don't want to catch you not telling us anything you've found out. I know that thing you do where you think you have the answer but you don't tell anyone because you haven't worked it out yet. I'm not talking about that. I'm talking about information. If you get any information, you pass it along to us. Even if it's not in the best interests of Tibor Kasparian."

"I think the truth will always be in the best interests of Tibor Kasparian," Gregor said.

"Don't bet on it," Dickson Greer said. "You never know what's coming out of the woodwork then."

"The next thing," John said, "is a technicality, but the law is full of technicalities. Unless you can get Tibor to talk to you and authorize you to act on his behalf, you *can't* go charging around telling people you're investigating for the defense. The operative word is 'can't.'"

"But I will be investigating for the defense," Gregor said.

"Not officially, you won't," John said. "Not unless you've been authorized by Tibor or Tibor's attorney. And as we sit now, Tibor won't even authorize an attorney."

"Don't you think that's very strange in and of itself?" Gregor asked. "Why won't he accept an attorney? Why won't he talk to Russ? Russ *is* his attorney, as far as he has one."

"That's the kind of thing we were hoping you could tell us," Dickson Greer said.

"I think it borders on being insane," Gregor said.

"I think it borders on being perverse," John said. "But here we are. George and Dick will take you to see some people. We'll give you all the information we've got, one way or the other. But we're all going to be breaking forty laws at once, and if we're not really careful, we're all going to end up in jail. We may all end up there anyway if Tibor turns out to be guilty. So watch your ass and try like hell to watch ours."

FIVE

1

Petrak Maldovanian didn't have an alarm clock. Instead, he had his aunt Sophie, who was to schedules what Genghis Khan had been to invading Asia. Petrak had never met anyone, ever, who could arrange her life so perfectly that it never deviated from the original plan. Even in an emergency—and Aunt Sophie had five children of her own—she seemed to be operating on some kind of flight plan.

There were definitely advantages to being as organized as Aunt Sophie was. Petrak had learned a lot since he came to live with her. His grades were better and his health was better and he was calmer than ever before. He'd even begun to lose the hair-trigger temper he'd been famous for back in Armenia. Before he'd lived with Aunt Sophie, he'd have said that a temper was something nobody could control. You *had* a temper, and you and everybody else had to live with it.

The problem with Aunt Sophie's organization was that it

didn't stop when you needed it to, and this morning Petrak very much needed it to.

He'd been afraid the barrage of inconvenient questions was going to start the night before, but Aunt Sophie had been almost completely silent from the time they came back from the courthouse to the time they went to bed. She hadn't insisted that Petrak double-check his homework. She hadn't even looked in on him to make sure he was doing it. There had been something eerie about the way she flitted silently through the apartment, hardly banging the pots and pans when she washed up after dinner.

She was banging the pots and pans now, though. Petrak had been listening to her for half an hour. First there'd be a *rustle-rustle-rustle* sound as she moved across the kitchen floor. Then there'd be a hard metallic *thwack* as she slammed a pan down on the stove. The first of the *thwack*s was the larger frying pan. The second was the smaller one. She must be making bacon and eggs.

"Petrak!" she called up in her flat American voice. "You can't waste any more time. You have to get to school."

Petrak did, indeed, have to get to school. With somebody else besides Aunt Sophie, he could have pretended to oversleep and then rushed out the front door in too much of a hurry to answer any questions. Aunt Sophie never overslept, and she didn't believe in other people oversleeping.

"Petrak!"

Petrak launched himself out of bed and headed for the hall. "Have to take a shower!" he called. Then he raced into the bathroom. He turned the water on. He threw his clothes on the floor. He'd barely managed to get his hair wet when she was at the bathroom door, pounding.

"Petrak, I want you out here right this minute. I want you downstairs so that I can talk to you."

There was, Petrak realized, nothing he could do. Aunt Sophie had never walked in on him while he was in the shower, but he wouldn't put it past her, and he could hear that she was scorching mad. This was his fault, but it didn't make anything any better.

"Just a minute," he said.

He applied as much soap as he thought he could get away with. Then he got out from under the water, turned it off, and wrapped a towel around his middle.

He was sure he would find Aunt Sophie in the hall when he got out, but he was wrong. The hall was empty. The sound of rustling and banging was coming up from the kitchen.

Petrak went back to his room, carefully selected perfectly clean clothes so that Aunt Sophie didn't have anything extra to yell about, and got dressed.

He appeared downstairs two minutes later, wearing a black and yellow rugby shirt that was going to make him a target at school all day.

He sat down at the little round breakfast table. "Good morning," he said.

She'd had her back to him as she was working at the stove. Now she whirled around and glared, and he realized that he had spoken in Armenian without thinking about it.

"I've *told* you," she said.

"Yes," Petrak said. "Yes. I'm sorry, Aunt Sophie. I'm a little tired."

Aunt Sophie turned back to the stove. "I left a message on Mr. Donahue's answering machine. So that we can find out when Stefan will have his new hearing. They can't keep him waiting in jail forever, even if somebody did die."

"Yes," Petrak said. There didn't seem to be any point in pointing out that it wasn't just that somebody was dead, but that somebody had been murdered.

Aunt Sophie got a plate from the cabinet and put it in front of him. She got one of the frying pans from the stove and dumped a pile of scrambled eggs out of it. She got the other frying pan from the stove and offered him the bacon.

Petrak took four pieces. Aunt Sophie was apt to go on about how he ate too much, but also about how he ate too little.

When she was done serving out his food, she sat down across from him. She already had a cup of coffee. He hadn't noticed it before. She held the coffee cup entirely surrounded by her hands and said, "Well."

"Well" was not a good sign.

"I don't think we have to worry about it taking forever," Petrak said, proceeding cautiously. "I think—"

"Where did you go when you left the courtroom?"

There it was. Here was something else about Aunt Sophie. She never beat around the bush. It was one of the phrases he thought of as "speaking American."

"Petrak," Aunt Sophie said.

"I went to look for Mr. Donahue," Petrak said. "He was gone so long."

"You went where to look for Mr. Donahue?"

It took everything Petrak had not to shrug. Aunt Sophie hated shrugs.

"I went out into the vestibule where the guard was."

"And that was it? You just went there? Because that's not what I heard from the police."

Petrak pushed food around his plate. "I went out past the

guard and looked around. There was a hallway with some people in it and I went down there for a while. Not very far. I really didn't go very far."

"You were in the room with Father Tibor before I got there," Aunt Sophie said. "I heard that woman screaming and I went looking for you and then the police stopped me, and it turned out you were in the room. How did you get in the room?"

"I heard the screaming, too. I was in the hall and somebody started screaming, it was around a corner in another hall, and everybody started running for there, so I went."

"Did it occur to you at all that it might not be a good idea to go running right for there? That if somebody was screaming, it couldn't mean anything good?"

"Maybe somebody was hurt," Petrak said. "Maybe they needed help."

"I'd like to believe that was your motivation, but I don't. You do understand that that place almost certainly had security cameras, and that you've got to be on them? In the wrong place at the wrong time. And you didn't find Mr. Donahue."

"I did find Mr. Donahue," Petrak said. "He was in the room with the screaming woman and, you know—"

"The dead body," Aunt Sophie said.

"There were a lot of other people there," Petrak said. "And there were a lot of people in the hallway in no time. They just came pouring in from everywhere. Except this one guy who went out a side door. I told the police about him. I thought he could be the murderer."

"A guy who went out the side door."

"I think he went out the door. He went around the corner to one of the back hallways. He was very strange."

"Very strange," Aunt Sophie said.

"I have to go to school now," Petrak said. "I don't think you have to worry about me. I don't think the police are going to think I killed that woman. Why would I kill that woman?"

"Because she was going to send your only brother to jail?"

"Tcha," Petrak said. "Mr. Donahue said we were going to find a way to stop that. She wasn't going to send Stefan to jail. And she can't do it now anyway, and maybe we'll get a better judge."

"Petrak."

"I don't care," Petrak said. "And I did see a man, a man in a suit, and he was going away. So if the police talk to me, that's what I'm going to say. And don't say they'll think I'm lying. I'm not lying."

"You lied about Stefan being here legally," Aunt Sophie said.

Petrak got up. He had to get out. He had to go to class.

"I'll go see Mr. Donahue when I'm finished at school," he said.

Then he bolted upright, grabbed his backpack from the kitchen counter, and bolted out the door.

2

Russ Donahue hadn't slept all night. He hadn't even pretended to sleep. He lay down in bed just for a little while, feeling Donna wide awake and trying not to be restless beside him. Then he got up and went into the living room to pace.

The living room of his house took up most of the second floor, leaving the ground floor to the foyer, the kitchen, and the dining room. From the big living room window, Russ could look down on Cavanaugh Street in the dark, and count the houses and apartments of the people he knew.

He'd moved onto the street when he'd married Donna and adopted her son, Tommy. He could remember almost everything that had happened in the years since. He and Donna had their own son now. He was very happy with that, even though he knew Donna would have preferred a daughter. There should be plenty of time for daughters. Donna was young. He was young. In the ordinary course of things, even the bills would clear up, go down, get better.

He couldn't get his mind off the fact that this was not the ordinary course of things. If the worst happened, if the *very* worst happened, if Tibor were convicted of murder and sent away to prison, or sent to the electric chair—

Russ didn't know how to calculate things like that. He would say them to himself the way he did with all his clients who were in serious trouble, but instead of thinking through the options, his mind just came to a stop. He kept seeing Tibor on the floor of that room with the gavel raised over his head. The blood was everywhere. The blood was on Tibor and on himself and on the furniture and on the books in the bookshelves.

And Tibor's eyes were staring right at him, absolutely flat, absolutely expressionless, absolutely dead.

Donna came out after a while and sat down in one of the big armchairs. She was good about things like this. She didn't nag. She didn't prod. She did worry, though, and Russ could feel it.

"You can't make this all your fault," she said to him. "If he won't talk to you, he won't talk to you."

"I know," Russ said.

"He won't talk to Gregor, either. I talked to Bennis. Gregor is going crazy."

"I know," Russ said again.

"You can't do this," Donna said. "You'll make yourself sick. What if you make yourself too sick to work and then he does want to talk to you? What will happen then?"

"He won't want to talk to me," Russ said. "You didn't see him. You didn't see his eyes."

"I saw that damned video," Donna said. "I saw that."

"You can't see his eyes in the video," Russ said.

And that was true.

But it didn't matter what was true.

And when morning came, Russ left the living room and went upstairs to the master bedroom and took a shower.

If he'd expected the shower to shake him out of the mood he was in, he'd have been mistaken. But he hadn't expected any such thing. He was numb from head to foot. He thought he could stick a needle into his side and not even notice.

When he came down from showering and dressing and be-having as if nothing were the matter, Donna was waiting for him in the kitchen with a cup of coffee, a glass of orange juice, and his briefcase.

"I didn't cook anything," she said. "You're acting as if you wouldn't want it. But I will cook something. You only have to say the word."

"I'm late for the office."

Donna kissed him. Russ was sure she had. He couldn't feel it, but he saw her lean over toward his cheek. The boys were not up. That was very odd. They usually woke very early, far earlier than he did himself. Of course, they had both been very restless the night before. Tommy had watched the news, and he was smart enough to understand it. The baby was just good at picking up signals that something was wrong, and when he did, he fussed.

Russ got out of the house as quickly as he could and into his car and then downtown, down to where the traffic was. He loved the sound of the traffic. It made him feel almost instantly better. The whole world had not stopped. There were still people going places.

When he got upstairs, the receptionist was at the front desk, looking bright and blond. The secretaries were typing away in the peripheral offices. The door to Mac Cafton's office was open, and Mac was standing at the side of his desk, waiting.

Mac Cafton was Russ's almost-new partner. They'd been together for less than four years, but before that, they worked together for years in a large multi-partner firm that they had both hated. When they had decided to go out on their own, going on together seemed a better idea than trying to fly solo. It had not, however, been easy, and Mac was always on the verge of bleeding ulcers.

Mac moved toward the reception area as soon as he saw Russ come in. Russ gave up any thought of getting into his own office without a conversation.

"Hey," Mac said.

"Hey," Russ said.

"You want to come in? I've been worried about you."

The receptionist flashed him yet another big smile. Russ made himself go into Mac's office.

Mac closed the door behind him. "I have been worried about you," he said. "You were a mess when you went home yesterday and you look like you're a mess now."

"I am," Russ said. "I'm sorry. I just can't wrap my head around it."

"You can go home for the day, if you want," Mac said. "Or just hang around here and take it easy. I can handle most of what needs to be handled. I don't know how your clients will feel about having to deal with me instead of you, but we can work around that if we're careful."

Russ shook his head. "No. Thank you, but no. I've got to snap myself out of this sooner or later. Donna asked me this morning what I would do if Tibor suddenly changed his mind and wanted to see me and I was too sick to do anything about it. I suppose she had a point."

"I tried to talk to Tibor myself about an hour ago."

"Did you? How did it go?"

"No joy," Mac said. "Got told by a very polite policewoman that he wasn't interested."

"You should have expected that," Russ said. "It's not just me he isn't talking to. He wouldn't talk to a public defender, either."

"I remember, but people can be odd about this kind of thing. I thought he might not want a public defender, because he didn't want a public defender. And I thought he might not want to talk to you because he was embarrassed."

"Embarrassed?"

"I know you're convinced that he couldn't have committed that murder, but there is an awful lot of circumstantial evidence, and some that's more than circumstantial. I thought maybe he just didn't want to talk to his friends, because he wasn't ready to make explanations yet. I thought maybe he'd take me as his attorney because I was somebody he knew but not somebody he knew well."

"Okay," Russ said. "I guess that makes some kind of sense. But he wouldn't talk to you."

"He would not."

"He can't keep doing this," Russ said. "There are formalities. There will have to be an arraignment—"

"In about an hour and a half," Mac said. "At least, that's when it's on the schedule. I've had Bonnie checking. Usually the guy has a lawyer and if there are people who are concerned, they find out the whens and wheres through him, but in this case—"

"Yes," Russ said. "In this case."

"You'd better be ready for the thing to be a zoo," Mac said. "Jenn's been fielding calls from reporters all morning. I saw Cavanaugh Street on the news last night."

"I didn't watch the news last night," Russ said. "There didn't seem to be any reporters there this morning. Maybe they were chasing after Gregor."

"Are you sure you're all right?" Mac asked.

"Yes," Russ said. He even felt a little all right. Only a little, but it was better than what he'd had up to now. "I'll be fine. There has to be work I have to do, whether Tibor is talking to me or not."

"There's all this stuff about that foreclosure case we've been working on," Mac said. "Your life may feel like it's stopped, but J.P. CitiWells is a machine. And the machine is moving. Go settle in and I'll bring you the stuff we've been looking at this morning."

"Right," Russ said.

"I know it sounds impossible, but they're actually foreclosing for real this time, and I'm still sure we can prove they don't hold the mortgage."

"Right," Russ said again.

Then he went out of Mac's office and across the reception area to the door to his own office. Everything looked perfectly normal. Everything looked perfectly sane. Mikel Dekanian needed a lawyer who was paying attention if he wasn't going to end up on the street with his entire family.

But Father Tibor's arraignment was in an hour and a half, and Russ intended on being there.

3

Halfway across town, Father Tibor Kasparian lay on the long hard cement cot that was what this jail cell had for a bed and wished he had a book. It could be any book. He didn't really think he could read right now, but it always made him feel better, and calmer, and more sane, to hold a book. He had never been able to understand people who did not read. He had never been able to understand how they held on to themselves.

Breakfast had been one of those infernal breakfast sandwiches. Tibor had never understood those either. Surely, there had to be something wrong with people who ate breakfast sandwiches.

Surely there was something wrong about people like Martha Handling, but that was another kind of puzzle. Tibor was always surprised at how casual and unassuming most real evil really was. He did not mean it was "banal." It was that so much evil was done as everyday business. People did enormous harm. They made each other suffer. They destroyed any respect they could have had for themselves and for other people. And it was nothing. It was just transactions. It had the same emotional force on their brains as going grocery shopping or getting an oil change for their car.

Surely there ought to be something else there. There ought to be a little spark of protest. There ought to be *something*. But there never was.

Tibor hadn't known the truth about Martha Handling until yesterday, although he had suspected it. He had reported his suspicions to Krekor, and then to all the people Krekor recommended he talk to. In the kind of novels he read, this would have led to his own murder at the hands of the evil corporation that was paying the bribes that were making Martha Handling do all those awful things.

But that hadn't happened, any more than what he had really expected to happen. The case was not immediately taken up by the authorities. Martha Handling was not immediately suspended from the bench.

As far as Tibor could see, nothing had happened.

Except this.

A policewoman came to the door and looked in through the small window. "Father Kasparian?" she said. "If you would please put your hands behind your back and then put them through the slot so that I can access your wrists."

Tibor got up and did as he was told. He found all these things they did to be—hyperbolic? He couldn't think of the English word. The American justice system, at least in Philadelphia, seemed to treat all prisoners as if they were dangerous animals.

The handcuffs went on. They bit him, as always. Tibor stepped away from the door and turned to face it just as the policewoman was giving him those same instructions.

The policewoman put her key in the lock and opened up. "You're due in court, Father Kasparian. We need to get you ready."

"Ready?"

"The van is already waiting," the policewoman said. "You'll be going outside, so you'll need leg irons. We've been told you won't need a jacket. We're having a very warm fall."

Tibor had no idea what to say to that. He moved along the corridor at the policewoman's side. Prisoners came to the doors of the cells along the way and looked out at them.

Everybody was bored. Everybody was mind-numbingly, intransigently bored. Maybe this was true everywhere in the system. Maybe the prisoners on death row did not have their minds wonderfully concentrated, but were only bored.

"If you'll kneel with your back to me on the bench, Father Kasparian. I'm told they've got a lawyer waiting for you at the court. You want a lawyer, Father Kasparian, even if you think you don't."

Tibor knelt on the bench and stared at the beige-painted concrete wall. The leg irons did not bite the way the handcuffs did, because he was wearing socks, and the socks kept the metal away from his skin.

That was the hardest thing to get used to.

The metal against his skin.

SIX

1

It was George Edelson who took Gregor across town in a city car, bumping through traffic with a speed and unpredictability that would have been terrifying if the streets had been entirely clear.

"The idea is that I'm already in as much trouble as it's possible for me to get into, so you might as well be seen with me as with anybody," George Edelson said. "And this is convenient. The juvenile court is only about a block away from where your Father Kasparian is going to be arraigned, and we assumed you'd want to be on hand for that."

"I definitely want to be on hand for that," Gregor said.

Privately, he thought the arraignment would be a good place to jump the gates and throttle Tibor where he stood. Tibor needed to be throttled. Even if he was guilty. Especially if he was guilty.

George Edelson was pulling into a tiny parking lot behind an enormous granite building.

"We're going to talk to a man named Sam Scalafini. He runs the security operations for all the court buildings in Philadelphia. At the moment, he's going to be lucky if he doesn't get fired. So I'm assuming he's going to cooperate."

"Security," Gregor said.

"Think security cameras," George Edelson said. "In the courts, as in practically every other place these days, there are security cameras."

They got out of the car and went to a small back door.

A tiny Latina policewoman was standing just inside it. When she saw George Edelson, she nodded and opened up. "Good morning, Mr. Edelson."

"Good morning, Betta. Is the court still closed?"

"For one more day, yes, sir. We tried to find some way we could open it partially, but there just isn't any way to secure all the possible entries to the crime scene."

"What about the cameras?"

Betta snorted. "I think they're working on it."

"They'd better be," George Edelson said.

He took Gregor down a corridor, around a corner, and then to a door that led to a staircase.

"Operations in the basement," he said. "We've had to retrofit all these old buildings. You wouldn't want to give them up. We'll never get architecture like this again. Watch your step. The public doesn't come down here, and neither do the judges. Well, except Martha Handling. She came down here often enough. Anyway, it's the last place to get repaired."

The stairs seemed to be in perfectly good repair, but the basement to which they led was a little . . . dank. It wasn't so bad that the walls were sweating, but it smelled rank, and it felt oppressive.

There were halls down here, too, but they were made of paste-board and stood on rollers. George Edelson crashed around them as if they weren't likely to fall over or skitter into the distance at any slight tap.

Gregor saw the big bank of screens before he saw or heard a person. A moment later, a head popped up and a thick man with dark hair waved at them.

"Sam!" George Edelson said, sounding sarcastic.

"I'm *working* on it," Sam said. "No matter what you guys think, it's not my fault if a sitting judge is a world-class nutcase who goes and gets herself murdered. I hope she's satisfied wherever she is right now. We told her it was for her own protection."

Gregor and George rounded the final gauntlet of pasteboard partitions and came to Sam Scalafini and his big bank of controls. Scalafini did not get up. His shirt was so tight across his upper body, it looked like his collar was strangling him. Gregor pegged him as someone who would not get up for anything short of a major natural disaster.

George Edelson did not sit, although there were chairs available. "Gregor Demarkian," he said. "This is Sam Scalafini."

"Yeah," Sam Scalafini said.

"Sam's going to tell you what he told us," George said. "About why we don't have viable security camera footage of the events preceding the murder of Martha Handling yesterday. Because, you know, keeping a viable security tape record of the events that go on in the courthouses is just, well, Sam's job."

"Fuck you," Sam Scalafini said. "And I apologize to Mr. Demarkian if he doesn't like the language. And I'll say it again. It's not my fault if there's a sitting judge who's a nutcase. Because that woman was a nutcase. And George here knows it."

"You're talking about Martha Handling," Gregor said. "She was a nutcase how?"

"A nutcase about security cameras," Sam Scalafini said. He let his hands flutter in the air. "Look, they all have a thing about security cameras. The judges and the lawyers both. They've all got a bug up their asses about confidentiality. We were going to put in microphones a few years ago, and the entire frigging bar had a hissy fit."

"Of course they did," Gregor said. "You can't record conferences between lawyers and clients, that's—"

"Yeah, yeah, yeah," Scalafini said. "That's all supposed to be secret. It's frigging insane, if you ask me. You should see the people we get in here. Juveniles, too. Anyway, they didn't want sound, they didn't get sound. The problem with Martha Frigging Handling is that she didn't want anything. The first big issue was her chambers, and that was enough to make us all nuts. There never were any cameras in the chambers themselves. We didn't even try that one. But she wouldn't believe us. No matter how many times we told her, she wouldn't believe us. I even took her down here a couple of times and showed her there weren't any images coming up from anybody's chambers. She just thought I was hiding something from her. A secret command post. That's what she called it."

"Martha Handling was an interesting person," George Edelson said blandly.

"She came down here and looked around on her own a couple of times," Scalafini said. "I found her creeping around. Gave me the frigging willies, let me tell you."

"I didn't think that tape came from security cameras," Gregor said.

"If you mean the tape of Father Kasparian, ah," George said, "ah, wielding the gavel—no, it didn't. For one thing—"

"There was sound," Gregor said.

"Exactly," George said. "But Sam's got more to tell us—don't you, Sam?"

Sam looked like he was ready to kill somebody. "Ms. Handling didn't like cameras anywhere," he said. "She didn't like them in the hallways. She didn't like them outside at the door or in the parking lot. She tried to get us to take them all down. And when she couldn't get away with that—"

"Even the defense attorneys weren't okay with that," George said.

"When she couldn't get away with that, she started 'fixing the problem' herself. She'd come in really early before anybody was here, take a can of black spray paint, and go walking around spraying the lenses. She made a mess, too, because the paint would drip. And drip. And drip."

"Spray paint," Gregor said.

"We kept catching her at it," Sam Scalafini said. "We kept seeing her—"

"But not at the time, Sam," George Edelson said. "You should have been looking at those damned monitors, and you should have been able to catch her in the act."

"I can't be six places at once," Sam said. "And sometimes there were issues."

"He means that sometimes one of the cameras went down and he didn't fix it immediately," George said. "Because he had issues."

"You can go crap yourself, George, you really can," Sam said.

"If I crap, Sam, it's not going to be on myself, it's going to be on you."

"Let me see if I understand this," Gregor said. "Martha Handling hated security cameras, so she would spray-paint the lenses. But didn't you clean them off? Even if you missed her in the act, you must have noticed that something was wrong with the pictures on your screen."

"Yeah," Sam Scalafini said. "We did sort of notice it."

"The first time," George Edelson said.

"George, for crap's sake. I did something about it the first six times it happened at least, and you know it. It's just that she was always checking, and you guys were being no help. I'm working security, for crap's sake. You know as well as I do that I can't go hauling off against a judge. It would have been my ass. And nobody would have been yelling about how I did the right thing, either."

"You could have cleaned the damned lenses off," George said. "Not the first time. Not the first six times. Every time."

"Yeah, and then what? Then a whole crapload of stuff wouldn't have gotten done and I'd've heard about that. And don't you think I wouldn't've." Sam turned to Gregor Demarkian. "She'd go around with the spray paint can. And there are lots of security cameras, so we'd get tape of her doing it. She'd cover about six of the things and then she'd go back to her chambers and go searching through it for cameras. Except it's like I said, there weren't any in there. After a while, I mean, what the fuck? We knew who was doing it. She wasn't going to go rob somebody or set a bomb off in the court or something. It wasn't a priority. It's damned hard to get spray paint off those lenses."

"Coffee breaks were a priority," George Edelson said.

Sam Scalafini flipped the bird. "You know what, George? You can kiss my ass."

"Let me just try to get this straight," Gregor said. "There's no security camera footage of what, exactly?"

"Of anybody going through the hallways leading from the back door, the one we just came through, to Martha Handling's chambers. And none from the hall leading from where Martha Handling's chambers are to the hall that leads to the front foyer."

"Okay," Gregor said. "So, there's a front foyer. There are security cameras there."

"Right," George said.

"And then," Gregor said, "there's some kind of corridor you can go down, and then—what? You make a turn? And when you make that turn, that's the corridor Martha Handling's chambers are on."

"Right," Sam said.

"So," Gregor said. "There are security cameras on the hall that leads from the foyer to the corridor that leads to the chambers, but the lenses on the cameras were blacked out on the foyer that leads to the chambers. But they were not covered in that first hallway."

"The last one before the end was," Sam Scalafini said. "You never knew how far Martha—Judge Handling was going to be willing to go. It changed."

"But wasn't there a security guard on duty?" Gregor said. "Shouldn't somebody have been patrolling the halls—?"

"Yes!" George Edelson said brightly. "Shouldn't someone?"

"Frigging A," Sam Scalafini said.

"The point of security is to provide security," George Edelson said. "That's why we have security. There is no point to a security system that is run for the benefit of people taking coffee breaks,

running out to pick up sandwiches at the all-night deli, not showing up at all and still mysteriously being signed in. Do you want
me to go on, Sam? Because I can go on all night."

"Frigging asshole," Sam said.

"I may be an asshole, Sam, but you're just one more train
wreck in the story of corruption in Philadelphia politics. Hell.
You ought to be in the Corruption Hall of Fame."

2

Gregor waited until they got down the street and into the other
courthouse before asking any of the obvious questions.

"You can't tell me," Gregor said, "with a straight face, that
that man has a chance in hell of holding on to his job after—
what was all that, exactly? Corruption? What was he corrupting?
He wasn't doing his job, that I can see, but—"

"The only reason he isn't already out of the building is the civil
service rules. John is on the warpath. Scalafini will be out on his
ear and worse before close of business today," George Edelson
said. "My God, have you any idea how hard John has worked, for
years, to clean up the mess in this city? And now this. Some two-
bit, punk-assed—"

The courtroom they were entering was one of the modern
ones, with the judge's bench backed by a flat wooden wall with
symbols on it meant to stand in for the old formalities of a court.
Gregor preferred the old Depression-era stone-and-solemnity architecture, the kind Bennis called "socialist humorlessness." They
might be humorless, but they gave the impression that somebody
was taking the law seriously.

The spectator's seats in the courtroom were not packed, but they weren't empty, either. People sat scattered, but in little clumps. There was a clutch of young men who looked both belligerent and already defeated. There was an elderly African American couple holding on to each other, the woman crying soundlessly with her head against the man's breast.

There was also Bennis, and Donna, and Lida Arkmanian.

"I think we should be over there," Gregor said, pointing to the three women. Bennis looked as belligerent as the clutch of young men, but not in any way defeated.

George Edelson let Gregor lead him to a pair of seats just behind the women.

"John had half the office going at it all last night," George said. "Scalafini has been passing out jobs to relatives like they were candy. Nobody was doing any actual work that we can see. And he's got to have somebody on the inside in human resources, and we haven't found that person yet. And the worst thing is, if this hadn't come up, we might never have found it. No, that's not true. Something as bad as this was going to come up sometime. John's ready to take his chances on justifiable homicide."

"So," Gregor said, "does that mean there aren't any usable pictures from the security cameras? We can't tell who was or wasn't in the hall?"

"We've got some blurry stuff. Sometimes the spray job was a little out of whack. She was a short woman and her aim wasn't always accurate. But she was doing it time after time. She wasn't even really checking to see if they'd been cleaned. She just brought the can and zapped them. But there's blurry stuff. We'll give you a copy of all that we have. And then there's the hall that leads to the hall. The last camera there was spray-painted, but none of the ones leading to the foyer was, so we've got all of that clear."

"But that's good," Gregor said. "We've got something then, we know who went into the hall that would at least lead him to the murder scene."

"Not exactly," George Edelson said. "At the end of that hall is where the restrooms are. Everybody and his brother went down that hall. And the usable footage stops just before you can tell who was going into the restrooms and who was making the turn into the next corridor."

"And I take it very few people *didn't* go down that hall," Gregor said.

"Half the population of Philadelphia went down that corridor," George Edelson said.

All three of the women had turned around. They were waiting patiently for the conversation to be over. Lida Arkmanian was not going to be patient much longer.

Gregor made the introductions.

"It's nice to meet you," Bennis said to George Edelson in her best Main Line debutante voice. Then she turned to Gregor. "Do not get started," she said. "It's a public hearing. Donna called Russ and asked about it. If it's a public hearing, we can be here."

"It's very important to let him know he has our support," Lida said. "Even if he thinks he doesn't want it. Even if, even if he did something—" She started to tear up.

Donna patted her on the shoulder. "He hasn't done anything," Donna said firmly, "except somehow get himself involved in a mess somebody else created. Just you wait. Gregor will figure it all out."

"It's definitely a public hearing, and I'm not in the least upset that the three of you are here," Gregor said. "If I'd thought of it, I'd have had you bring half the membership of the church. I'm for putting as much pressure on him as possible. He's going to have to start talking to somebody sometime. It would be better sooner rather than later."

The big swinging double doors at the back of the courtroom opened, and after a bit of shuffling Tibor came in, handcuffed and shackled, dressed in a jail uniform, and flanked by two guards. Gregor saw Bennis tear up and then push the tears back by sheer force of will.

"I thought they didn't allow that anymore," she said. "I thought the Supreme Court said the defendant had to be in ordinary clothes."

"That's for the jury trial," George Edelson said helpfully. "The court was afraid that prison clothes would prejudice the jury. They're prejudiced enough as it is, if you ask me."

Tibor did not turn to look at them. He stared straight ahead until he got to the defense table. A young, harried-looking man was sitting there. Gregor assumed he was from Legal Aid or the Public Defender's Office. Tibor sat down next to him and shook his head.

"What's that?" Bennis demanded.

"My guess is that Tibor is refusing the services of yet another attorney," Gregor said.

"He turned me down yesterday," George Edelson said.

"He should have Russ," Donna said. "He's always had Russ for everything. He's got to know he can trust Russ no matter what's going on."

"He couldn't trust Russ to plead him guilty to something he's not guilty of," Gregor said. "And he couldn't trust Russ to hide anything that the court needs to know."

"Do you think he's going to plead guilty?" Bennis asked. "Do you think he'd really do something like that?"

"There isn't a deal on the table," George Edelson said. "And it's a capital murder case."

Lida Arkmanian blanched.

Gregor explained. "Most judges won't let a defendant plead guilty to a capital murder charge if there isn't a deal on the table to forgo the death penalty. You don't want—"

The bailiff was suddenly at the front of the court, droning out a string of words and numbers that went by without Gregor being able to take them in.

Then the bailiff said, "All rise," and everybody stood up.

The judge who walked in from behind the bench was an older man, tall and broad but also a little stooped. The bailiff announced him as "the Honorable Roger Maris Oldham presiding."

The judge sat down. Everybody else sat down.

Bennis turned around and leaned as close to Gregor's ear as she could get. "I know him," she said. "He went to school with Bobby and Chris. Not that he could stand either of them, mind you, because he was Dudley Do-Right and they definitely weren't."

"He's very fair," George Edelson said.

The bailiff was glaring at them. He'd already read out a stream of numbers and case codes. Gregor gestured at Bennis frantically. He did not want them all removed from court.

Bennis turned forward again. Roger Maris Oldham leaned over the bench and asked, "Is that Mr. Hernandez? You're appearing for the defendant?"

Mr. Hernandez stood up. "Excuse me, Your Honor. I don't know that I am."

The judge got a half-bemused, half-furious look on his face. "Well, Mr. Hernandez," he said. "You were sitting at the defense table. You rose to talk to me from the defense table. On most occasions, those would be clear indications that you were speaking on behalf of the defendant."

"Yes, Your Honor. I did come here this morning to speak on behalf of the defendant. But Mr.—Father Kasparian has indicated to me since I got here that he does not want me to appear on his behalf."

The judge sat back. "I've been hearing about this all day yesterday," he said, "but I wasn't sure I believed it. Sit down, Mr. Hernandez. Father Kasparian, if you would please rise."

Tibor stood up. Gregor spent a useless moment trying to gauge his mood. There didn't appear to be any mood to gauge.

"Father Kasparian," the judge said, "you are within your rights, of course, to serve as your own counsel, and to defend yourself. I will say that I find the idea of doing so in a capital case to be completely insane. You may be a very intelligent man. You may be justifiably convinced of your own innocence. But the law is not a game. There are no automatic do-overs if you get things wrong. And if you get things wrong in this matter, the consequences could be literally a matter of life or death. Do you still insist that you want to act as your own counsel?"

"Yes, Your Honor," Tibor said.

"Very well, then," the judge said. "But I want to tell you something else. I have heard all about your behavior since your arrest yesterday, and I want you to understand, without ambiguity, that I will not stand for it here. This is an arraignment. It is not enough

123

for you to stand on the Fifth Amendment here. Nobody is denying your right to refuse to incriminate yourself. Such right notwithstanding, you are required to enter a plea to this charge. Do you understand that?"

"Yes, Your Honor."

"The charge is one of capital murder, willful murder in the first degree. The State will contend that you did willfully and with malice aforethought bring about the death of the Honorable Martha Handling on the ninth of September in this year. Do you know what that means?"

"Yes, Your Honor," Tibor said.

"Is there any reason for this court to be concerned about your ability to speak and understand that English language? Do you need an interpreter?"

"No, Your Honor. I have lived in Philadelphia for many years. I am competent both in speaking and understanding English."

"All right," the judge said. "Then we'll begin. Please sit down, Father Kasparian. If the attorney for the Commonwealth will please rise."

The attorney who rose from the prosecution table was not somebody Gregor recognized, but it hardly mattered. He kept staring at Tibor's back. Now that he was seeing Tibor in person, this whole thing made even less sense than it had when he'd only heard about it.

Gregor wasn't sure how he would have expected Tibor to behave if he'd actually been guilty of a murder, but this was not it. The problem was, it wasn't the way he'd have expected Tibor to behave if he had been wrongly accused, either. The back was straight and unbending and without a hint of compromise. Tibor's voice, when he spoke, was dead flat and without affect.

The attorney for the Commonwealth had sat down. Tibor was standing up again.

The judge said, "You have heard the charges against you. How do you plead?"

Bennis sat forward on her chair, tensed. Gregor couldn't help himself. He sat forward, too.

Tibor's back did not bend or shake, or even stoop. His voice, when it came, was clear and almost without accent.

"If it please the court," he said. "I plead nolo contendere."

PART TWO

ONE

1

There were reporters in the court. Of course there were. Gregor didn't know why he hadn't thought of it before. Cameras were barred, except by special permission of the judge, but reporters came in like the rest of the public, and there was no chance they would have skipped this particular arraignment.

It wasn't only the reporters who were making a fuss, however. They were restricting themselves to scribbling furiously on notepads. The guard at the door had collected cell phones, probably to ensure that there were no phone pictures of the arraignment.

Lida Arkmanian didn't need a cell phone to cause a disturbance, and although Bennis and Donna were better, they weren't exactly quiet.

"What does it *mean*?" Lida wailed, and kept wailing, minute after minute, while the judge brought his gavel down over and over again.

Gregor tried not to think of what that gavel pounding reminded him of.

Bennis turned around and said, "He can't do that, can he? He can't plead nolo contendere to a murder charge."

"For God's sake," George Edelson said. "What the hell does he think he's doing?"

That last thing was the most important question. If Gregor could have gotten close enough to Tibor to shake him, he'd have asked it himself.

The judge's gavel started to do some good. The crowd began to quiet down. Gregor realized the bailiff was bellowing, and hadn't been heard over the rest of the din. The judge looked as if his patience had been tried, found wanting, and thrown in a ditch.

"Watch out," George Edelson said. "I think the excrement is about to hit the fan."

The judge waited until the courtroom was entirely quiet. Then he looked at Father Tibor and said, "Father Kasparian, do you have any idea what you're talking about? Do you know what nolo contendere means?"

"Yes, Your Honor."

"Fine," the judge said. "Explain it to me."

Gregor had no doubt that Tibor knew what the phrase meant, but, like the judge, he wondered what the man was trying to do. It would help if Tibor would show some emotion. Instead, his back was straight, his voice was colorless, and he was calmer than anybody else in the room.

"To plead nolo contendere," Tibor said, "means that I acknowledge that the police have enough evidence to arrest me, and the prosecution has enough evidence to convict me, but I do not plead guilty, and I do not admit to any guilt."

The judge sat staring for a while. He was as clear of emotion as Tibor had been—except, Gregor thought, that he looked interested.

"Do you understand, Father Kasparian, that you are here charged with capital murder? That as a capital case, the result of a conviction, by whatever means, could result in the death penalty?"

"Yes," Tibor said.

"Did I notice a little hesitation, Father Kasparian? Because if I were in your position, I'd be showing a great deal of hesitation right now."

"I am not hesitating," Tibor said.

"Are you prepared to be executed?" the judge said.

This time, Tibor did hesitate. "From my understanding," he said, "it is not usually the case that men are executed in this state except after a jury trial."

The judge suddenly seemed to unwind. "Ah," he said. "I see. You hope that by entering such a plea, you will avoid a death penalty that might be imposed after a trial."

"No," Tibor said.

"No? But you just said that was what you were doing."

"Please excuse me, Your Honor," Tibor said. "You asked me if I was prepared to be executed. I only said that, as I understand it, that would not be a plausible outcome for this kind of plea."

"And you're willing to trust in the plausibilities?"

"I think it is too early to think about it."

The judge stared over his desk at Tibor. The stare went on for a long time, second after second. For once, everybody in the courtroom was absolutely silent.

Then the judge leaned even farther toward Tibor, so far that his body stretched almost across the desk. "Father Kasparian," the judge said, "I have no idea where you heard about the plea of nolo contendere. You're not a lawyer, you're not even willing to speak to a lawyer. But a lawyer could have told you what I'm going to tell you now, and saved both of us a lot of trouble. I will not accept a plea of nolo contendere in this case. It is not a proper plea to the charges here made, and would not be acceptable to any judge in any court in the Commonwealth of Pennsylvania. I will ask you now, one more time, to enter a proper plea to these charges before this court. Guilty or not guilty, Father Kasparian. Take your pick."

Tibor seemed to sway a little. "I have the right to remain silent," he said finally.

"I've told you before, Father Kasparian. You do not have the right to remain silent in the matter of a plea. Guilty or not guilty, Father Kasparian?"

Tibor stood where he was, not budging.

"All right, then," the judge said. "I hereby enter a plea in this case of not guilty."

"I have not said it, Your Honor," Tibor said.

"It doesn't matter if you've said it or not," the judge said. "A plea must be entered, and I cannot enter a guilty plea for you. But here's what I can do: I am recommending to the court that will try you that your right to represent yourself be revoked. It is my considered judgment that you're either incompetent to represent yourself or attempting an elaborate maneuver to evade justice. Whichever one it is, you won't be getting away with it any longer. The plea in this case has been entered as not guilty. This hearing is over. Gentlemen, please return Father Kasparian to his jail cell. Maybe if he sits in it long enough, he'll appreciate the wisdom of getting himself a lawyer to get himself out of it."

And then, just like that, it was over. The bailiff said, "All rise." The judge and everybody else rose for a single ceremonious second. Then Tibor was handcuffed again and led out of the room in shackles.

"For God's sake," George Edelson said again.

"Gregor, what's going *on* here?" Bennis demanded.

"Out in the hall," Gregor said.

They all trooped out into the front foyer, passing other people coming in, another prisoner being led through in handcuffs and shackles. Gregor made a quick look around, but Tibor was already gone.

"Gregor, you can't just keep shutting me up," Bennis said. "What just happened in there? What in the name of hell is going on?"

"He got that judge angry," Donna said. "I could see it. It can't be a good idea to get the judge angry."

"Gregor, there's got to be some explanation for what he's doing. Either that, or he's gone completely insane," Bennis said. "I think he's going completely insane. What could that possibly have been in aid of?"

"He couldn't have thought he was going to get away with that," George Edelson said. "Not if he's got half a brain in his head. I've met him. He's got half a brain in his head."

Gregor stood still in the eddy of people that moved continuously and never went anywhere. The alarm bells that had been going off in his head since this whole thing started were now on full alert. It wasn't just that something was wrong. It was that something was very, very wrong and getting wronger by the minute.

"I don't think he knew what was going to happen when he did that," Gregor said. "I think he was taking a shot."

"But why?" Bennis demanded.

Gregor didn't know.

2

Out on the courthouse steps, Gregor Demarkian tried to tear his mind away from what had gone on in the courtroom to figure out what he ought to do next. It was not so easy to know as it ought to have been. Gregor had been investigating murders of one kind or another for decades. He understood procedures and the need for them. He understood that every investigation required an order, and that there were very few orders to choose from.

In this case, no order seemed to be available. He wasn't imposing any. The police, as far as he could tell now, weren't imposing any. And no order was arising spontaneously from the evidence so far.

Everything was just lying around in a jumble.

It was cold on the courthouse steps. Gregor found himself wishing for a coat. Bennis was shivering, but she never wore one.

"Well," she said. "Now what are we going to do? We promised to go back to the street and tell everybody about everything, but what are we going to say? Hannah Krekorian is going to have another attack of the vapors. And that's just to start."

"We're supposed to have lunch at the Ararat," Donna said miserably.

Lida Arkmanian was not shivering. She was wearing the same three-quarter-length chinchilla coat she wore everywhere, winter and summer, no matter what. Gregor didn't know if it was more surprising that she had never collapsed from heat poisoning, or that she had never been doused with paint by animal rights activists.

"We'll just have to tell them what happened," Lida said. "Maybe one of them will think of something we haven't. Maybe one of them will be able to make sense of it."

"We went to school with Hannah Krekorian," Gregor said. "Has she ever made sense out of anything?"

"Maybe not," Lida admitted.

"Well, we've got to get back, whatever else we do," Bennis said. "They're all probably sitting there at the Ararat waiting. They're going to think there's been a shooting or something. Linda Melajian is going to be checking the news every twenty seconds."

"The news," Donna said. "Do you think this is going to be on the news? What will they say?"

"This is going to be all over the news everywhere," Bennis said. "We'd better give up any thought of getting away from it. For all I know, the news vans are going to be back on Cavanaugh Street, and I don't think Linda can keep reporters out of the Ararat. Maybe we should give Hannah a call and have her bring everybody over to our place so we can talk in private."

"I've got a bigger living room," Lida said.

"I've got to call Russ," Donna said. "He's a lawyer. He'll know all about this 'nolo' thing and whatever it's supposed to mean—"

"Nolo contendere," Bennis said. "No contest."

"The judge tried to explain it," George Edelson put in helpfully.

The women turned to look at him in a way that made it clear they'd forgotten he was there.

"I'm sorry," Lida said automatically. "We did hear the explanation, but I for one am very stupid."

"You're not being stupid," Gregor said.

They all stood there for a minute, then, awkward.

Finally, Bennis shook herself back to an operational mode. "I'll go get the car," she said. "I'll pick you two up in a minute and we can talk on the way back. But you know what I'd like to know? Why would Tibor have wanted to kill this woman anyway? I mean, why would he have bothered?"

"But we know that," Donna said. "She's the judge who's always sending children to juvenile jail even for small things and sentencing them to years when any other judge would have given them probation, and Stefan Maldovanian was one of his personal projects and he thought Martha Handling was going to send him to jail and have him deported over—"

"Stop for a minute," Bennis said. "Does that make any sense to you? I mean, really. Why go to all that trouble over an issue like that? What would he have expected to get out of it?"

"Well—" Donna looked puzzled. "Well," she said again, "maybe he hoped that, with this Judge Handling gone, Stefan Maldovanian would be assigned to another judge, and that judge wouldn't be so harsh."

"And for that he'd have killed the woman?" Bennis said.

"Maybe he was just very angry," Lida said. "That thing, that video, he was pounding and pounding and when I saw it, I thought he might be very angry, he might have lost his temper because of something this woman said, or—"

Lida stopped. She looked puzzled, too.

"Exactly," Bennis said triumphantly. "I know we all hate looking at that damned clip, but I spent hours looking at it this morning and if you do the same, you'll see the same. It's not just that Tibor never loses his temper, although he never loses his temper. It's that he's not angry in that clip. He isn't. He's supposed to be pounding away at someone's head, but he's acting like he's pounding a nail into a two-by-four. He's not angry. He's not even upset. He's just doing it."

"But he couldn't do that," Donna said. "He couldn't pound in somebody's head just calm and collected like that."

"Then maybe he isn't pounding somebody's head in," Bennis said. "As everybody keeps mentioning and then forgetting, there's no sign of a head in that clip, except for Tibor's. Maybe he's pounding something else."

"But," George Edelson said.

Bennis had her keys out of her oversized shoulder bag. "No buts," she said firmly. "There isn't a ghost of an idea of why Tibor would have wanted to kill that woman in the first place. And as far as I can tell, not a single person, not even Gregor and Russ, have suggested a possible motive. Never mind a plausible one."

"Interesting," Gregor said.

"I'm always interesting," Bennis said. "You two stay still. I'll have the car here in a second." Then she took off down the courthouse steps to the street.

3

Gregor and George Edelson waited until Bennis came around to pick up Lida and Donna, and while they did, they said not much of anything about anything. Lida and Donna seemed exhausted by the subject. Gregor didn't blame them. The wind was picking up. Lida kept wrapping her coat more tightly around her chest.

When Bennis had come and the women had gone, Gregor turned to George Edelson.

"You know," he said, "Bennis is right. There isn't a plausible motive."

"Motives don't have to be that plausible when we have something like that clip," George said. "And I don't know what to make of that thing about Father Kasparian not looking angry on it. I mean, maybe he did or maybe he didn't, but it's hard to tell anything on those phone videos."

The two men started walking down the steps to the street.

"Let's let that go for the moment," Gregor said. "Do you know what I think is strange? We've been talking all day, I talked to everybody except Tibor yesterday, everybody on the Cavanaugh Street end. We talked about the clip. We talked about who saw what in the corridor and the judge's chambers. You and John and I talked about what I could and couldn't get away with making a private investigation of this murder. But none of us, not once, ever talked about Martha Handling, except for the security guard—"

"Sam Scalafini."

"Sam Scalafini," Gregor repeated. "My point still stands. People don't get murdered out of the blue. There's almost always a reason for it. And the reason is almost always either part of the person's character or part of his situation. Her situation, in this case. Does Tibor, or anybody, bludgeoning a person to death because she might send a kid to do a lot of juvenile jail time make sense to you?"

"It would with a certain kind of person," George Edelson said. "I've seen a lot of rage in my time. Rage can do amazing things."

"I'm going to have to look at the clip again," Gregor said, "but

I think Bennis is right. I think Tibor isn't showing any rage in that clip."

"It's like I said," George said.

"I know," Gregor agreed. "There's only so much you can tell from a phone video. Did you find the phone the video had been made on?"

"I don't think so," George Edelson said. "I've got a bunch of notes in my briefcase that I'm supposed to give you before we're done. And we're going over to Homicide, and they know all that."

"But it was a phone video?" Gregor asked. "It wasn't a security tape."

"No, we told you," George said, "there aren't any cameras in the judge's chambers."

"So now we've got another problem," Gregor said. "Assuming that is a clip of Tibor murdering Martha Handling, then not only was Tibor murdering Martha Handling, but somebody was standing by recording it. If Tibor was in some kind of frenzy, he might not have noticed that. But what about the person making the video? Why wasn't that person running off somewhere to call for the police?"

"All right, yes," George Edelson said. "That occurred to us. Lots of us. Homicide, too."

"I take it the police have checked the phones of the people found in the chambers when they got there, at least?"

"The clip didn't come out until a couple of hours after—after. The cops didn't even know about it when they sent everybody home."

"So the police haven't looked at them?"

"No, not that," George said. "They did get onto it—it's just that it had been a while. And they're checking it out. But if they came in the front door, their phones would have been confiscated. And most of them came in the front door. We do have security tape footage of that."

"Of course," Gregor said, "given a couple of hours, someone who understood how those things worked could have deleted the video from the phone."

"Those things are retrievable," George said.

"With some work, an expert, and a court order," Gregor said. "Well, you shouldn't have too much trouble getting the court order. And assuming the person who took the video didn't just throw his phone away. And assuming that the person who took the video is one of the people who was found in and around the judge's chambers when the police got there. Do you see why it's so important to understand the victim?"

"Understanding the victim will tell us who took the phone video?"

"Maybe," Gregor said.

They had walked down the street some ways, and Gregor saw they were standing across from the courthouse where the murder had taken place. People were going in and out of it. It was not entirely shut down. There were extra police on the steps and at the door, and Gregor was sure that if he went inside, he would find the corridors leading to the judges' chambers blocked off in all directions. He could just imagine how the other judges were taking that.

"I'm surprised the police didn't shut down the whole building," he said to George.

George shrugged. "They shut it down yesterday," he said. "Then they spent the whole night in there. You want to go back and talk to Sam again?"

"Not now, no. Did you know Martha Handling? Personally?"

"Everybody in city government knew Martha, more or less," George said. "I didn't know her well, if that's what you mean."

"Did you know her well enough to tell me if Sam Scalafini's description of her was correct?"

"You mean about her being crazy?" George said. "I don't think I'd have said crazy as much as I'd have said bitch. I knew about the thing with the security cameras, though. Everybody knew about it. The first three or four times she pulled it, Scalafini got in touch with the mayor's office and we looked into it. I got sent down to tell her that her chambers had no security cameras in it and the other security cameras were none of her business."

"And?"

"And," George said, "*she* gave *me* a lecture on how she knew what we were up to and how we couldn't fool her no matter how hard we tried and how she had ways to make us look bad, and on and on and on."

"That sounds like Scalafini's description."

"I guess," George said. "It was just—less Looney Tunes and more Axis of Evil, I guess. She really was a bitch, Mr. Demarkian. A world-class, down-to-the-bone bitch. And that's before you even consider the possibility that there was corruption going on. That she was selling out to Administrative Solutions of America."

"But," Gregor said, "you haven't proved the allegations of corruption as of yet."

"No," George said. "We keep thinking we're getting close, and the feds keep thinking we're getting close, but it all keeps sort of falling apart. There's enough on the table now to be pretty sure that something was going on, but we can't nail just what. Or maybe not. Because that's another aspect of this. I can't help thinking that it might have been something else."

"Like what?"

"Like sheer mean," George said. "She really, really, really was a bitch, Mr. Demarkian. She set out to hurt the hell out of people. In little things as well as big ones. And for no discernible reason. If she knew you were vulnerable somewhere, she went right at you. She even went after John."

"John? I wouldn't think John had a lot of vulnerable points by now," Gregor said.

"I wouldn't have either," George said. "And I didn't get the reference. Something about a woman, I think, but I didn't ask and I'm not going to. Anyway, John is not your standard victim. He let her have it, and as far as I know, she never tried anything on him again. But it goes to show, if you get my meaning here. The woman couldn't keep an assistant for a year, and even the ones that lasted a year were few and far between."

"And somehow this means she was less likely to be involved in corruption than otherwise?"

"Not that she'd be less likely to be involved in corruption," George said, "just that the long sentences she kept giving those kids are less likely to be proof of anything except how unbelievably vile she was. She always gave harsher sentences than anybody else, even before we had privatized prisons."

"As long as the ones she'd been giving after we got privatized prisons?"

"I don't know off the top of my head," George said. "But if I were going to go after somebody to bribe, Martha Handling would be the one. With other people, if they started to give out those long sentences, you'd be surprised. But nobody would be surprised with Martha. It would just look like business as usual."

"You said we had an appointment to see people at Homicide?"

"Yeah," George said. "We do. Are you feeling all right? You look kind of funny."

TWO

1

Janice Loftus was as angry as she had ever been in her life, so angry that she was having a hard time keeping it from affecting her teaching. Janice didn't believe in anger, any more than she believed in hate. They were useless emotions. They cluttered up your life. They imprisoned you in the past and cut you off from the future.

Today, though, no matter what they did, Janice found it impossible to keep clear of them. She was beginning to wonder if she had somehow become trapped in the patriarchal paradigm. Aggressive emotions were always patriarchal. Women were oriented toward cooperation, the way all oppressed peoples were, and they were now living in a world where only cooperation would work.

But there was no cooperation, not from anybody. Even Kasey Holbrook was not cooperating, and that was her job.

"I want you to stay out of it," Kasey had said yesterday, when Janice had been trying like mad to make her make sense. "This is a murder case. It's a spectacular murder case. It's all over the news. It's going to be all over the national news in no time flat. It wouldn't be good for the organization and it wouldn't be good for you to be right in the middle of it."

Janice had begun to feel her head throb, right then and there.

"But we can't pretend I'm not in the middle of it," she said. "I found the body, everybody knows that. I was interviewed on the local news. They'll play it over and over again."

"That's no reason for you to make your part bigger than it has to be," Kasey said. "All I'm saying is to lie low and stay out of it as much as you can."

"But I can't stay out of it," Janice said, the first of a whole series of ugly suspicions blossoming in her brain. "You must be able to see that. I'll have to testify at the trial—"

"If there is a trial," Kasey said, "and even if there is, it'll be months away. Maybe even years."

"But I'll still have to testify," Janice said. "And of course there'll be a trial. That man is a friend of Gregor Demarkian's. Do you think Gregor Demarkian is going to let him plead guilty? And I don't see the point of shutting up for a year or two. Don't you see what an opportunity this is? We've been talking about Martha Handling for years. And now we've got her. We've got everything. The bribe taking, the sentences that went on forever—"

"We don't actually have any proof that she ever took bribes," Kasey said, "and everybody's known about the sentences for as long as Handling was giving them. Nobody cared, in case you didn't notice. Harsh sentences are politically very popular with just about everybody but the families of the inmates, and practically nobody will listen to them."

"But this is different," Janice insisted. "She's a big noise in the news now. Everything about her will come out and be in the papers. Things we couldn't get any traction on before will be news. And the news will make all the difference."

"No," Kasey said. "It really won't."

That was when Janice realized what was going on. It was a disease, power was. Kasey had it. Kasey was used to getting all the publicity and attention for herself. She was used to making all the waves and seeing herself on the six o'clock news. She obviously hated the idea of anybody else getting a little attention.

Really, Janice had thought when she finally got off by herself and was able to think. She should have known it all along. She really should have. Kasey had been showing all the signs for years. All that talk about "collegiality" and "leading by consensus." It was just a lot of words to mask the grab for power. And the power was a soft power because only with soft power could you go on pretending as if you really believed in equality.

It happened to all of them. It really did. Janice had never belonged to any organization anywhere that was any different.

By the next morning, she'd managed to calm herself down. She'd gone in to school and taught her first class. She'd answered a few questions from fellow faculty members and one from a student. Most of her students never watched the news, so they knew nothing about the fact that Janice had become the pivotal element in the country's most famous murder case.

Most famous at the moment, Janice reminded herself when she went into her office for office hours.

She didn't know what she'd expected when she turned on her computer. She did know that the arraignment was supposed to be today. That had been on the news last night, even though cameras were not being allowed in the courtroom. Cameras in the courtroom were something Pennsylvania Justice strongly supported. The more a record existed of every phase of a case, the more likely it was that they could get innocent people out of jail once the injustice had been done.

At least, that was the theory. Janice was now fairly sure that Pennsylvania Justice supported cameras in the courtroom because Kasey liked to see herself on television. Some people just couldn't get enough of being made a fuss of. You saw that with Kasey all the time. She had to be the queen bee at every party. She had to be the person who stood up at the microphone and announced policy at press conferences, and announced the results of investigations, too.

Somebody else might have given the spotlight to one of the people who did the really important work, but not Kasey. No matter how many hours the volunteer lawyers spent working on cases, no matter how many mountains of material the volunteer researchers looked through to find the kink in the armor of conviction, no matter how much work *other* people did, it was always Kasey up there, being the Public Face of the Organization.

Well, Janice thought, that kind of thing always ended badly. That kind of thing ruined organizations. It put an end to all the good work. Janice knew that for certain, because she'd seen half a dozen organizations come apart.

The first of the Web sites Janice managed to get to load was WTFX, which was, of course, Fox. Janice never watched the Fox News cable channel, because it was nothing but lies and propaganda, but she watched all the local channels in turn, because no single one of them ever seemed to have what she needed for weather.

She made a face at the Fox local anchor and tried again. This time, the Web site for WPVI actually managed to load.

And although ABC was nothing more than the usual patriarchal imperialism, it had a few things going on.

What was on WPVI was the arraignment, which was what Janice was looking for, but it wasn't the arraignment she had been expecting.

She hated to admit it, but Kasey had made one relevant point. If that priest pleaded guilty, there would be no trial. And if there were no trial, that would be the end of any publicity Janice could get on the subject of the betrayal of juvenile justice.

Kasey Holbrook might be willing to use up all the leverage she had just to get a bit of publicity for herself, but Janice was not. The world was full of injustice, and it was going to stay that way if people didn't get out and do something about it.

Janice had always had a picture of herself getting out and doing something about it.

She settled in to read the news story on the arraignment—it was the lead story; of course it was—certain that she was going to find a recap of the whole case. Instead, she found a long, rambling piece that made no sense to her at all, all about pleas and what you couldn't plead to and how the judge had been very angry with Father Tibor Kasparian.

Of course the judge had been angry with Father Tibor Kasparian. Judges were always angry with priests when priests ended up in court. That was because priests and judges were icons of the patriarchy, and when one of them got arrested, it threatened the entire power structure.

Janice read through the piece all the way to the end. Then she read through it again. Then she rechecked the home page. There were no other stories about the case.

By then, she could feel the steam coming out of her ears, but she held it back. She needed to be calm. She needed to be clear-headed. She brought up CNN. It had a story about the case, too, and right on the home page, but like the one on WPVI, it said nothing about the background and nothing about Martha Handling.

Janice closed her eyes and tried to think. It seemed impossible, but there it was. They were missing the entire point. They were wandering around talking about trivialities, and the real story was right under their noses. They were doing that even though Janice herself had tried to tell them, just yesterday, what it was really all about.

The least she had the right to expect was a whole slew of stories that exposed Martha Handling for what she had really been. Janice had counted on those stories. Without those stories, there was no point at all to anything that had happened.

The steam was rising and rising. Janice thought her head was going to explode—literally, right there in the office, sending blood and bone and brains all over the office walls.

She hadn't bothered to unpack her tote bag when she came into the office. It was sitting on the floor at her feet. She picked it up and got to her feet. She was supposed to log off the computer when she was finished with it, but she didn't have time. She held down the Start button until the machine kicked off. Then she held down the Start button again until it started to reboot.

She'd wanted to rush right out of the room without paying attention to any of it, but she knew what the result of that would be.

Men were always trying to undercut women in positions of power and responsibility, and that was especially true of the men in the IT department.

2

Petrak Maldovanian had known, from the moment he first saw Martha Handling lying there dead, that he was going to have to find a way to talk to Stefan alone. Talking to him was not so difficult as Petrak had expected it to be when Stefan was first taken into custody. Since no "disposition" had been made in Stefan's case, there were generous visiting hours available at the Juvenile Detention Facility, and the lawyers could come and go almost as they wanted.

At least, the hours were generous from Petrak's point of view. Back in Armenia, if they locked you up, they locked you up. If you happened to be of the wrong race or religion, they locked you up for a good long time before they got around to doing anything about you. When the old Soviet Union fell—Petrak didn't know this from experience, he wasn't born yet, but he'd heard all about it often enough so that he felt as if he'd been there—

When the old Soviet Union fell, everybody thought the disappearances and show trials would be over, but it hadn't turned out like that. In some ways, thing were better. In some ways, they were actually worse.

Things were certainly better in America. Petrak could testify to that, because in just ten minutes, he would be allowed to talk to Stefan in a secure little room at the back of the building. He had rushed down here as soon as his College Algebra class was over. He had been almost rude to Professor Loftus when he passed her in a corridor. She looked all worked up and flustered, which was not usual for her, but he did not stop and ask her why.

The real issue here, Petrak knew, was not getting in to see Stefan, but getting to talk to him alone. Aunt Sophie was very conscientious. She went to see Stefan at every opportunity. She even used her lunch hour to do it. Her lunch hour, though, was more restrictive than the visiting hours. That meant that Petrak had a chance. If he got to the JDF early enough, he would have some time alone with Stefan before Aunt Sophie came along and insisted that everybody start speaking English.

Petrak knew that everything was better in America, but he was not naïve. They said that the visiting rooms were secure and that nobody listened in on private conversations, but he didn't believe it.

Most of the people who worked at the JDF were women. The woman on the intake desk when he arrived was very small and frail.

Petrak tried to look humble. It was very important to look humble in front of Authority.

"Please to ask," he said, thickening up his accent and trying to be as awkward as possible. "My brother, he is doing well?"

"He isn't giving *me* any trouble," the little woman said. Then she spoke into her phone, waited for a reply, and hung up. "They're bringing him over. You can follow me. Where's your mother this morning?"

Petrak was momentarily stumped. His mother had been dead for seven years.

"Ah," he said finally. "This is my aunt, the woman I usually come with."

"I'm sorry," the little woman said. "It's mothers we get, usually. Fathers, not so much. Grandmothers, a lot of the time. You know the drill, right? You have to let the guard check you over."

Petrak knew the drill. He waited at the cage gate while the guard patted him down and then went up one side of his body and down the other with a wand. This guard was male, and looked menacing.

The little room for visiting was all the way at the back and did not have the bulletproof glass partitions that Petrak had seen on television shows set in adult prisons. Stefan was already waiting for him, sitting on a bench on one side of a wooden table. He was wearing the bright orange sweat clothes that were the juvenile system's answer to the bright orange jumpsuits for adults.

"Barev dzez," Petrak said, sitting down across from him.

"Barev dzez," Stefan answered, looking surprised. But he did what Petrak wanted him to do. He went on in Armenian. "Why are we being so formal?"

Petrak went on in Armenian, too. "I wanted you to speak in Armenian, this is all. For once I would like to have a private conversation."

"Where is Aunt Sophie?" Stefan said. "Aren't you early?"

"I came before Aunt Sophie could be away from work," Petrak said. "Like I said. I wanted us to have a private conversation."

"Can we have a private conversation here? Maybe it's like in that movie. Maybe the walls have ears."

"Maybe the walls have ears, but I don't think the walls speak Armenian. Almost nobody speaks Armenian."

"What is going to happen next?" Stefan said. "I have asked about another hearing, but they won't say anything. They say my lawyer will tell me."

"Aunt Sophie said she would talk to Mr. Donahue today," Petrak said. "Maybe she will have the news when she gets here."

"She is coming?"

"She always comes," Petrak said. "She will come and think I am not here, because I will not be waiting for her in the lobby. Then she will be surprised to see me when she comes in. Or they will tell her at the desk. I don't know."

"It is good to see you, in any case," Stefan said. "It is good to have a visitor without the yelling."

"I could be yelling," Petrak pointed out. "I've got every right to yell. It's your own fault you are sitting where you are sitting. What were you thinking about? First cutting school and then shoplifting CDs and video games? And no attention to the security cameras at all. *Tcha.* If you have to turn yourself into a thief, do you have to turn yourself into a stupid thief?"

"I told you, I have not turned myself into a thief. It was an initiation."

"An initiation into what? The worldwide stupid society?"

"I have told you before, it is a club for the best—"

"Stop," Petrak said. "You have told me before. You have told Aunt Sophie. You have told Mr. Donahue. It is still completely senseless."

Stefan looked away. "There are people here who say that the priest killed the judge because of me. That Father Kasparian killed her because he thought she was going to have me sent away to prison for a long time."

"They are saying the same thing outside, but I do not think it is true. It does not sound like something somebody would do."

"Maybe the priest is what they say he is," Stefan said. "Maybe he is some kind of saint. They said that at home. That he was some kind of saint."

"Even saints don't have to be idiots," Petrak said. "What sense would such a thing make? This judge is now gone, and that means some other judge won't give you so much prison time? Even if that is true—*tcha*. It is a story for children."

"You want to talk to me alone," Stefan said. "This is what you want to talk to me about?"

Petrak shook his head. "In a way. In a way not. I need to know for certain. You did not leave the courtroom yesterday before they took you away officially?"

"I could not leave the courtroom," Stefan said. "There were guards at both the doors. And guards outside. And I was wearing this."

"And you will be on the security cameras?" Petrak asked. "There was something wrong with the security cameras. Some of them were not working. I didn't understand it when I heard it on the news. So maybe you will not be on the security cameras."

"Aunt Sophie was there," Stefan said. "She never left the seat next to me."

"Good," Petrak said. "That will help."

"You were not there," Stefan said. "You left and then you were gone a long time."

"I went to look for Mr. Donahue," Petrak said. "*He* was gone a long time. And then everything got crazy."

"I think the best news would be if everybody were missing for a long time," Stefan said.

Petrak looked up at the clock on the wall. He didn't have much time. "I found something," he said. "I found it in one of the side corridors. I went to the toilets and looked there for Mr. Donahue, and when he wasn't there I went on to the back, but it was confusing. There were hallways and they went everywhere."

"If you are going to tell me you killed that woman, I am not going to listen to it. I don't want to hear it. I don't want to know it."

"No, no," Petrak said. "It's not that. It's that I found something. And I do not know what to do about it."

"What did you find?"

"It was a cell phone," Petrak said. "The corridors were confusing and I went through them and then I was outside, and then I came back in again, and it was there lying in a doorway and I just picked it up. It was lying there and I picked it up. And then all the crazy things started to happen and I forgot about it. But it was in my pocket. And so I looked at it last night and I saw what it was, and I don't know what to do about it. But first I had to talk to you."

"Why would you have to talk to me?"

"Because there were pictures of you on it," Petrak said. "Only two. But they were there. And there were pictures of other people, also. And the pictures are strange. They are very . . . blank, I think. The people in them look dead. You look dead."

"I am not dead," Stefan said.

"Yes, I know that," Petrak said. "But I thought, if there were pictures of you on this phone, then maybe the phone belongs to you, or maybe it belongs to one of your friends. Maybe one of your friends in this club that wants you to shoplift for an initiation."

"How could it be my phone?" Stefan said. "They do not allow you to keep your phone in this place. They took it away from me as soon as I walked in here."

"That is not the same as saying no," Petrak said.

"Then I am saying no," Stefan said. "Maybe if somebody stole my phone from the place where they keep the things here, maybe somebody could have dropped it in the corridor. I did not. And you know my phone. You should know if this phone is mine."

"This is not your regular phone," Petrak said.

"There, then. *Tcha*."

"This is a phone with nothing on it," Petrak said. "There are no games and no music, and there is nothing on the—" He struggled to find the word in Armenian, and didn't know it. "—on the telephone directory," he said finally. "It is like on that television show. I think it is a burn phone."

"And you think I have a burn phone?" Stefan demanded.

"This club," Petrak said, "how am I supposed to know what goes on in it? How do I know what it is making you do? It is already getting you arrested."

"It's a club, Petrak. It's just a club. It's not a criminal conspiracy."

"A club can be anything," Petrak insisted.

Stefan gave it up. "What would it matter if it was my phone?" he said. "If it's a burn phone and there's nothing on it? Except the pictures. You said there were pictures. So there's something on it."

"There is also a video on it," Petrak said.

"A video," Stefan said. "And is this video also about me?"

"No," Petrak said. "It's that video. That video—"

Stefan finally looked interested. In fact, Petrak thought, he looked stunned. "This is not good," Stefan said.

"I know it is not good," Petrak said. "I don't know what to do with it. I don't want to bring it in to the police, in case they think I was the one, the one who took the video. But I also did not want to do anything unless I knew that you did not take the video."

"I could not take the video," Stefan said. "I've already told you. I was under guard."

"Or one of your friends," Petrak said.

Stefan let out a string of profanity that made Petrak blush until he remembered that nobody around them could understand it.

"I will say it again," Stefan said. "It is only a club. It is not a gang. It is not about drugs or having weapons. It is not about anything you have to be worrying about."

"It has pictures of you on it," Petrak said. "Two pictures of you on it."

Stefan let out another stream of profanity and then stopped, dead, mid-syllable.

Petrak turned around and saw Aunt Sophie coming toward them at full steam, looking at least as angry as she had this morning. He didn't think Aunt Sophie could understand Armenian profanity, but you could never tell.

"You were supposed to wait for me," Aunt Sophie said as she reached the table. "I spent fifteen minutes out there, expecting you to show up, and I'd still be there if that nice woman at the desk hadn't figured out what was going on and told me you were here. What are the two of you doing? Why are you speaking Armenian?"

"Sometimes it is easier to speak in Armenian," Petrak said. "It's the language we are used to. We have to work at it to speak in English."

"Sometimes I am too depressed to speak in English," Stefan said.

Aunt Sophie looked from one to the other. Petrak could tell she wasn't really buying this. She almost never bought anything they said, even if it was true.

Petrak started to try to think of some way to explain what they had been doing if she insisted, but she didn't. She just sat down and gave up on it, at least for the moment.

"I've got some news about what's happening with your hearing," she said.

Then she began to unpack things from her shoulder bag.

THREE

1

Gregor Demarkian had spent his entire adult life working in law enforcement in one capacity or another, and he knew how homicide detectives tended to think. The very first priority was a kind of tribalism. That was why Gregor had been very careful never to get a private investigator's license. Too many books and too many movies had made private investigators the Enemy in too many police departments, and especially in the larger cities. The entire profession had been professionalized out of all recognition in the years since Gregor retired from the FBI. Forensics had gotten more elaborate and more technical and more accurate. Methods of investigation had been refined and codified and then refined again as the court cases rolled on, telling cops and agents what they were and were not allowed to do. There was a distinct air of Sacred Secrets about the whole thing. Outsiders were not only resented for being outsiders. They were also despised for being amateurs, even when they were being paid.

Gregor's response to this had been practical. He only involved himself in cases where the local law enforcement had asked him in and paid him for coming in. That did not make him an instant insider, but it at least gave him an official standing. It meant that the local police were obliged to talk to him, and the local suspects were obliged to take him seriously.

And then, in spite of all those precautions, he still often found himself in the position of being resented and obstructed at every turn.

This afternoon, Gregor was more than aware that he had no official standing, at least not publicly. And he didn't kid himself about what his unofficial standing would bring in its wake. He was, in this case, everything he shouldn't be: He was a close friend of the prime suspect. He was a close friend of the mayor, which made him a representative of an interfering outside political force. He had a big public reputation, which made him a glory hound. He was the last person Homicide would want to see.

Gregor said none of this to George Edelson as they crossed to the building where they were to have their appointment with the two detectives who had been handed the case, but he would have been very surprised if it hadn't occurred to Edelson himself.

"They're good men," Edelson kept assuring him. "First-rate professionals. Lots of experience."

Gregor made a noncommittal noise. He'd have preferred two men with less experience and no bullheadedness, but the chances that he would ever have gotten something like that were nearly nil. You didn't put two new men on a case that was going to suck up national attention.

"I know you probably feel that they're jumping to conclusions," George said, "but I can assure you, they are not—and they

160

never have done any such thing. It's just that this case, well. This case does look—"

"Open and shut," Gregor said. "I know."

Gregor thought he was ready for what he could expect, but he let Edelson lead him through the long corridors of the Homicide Division without protesting. When had every police department and Social Services office and Department of Motor Vehicles building become a warren of corridors made out of pasteboard and put up on rollers? Had something happened to architecture and aesthetics when he wasn't looking?

Gregor followed Edelson into an actual corridor, with real walls, and then down a single flight of heavily fire-protected steps to an open area full of round tables with laminated tops that were peeling in every direction.

"It's what passes around here for a lunchroom," Edelson explained. "You've got to bring your own."

The room was empty except for two young men sitting at the back. Both of them were thin, short, and dark. Both of them were very upset.

"There they are," Edelson said.

Then he walked himself and Gregor up to the table where the two young men were sitting and said, "Tony, Ray, this is Gregor Demarkian."

Tony and Ray looked up from where they were sitting and made noncommittal grunting sounds. Gregor had no idea which one was which.

"So," George Edelson said. "We should get started. You two are busy. I'm busy. Mr. Demarkian is busy."

This time, there wasn't even a noncommittal grunt. This was much worse than Gregor had been expecting.

George Edelson pulled out a chair. Gregor stopped him before he could sit down.

"Do us both a favor," Gregor said. "Go wander around someplace for half an hour."

George Edelson looked startled. "I don't think that would be a good idea, do you? John said—"

"I can guess what John said," Gregor said, "and he means well, but the best thing you can do right now is to get lost for half an hour. Or forty-five minutes. Go wait for me somewhere. Play something on your cell phone."

Tony and Ray were watching all this very carefully, but they were not moving. They weren't even blinking.

George Edelson looked from one to the other and then at Gregor. He looked resigned. "All right," he said. "If that's the way you want to play it. I think you're wrong."

"If I'm wrong, I can always come and get you and we can start all over again."

"Right," George Edelson said. "But I know *these* two, and you don't." Then he took himself off, moving very slowly, as if he expected to be called back any minute.

Gregor waited until George Edelson was all the way out the door, and then turned to Tony and Ray. "Which of you is which?" he asked them. "Tony who, and Ray who."

The slightly shorter one stirred. "Tony Monteverdi," he said. "That's Ray Berle."

"Fine," Gregor said. He pulled out one of the molded plastic chairs and sat down. "Do you think we can cut through the horse manure right away and then get down to business? You two don't want me here, you don't think I should be here, and you resent like hell the implication that the mayor doesn't think you can do your jobs."

Ray looked more surprised than George Edelson had when Gregor told him to get lost.

Tony looked skeptical. "If you think you can pull bull like that and smooth this over, you're wrong," he said. "We know who you are. We know what your reputation is. At least you're not some kind of frigging amateur. But you don't belong here. It's just wrong."

"I agree," Gregor said.

"Then you're going to go?" Tony said.

"No," Gregor said. "The man who is probably my closest friend on earth has been arrested for murder. He's behaving like—"

"A world-class asshole?" Ray suggested.

"A something," Gregor admitted. "A lunatic, maybe. And not like himself. He's been accused and he's behaving erratically, and I don't know why. You think he's guilty. I don't. But it doesn't matter which of us is right. In either case, I'd still want to know what was going on."

"What bugs me," Tony said, "is the only reason you think he isn't guilty is you've known him forever and you think he couldn't do something like this. But you're wrong. We see it every day. Almost everybody who murders anybody has a pack of relatives and friends who say he couldn't have done it, no way. People do things nobody would expect them to do. They do them all the time."

"And if he did this," Gregor said, "I'll find out about it. And then I'll know. But I can't know if I don't have the facts."

"Honest to God," Ray said. "I'd have thought that video would be enough for anybody."

"Do me a favor," Gregor said. "Skip the video for a moment. Explain the times."

Tony shifted in his seat. He looked a little less rigid. Gregor mentally crossed his fingers.

"All right," Tony said. "What about the times?"

"Start with the basics," Gregor said. "The judge was in the courtroom originally? She was in the courtroom when Tibor Kasparian got there?"

"No," Ray said. "She had an earlier case. She heard that case and she finished early, but they hadn't brought the Maldovanian kid over yet. They usually bring them all over together, it's more efficient, but that day there was some holdup. I think it had something to do with the Maldovanian kid and Immigration. Handling finished her first case and couldn't call the second one, because the kid wasn't there, so she went to her chambers."

"Her chambers is the room she was killed in?" Gregor said.

"Yeah," Tony said.

"And that was when, exactly?" Gregor asked.

"About ten thirty," Ray said.

"About ten thirty," Gregor repeated. "And her body was found when?"

"Eleven forty," Ray said.

"So, we've got about an hour and ten minutes where we don't know what was happening to her."

"We know she was being murdered, Mr. Demarkian," Tony said. "I get the reasonable doubt thing, but we definitely know she was being murdered."

"We know she was being murdered," Gregor said, "but you

know as well as I do that we can't pinpoint time of death even as close to an hour and ten minutes. The best we can do here is say she was killed between ten thirty and eleven forty, because at one end of that time she was seen alive, and at the other end of that time she was found dead. Do you know who was in the building at ten thirty?"

Tony looked indignant. "*Dozens* of people were in the building at ten thirty. It's a courthouse. And it's a courthouse for juveniles, so there are social workers and child psychologists and I don't know who else all over the place."

"All right," Gregor said. "Let me put it another way. There were security cameras?"

"Some," Ray said. "Not as many as you'd think. There are a lot of privacy issues with juveniles. So there's a security camera right at the door, that tells you who goes in and out. And there's one in the foyer right at the start of everything. And then there's one in each of the corridors to the right and the left. There's also one at the end of the corridor to the right, because that's where the restrooms are."

"People think they can do all kinds of fancy stuff in the restrooms," Tony said.

"And?"

"We have pictures of about forty people who came in through the front door that morning and who then went down the corridor to the bathrooms," Ray said. "The way the cameras are positioned, you can't actually tell who goes into one of the bathrooms and who just keeps going into the next corridor, and unfortunately—"

"The camera in the next corridor had been tampered with," Tony said.

"We do have some blurry stuff from that camera," Ray said. "We think a total of seven people went down that corridor. Not including Judge Handling. She didn't use that corridor, as far as we can tell. There's a door behind the judge's bench in every courtroom and it leads directly into the corridor where the chambers are."

"And you could see, clearly, that Father Tibor Kasparian used that corridor?" Gregor asked.

"Hell, Mr. Demarkian. Everybody used that corridor," Ray said. "Father Kasparian. The Maldovanian kid's brother. That woman who started screaming and brought the police down on the scene."

"Janice Loftus," Tony said.

"Yeah, Dr. Janice Loftus," Ray said. "There's a good two dozen people we don't know who they are yet. There are other people we know who they are but we don't think they matter. Attorneys. Law enforcement and court staff."

"But you are sure that Father Tibor Kasparian was one of these people," Gregor said.

"Sure," Ray said. "He's one of the ones we've got twice. The first time was at ten forty-two. The second time was at eleven fifteen."

"What about coming back?" Gregor asked. "If the camera caught people going to the bathroom, wouldn't it catch them leaving?"

"Leaving can be harder to figure out," Ray said. "The camera's pointing the wrong way. You get people's backs. Sometimes you can recognize them, but sometimes you can't. If they're dressed in a sort of nondescript way, and there are a lot of people milling around, it can be hard to pick out particular people and be sure of it."

"We've got Father Kasparian pegged going down the corridor the first time," Tony said. "Then we've got him going down it again the second time. But we can't find him coming back up after the first time. That's going to be a windfall to discovery, if Kasparian ever gets his act together."

"Unless he pleads out," Ray said.

"He's not going to plead out," Tony said. "He's already said he isn't going to plead out. He doesn't want to plead at all."

"Still," Ray said. "I bet it's coming."

"This is what I want you to do for me," Gregor said. "I want you to list everybody who appears on that camera starting at ten thirty and going all the way to eleven forty. Every single person. Even if you can't identify them. Then I want you to get me—can you send me the video from the camera? That's possible, isn't it?"

Tony and Ray gave Gregor a look that said, plain as day, it was possible, but neither of them had the least idea of how to do it.

2

They went back upstairs to the Homicide Division proper, and found George Edelson waiting patiently on a chair in the corner. On second thought, Gregor decided that Edelson was not being so patient as he seemed. His fingers were drumming against his knees. His feet were pumping up and down on the balls, making his knees look like pistons.

"Well?" he said when Gregor came in behind Tony and Ray.

Tony explained in just enough words to convey the nature of the operation, but not quite enough to make it clear. Then he went over to a cubicle and sat down. "This is mine," he said. Then he logged in to his computer.

The cubicle was stacked with files, on the sides of the desk and on the floor. There was a small old-fashioned filing cabinet in one corner. The top of the CPU was also covered with files. The monitor, being a flat screen, couldn't hold them.

"The best way I can figure how to do this," Tony said, "is to forward the video to your phone. I can do that with videos on my phone. I don't see why I couldn't do that from this computer. It occurs to me, though, that there's something else you might want to see."

"What's that?" Gregor asked.

"We've been putting together a minute-by-minute schedule of everybody who came in and out of that corridor, to the extent that we know who they are," Tony said. "We haven't gotten very far yet, and it's taking frigging forever—"

"We were talking about it right before you two showed up," Ray said. "We thought we'd get some people to help us with it."

"Over here," Ray said, pointing to the next cubicle.

There was a picture next to the computer monitor of Ray with a young woman and two young boys. Gregor presumed they were his family.

Ray logged on to his computer and then brought up a file.

Even with a truly spectacular level of computer illiteracy, Gregor could tell when something was taking forever to load, and the document Ray was trying to bring up was taking forever. Ray seemed to be no more patient about it than anybody else.

"We turned it into a PDF file," he said. "I hate PDF files."

"You didn't put it up as a PDF file," Tony said. "You put it up as a docx file. Got it. Now I just need to send it."

Gregor went back to Tony's booth. What showed on the screen was a single still picture, blurry and indistinct, of a lot of people in a corridor.

"Anybody we know?" Gregor asked. There wasn't anyone on the screen he could recognize.

"There isn't anybody on this frame," Tony said. "But if you look through the entire tape, you'll find a few. You'll find Father Kasparian, twice. There's the brother of the kid that was on trial. And there's the lawyers, the prosecutors, and what's his name, the one who wanted to be the lawyer for Father Kasparian—"

"Russ Donahue," Gregor said.

"Right," Tony said. "We're going to have to go and try to identify everybody we can, but just looked at the frame. There are dozens of them. And they're moving every minute. We did get a couple of interesting outliers, though."

"Got it," Ray said.

Gregor went back to Ray's cubicle. On the screen was an enormous list of numbers printed in a column, and next to them, every once in a while, were names.

10:30   Russell Donahue
           Catherine Arnold
           John Richard Magnini
10:31   Janice Loftus
           Martin Seligman
           Marlynne Cole
           Co'Dann Jackson
10:32   Stuart Creel
           Lorraine Czelowski
           Mark Granby
           Susan Chen
           Sharon Chen

Gregor sat back. "What is this thing?" he asked. "You're looking at the tapes and listing everybody you see minute by minute?"

"That's the idea," Ray said.

"You're right, it is going to take forever," Gregor said. "And does it make any sense? Granted it's thorough, but it hardly seems worth the effort. Tibor's already been arraigned. You're in the business of supplying evidence to the prosecutor's office. Why would you—?"

"Got it," Tony said. "The video should be on your phone." He slid backwards in his chair until he got to Ray's cubicle. "We started off fooling around with it," he said, "and if we'd come up completely blank, we'd have quit. But it's like I said. We found some interesting outliers."

"Right off the bat," Ray said. "In the first couple of minutes."

"So what are you trying to tell me?" Gregor asked. "You've changed your minds? You're not sure Tibor murdered Martha Handling?"

"Whoo boy," George Edelson said.

"We're as sure as we can be that Tibor Kasparian murdered Martha Handling," Tony said, "but we aren't the kinds of sons of bitches people make us out to be. We want to be thorough. We want to be right. And, like I said, we did come up with a couple of outliers."

"And we aren't close to having everybody identified yet," Ray said. "There are an awful lot of people going down that hallway and disappearing for minutes at a time, longer than that, even disappearing forever. Without the backup from the other cameras, we just can't be sure. So here we are."

"And where are we?" Gregor asked.

Ray tapped the screen. "There's Janice Loftus, for one thing," he said.

"And who's Janice Loftus?" Gregor asked.

"She's a professor at Philadelphia Community College," Tony said. "She's also the person who started screaming bloody murder that brought everybody in to find the body."

"Okay," Gregor said. "Why is she an outlier? Wouldn't you expect to see her picture on the security tape? She had to get to Martha Handling's office to find Tibor and the body."

"Yes, she did," Tony said. "But look at the time. Ten thirty-one. She didn't find the body and start screaming until eleven twenty-two. That's nearly an hour. What was she doing for an hour?"

"All right," Gregor said. "Interesting."

"More interesting than you know yet," Ray said. "There's a connection. There are a couple of connections. Loftus is a member of this group called Philadelphia Justice that tries to get cases reconsidered they think were wrongly decided. Sort of a local version of the Innocence Project."

"Those aren't bad ideas," Gregor said. "People do get wrongly convicted."

"To hear them tell it," Ray said, "people get wrongly convicted because people like me are racist crapholes who do it on purpose."

"And you think she may have murdered Martha Handling for handing out long sentences to juveniles because—" Gregor stopped. "I don't think that makes any sense when you're trying to use it for a motive for Tibor."

"There's something else," Ray said. "We didn't know it until this morning, or we'd have held her longer yesterday. It turns out there's another connection, and this one is a lot more interesting."

"And what's that?" Gregor asked.

"Janice Loftus and Martha Handling were roommates back in 1979, when they were freshmen at Bryn Mawr College," Ray said.

"So we Googled it just to see what we could get. And we didn't get much, but we did get the information that the two of them were fighting all the time and then ended up being split up for the second semester."

"It still sounds very thin," Gregor said.

"Right, it is," Tony said, "but it's a connection. But the other one's better. Look at ten thirty-two. Mark Granby."

"Oh, God help us," George Edelson said. "Here we go."

"Who's Mark Granby?" Gregor asked.

"Mark Granby is the local representative of a company called Administration Solutions of America," Ray said. "It's the company that now runs most of the prisons in the Commonwealth of Pennsylvania, including the juvenile prisons."

"Remember how we were talking about the rumors about Martha Handling taking bribes?" George Edelson said. "These are the people she was rumored to be taking bribes from. The general idea was that she took money and gave longer sentences so that the cells would be full and Admin Solutions would get more money. The Commonwealth pays them per prisoner per day served. More prisoners with more days served, more money."

"I did understand that," Gregor said. "And I can tell you what I thought of that from the beginning."

"The thing about Mark Granby is that there's no reason for him to be there. Absolutely none."

"And there was reason for Janice Loftus to be there?" Gregor asked.

"Yes," Ray said. "Janice Loftus drove Petrak Maldovanian to his brother's hearing. Janice Loftus is Petrak Maldovanian's professor of something or other—"

"American Government," Tony said.

"American Government," Ray repeated. "Petrak Maldovanian was just getting out of that class and he was worried about making the hearing on time, so Loftus gave him a lift over to the courthouse. Maybe that was some kind of a setup and she was just looking for an excuse to get to Martha Handling, but at least it's a reason. As far as we know, there's no reason for Granby to be there at all."

"Have you talked to him yet?"

"We were trying to work up an excuse," Tony said, "but we think it would be better if you talked to him. Assuming you can get him to talk to you. But technically, we're done with this."

"There's a suspect in custody," Ray said. "And the prosecutor is concentrating on the suspect."

"So is CNN," Tony said.

"Well, I'll be damned," George Edelson said.

Tony Monteverdi looked like he had something to say to that, but he didn't, and the two detectives began to print out material they knew Gregor had to have.

There was a lot of it.

3

Twenty minutes later, Gregor was back out on the street, carrying what felt like a twenty-pound weight.

George Edelson was carrying nothing, but he was visibly stunned. "I don't believe it," he kept saying. "I really don't. There really is material in this case for you to work with."

"I don't find that all that remarkable," Gregor said. "From the little I've been able to find out about this woman, she was in a position of power, she was generally disliked, and she didn't mind throwing her weight around. We were almost certainly going to find something somewhere if we looked long enough."

"We barely had to look at all," George said. "They picked that up just poking around. And if it does turn out that Martha Handling was taking bribes—"

"I think we have to assume she was taking bribes," Gregor said. "There's too much smoke in too many places for that one to be without fire. I think the real question is whom she was taking bribes from."

"But that's obvious," George said. "From Admin Solutions."

"I agree," Gregor said. "That's almost certainly going to turn out to be true. But just because she was taking bribes from one source doesn't mean she wasn't also taking them from another. We need to look into—I need to look into—what else she might have been up to. Because the more I hear about Martha Handling, the more she seems to have been up to."

"I was a prosecutor once," George Edelson said. "You don't want to get me started. It's why I quit, to tell you the truth. I hated being that way to everybody—"

The man who plowed into George Edelson seemed to come out of nowhere, as if he were running. The two men collided and they both went down. Gregor's first thought was that the man was running from the police, but no police were following, and in the tangle of the two bodies on the ground, the running man had come to a full stop."

"What the hell do you think you're doing?" George Edelson demanded. "I could have you arrested for this—"

The running man was on top, so Gregor held a hand out to him first. The running man stood up, and Gregor was shocked.

"Mikel?" he said. "Mikel, what are you doing here? And why were you running? You could have hurt somebody."

"He hurt me," George Edelson said as he got to his feet. "And he ruined this suit. It's got a tear in the jacket sleeve, would you look at that."

"Please," Mikel said, "I am very late. I have an appointment and I will not be on time and if I'm late, I may lose the house. I have to go."

"Tell me you don't have a meeting with somebody Russ knows nothing about," Gregor said. "You do understand that you don't understand the law—"

"Please," Mikel said. "Excuse me very much," he said to George Edelson.

And then he took off.

Gregor and George Edelson watched him go.

"I could have him arrested," Edelson said.

"Don't do that," Gregor said. "He's in the middle of some kind of unholy mess with his mortgage and he spends all his time worried he's about to be thrown out of his house."

FOUR

1

Father Tibor Kasparian trusted himself in almost everything, but he was beginning to find that he was not able to tolerate boredom. It was also true that he had not expected to be bored. He blamed himself for that. He usually had more foresight. Still, the way things had been, with the woman lying dead there on the floor, and everything he knew, and everything that had to be done— well, it hadn't occurred to him that he would have time to be bored, or mental space that wouldn't be occupied by the whole teeming mess of it.

This was the kind of thing that happened to you when you didn't think ahead. And nobody ever thought ahead in an emergency.

One of the things he had thought ahead about was what he would have to do while he was in custody, and that was not to talk to anybody he knew, ever. In a case like this, your best friends became your worst enemies, because you couldn't lie to them, and you didn't even want to. It had been almost more than Tibor was capable of to keep his head turned away from the crowd in the courtroom.

There they were, sitting in a little row: Bennis and Donna and Lida Arkmanian. There was Gregor, in a seat just behind them. If it had been anything else that happened, other than this, he would have discussed all his options with Gregor before he'd done anything at all. Then he would at least have known whether what he was going to do had a chance in hell at working.

The way things were, he had to keep his fingers crossed and hope. He was not an idealist, and he was not an innocent. He did not expect people to be naturally good at heart. He did not believe that there was no evil in the world. He most certainly did not believe that justice would always be done.

What he couldn't get past was that he was not only bored, but lonely, too. He was so lonely, his head felt empty of everything, and he didn't think he could fill it with books, even if he had any. The essential knot was untie-able. His only hope was not to say anything to anybody. His only chance of a way out of this mess was to let nobody know anything. And all the people he wanted to talk to would want answers to exactly those questions he did not want anybody to ask.

Even so, the cell was small, and it was very empty. He didn't understand why jailers everywhere always did this. Cells could be small. That didn't matter. But cells should not be empty. Even very stupid people could get bored with nothing to occupy them. And boredom always caused trouble.

He had gotten to the point where he was repeating nursery rhymes in his head when the guard came to tell him he had a visitor, and the visitor was not somebody he had expected. He had started by repeating Armenian nursery rhymes to himself. Then he had gone on to English. Then he had gone on to French. French was not a language he had ever been completely easy with, at least in its spoken form.

When the guard asked him if he wanted to go downstairs and talk to his visitor, Tibor had a moment of complete frozenness. Hannah Krekorian was down there. She had come to him all on her own, as if she had a plan. Hannah Krekorian never had plans, not real ones. She had vague intentions, and a lot of emotions, and a world's supply of intellectual confusion. She was a nice woman. She was not a threat.

The nursery rhymes were driving him crazy. He made up his mind before he'd had a chance to think it through.

"Yes," he said. "Yes, I will come."

Coming was a mass of complications: handcuffs, leg irons, orders. Tibor let it happen. If you got upset about these things, they wore you out. He also didn't entirely blame them. They would have seen that video just like everybody else. He hadn't seen it, but he could imagine. He probably looked like a crazed animal with no restraint.

They brought him to a room with a line of booths against one wall. The booths had seats and little shelf desks and phones, and one of the sides was faced with thick glass. Tibor had seen this on TV. He didn't know if the glass was so thick, it was impossible to hear through it, or if it required so much in the way of shouting that nobody wanted to do that. They wanted their privacy. They used the phones instead.

Hannah had been crying, and that was not a good thing. She

had never been an attractive woman, even when she was younger. Crying made her face go red and her eyes puff up and her nose run. Tibor wanted to put a hand through the glass and pat her head to make her feel better.

Tibor was more relieved than he wanted to admit that he had no sudden urge to start talking. Instead, he sat down and picked up the phone on his side of the glass and waited for Hannah to pick up hers.

She did pick up her phone, but instead of holding it to her ear, she put her face into an already sodden handkerchief and started to cry.

Tibor made motions telling her to put her phone to her ear, because they really weren't going to get anywhere if she didn't do that.

Hannah did it, and the first thing she said was, "I'm sorry I wasn't there this morning. I meant to be. Lida came to pick me up. But at the last minute, I couldn't handle it."

"There was nothing special about this morning," Tibor said. "You were better to stay at home."

"That's not what I hear," Hannah said. She'd gone from crying to indignant. "Lida has been talking about it ever since they came back. You did something stupid. Or you did something worse. You did something dangerous. Bennis called a Supreme Court justice to ask about it."

This was probably garbled. Tibor wondered whom Bennis had actually called, to make Hannah think it was somebody on the Supreme Court.

"I was sorry I hadn't been there," Hannah said. "If I'd been there, I would have known. So I thought I would come down here.

They were saying you wouldn't talk to anybody, you wouldn't even talk to Gregor, but I thought I'd come."

"Well," Tibor said. "I am talking to you. You can see there is nothing wrong with me."

"There's *everything* wrong with you," Hannah said in a wail. "Just look at you. And look at this place. What are you doing in this place? And that video. Have you seen yourself in that video? It's impossible."

"No, no," Tibor said. "I have heard about the video, yes, but I have not seen it. I do not have a cell phone here."

"I'm not completely stupid," Hannah said. "I know there must be something going on you're not telling anybody. I know there must be some reason you're not talking to Gregor, and it's not because you killed some silly woman you didn't even know. And I know that what you're doing is wrong, Tibor, I know it. I was suspected of committing murder once. This is not what you are supposed to do."

"No, no," Tibor said. "I am not doing anything. I am only telling the truth."

"Telling the truth to say you killed that woman?" Hannah said. "Telling it to a judge in court? I don't believe it."

"No, no," Tibor said again. "I did not tell anyone that I killed someone. You must understand—"

"Bennis said that after what you said in court today, they could send you away to jail forever. I understand *that*."

"No, no," Tibor said again.

But it felt hopeless. Hannah was sitting over there on her side of the glass, glaring triumphantly, and he couldn't think of another word to say.

And this had not relieved his loneliness.

It had made him feel as if he were the only person left on the planet.

2

Mark Granby had never liked his office in Philadelphia. There was something raw about it, as if it had never really been finished, or as if it was a sham, meant to fool people into thinking he was "an integral part of the Administrative Solutions family."

That last bit came from the little brochure they gave everybody who showed up for orientation. They gave it to the incoming receptionists and the incoming secretaries and the incoming middle management. They even gave it to the hires they were serious about. Mark had thought, from the beginning, that it was as if the company wanted to pretend to be making a sitcom about an office, as if they wanted to pretend they weren't doing the work they were doing.

The raw unfinishedness of the office always made Mark pause when he walked in. It practically screamed that he was expendable. If he had really been an important part of the Administrative Solutions family, his office would have been in Harrisburg, and it would look solid as a rock.

Mark had never liked being expendable, but he hadn't really *minded*. You took what you could get these days, and if you worked hard enough, you could find yourself moved into the category of essential personnel. Then you could sit back and let other people take responsibility for your mistakes.

The present situation, however, was not his mistake. It was

company policy, even though it was written down nowhere. Carter Bandwood had been completely clear about that. What Mark hadn't quite figured out at the time was that the way this thing worked, the only paper trail anybody would ever find would lead directly to Mark Granby, and nobody else.

That was why, when the call came, Mark had almost lost his lunch. For a couple of minutes after he was sure he knew what it was, he'd had the impression that the caller was speaking a foreign language. It was only a foreign accent. It was thick, and the man's syntax was too formal. It was not Spanish.

"There is your name here," the man said. "In the contacts list. There are voice mails with your name on them."

Why was it that the people who did these things were always so stupid? Not the man. Mark didn't know if the man was stupid or not. It was Martha Handling he couldn't believe. There she was, taking his advice, buying a prepaid cell phone that nobody could trace, buying half a dozen of them and throwing them out after a day or two. There she was, going to all that trouble, and then what did she do? She put his name in the contacts list for anybody at all to find.

At first, Mark thought that he ought to meet the man somewhere out of the office. They could run into each other at Starbucks. They could meet in a park with a bench. His mind kept racing through the possibilities as the man went on talking.

Then he realized that the one thing he could not do was to meet the man someplace else. If he was being watched, the implication would be that this was a clandestine meeting. He could almost hear some idiot in a courtroom somewhere, describing how he'd been skulking around, making it seem as if he were doing something wrong.

And he was doing something wrong. That would make it even worse.

He assumed that the man on the phone wanted money. People like that always wanted money.

At the moment, Mark didn't have any money. And he had the distinct feeling that if he called Carter Bandwood, he wouldn't get any.

He told the man to come by the office. He sat down behind his desk and looked at papers. There really wasn't much in the way of work that needed to be done. When things were going the way they were supposed to be going, Mark only had to keep track of the up-coming cases throughout the Commonwealth of Pennsylvania and make sure the management at the prisons knew what to expect.

And, of course, he had to talk to the judges, and to make sure they were happy.

Waiting for the man to show up, he imagined all kinds of things. He imagined himself right into an episode of *The Sopranos.* He thought about all the stories he had heard about the Russian mob, and Bruce Willis movies, and Arnold Schwartzenegger—but no, the accent had not been German. He couldn't really peg just what it was, but it definitely had not been German.

He left his door open while he waited, so that he could see who came in the door. And when the man did come, Mark was almost sure that he couldn't really be the man. Because when the man did come, he was a boy.

He was a boy Mark recognized.

Mark thought he was going to die on the spot.

The rule of thumb was simple. If you could see them, they could see you. He had seen this boy at the courthouse on the day Martha Handling was killed. He had seen him twice. The first time had been at the very beginning, when Mark came up the front steps. The boy had been with that ridiculous woman who carried signs at demonstrations. It wasn't the important woman, who was the head of Philadelphia Justice, but the squat little one who shrieked a lot. She had gotten through the first barrier, only to be stopped at the courtroom door, because the court was not going to allow her to be a spectator. She talked to the boy. Mark had thought he knew what she was doing. She was trying to get the boy to tell the guard at that door to let her in. The boy was not cooperating.

The second time Mark saw the boy had been later, downstairs, in the corridor where Martha Handling's chambers were. That was the time Mark thought the boy might have seen him. At the courtroom door, the boy had been too preoccupied with dealing with the squat woman. In that back corridor . . .

Well, in that back corridor, a lot had been going on. Martha Handling was already dead.

Mark got up out of his chair and went to the door of his office. The boy was talking to the receptionist. He looked up and stared right into Mark's face, but he didn't look as if he'd recognized anybody.

"I'm Mark Granby," Mark said, holding out a hand. "Why don't you come in where we can talk? I liked your résumé very much. I think we have some real possibilities here."

The boy looked confused. The receptionist also looked confused. Mark practically dragged the kid out of the front room and into the office. Then he closed the office door and locked it.

"Sit down," he said, not sounding as happy-crappy as he had outside. "I know who you are. You're the brother of the kid whose case was on when Martha Handling got killed."

The boy was looking around the office, unhappy. "It looks like the office of a bureaucrat," he said. "It should look like the office of a capitalist."

Mark knew what the kid meant.

"I'm Mark Granby," he said, "like I told you outside. Who are you? And don't tell me you aren't going to give me your name, because I can find it out."

"I am Petrak Maldovanian," the boy said.

Then he didn't say anything else. Mark stared at him. Petrak stared at the room, at the walls, at the desk, out the windows. Mark thought if this kept up much longer, he would scream.

"Listen," Mark said. "If we're going to do business, we should do business. It's not going to make much sense saying this was a job interview if we take forever. People will know something is up. Especially since I don't actually have a job opening and I'm not going to hire you for anything. What do you want?"

Petrak looked down at his hands. "I found a cell phone," he said.

"You told me that on the phone."

"It was not an ordinary cell phone," Petrak said. "It was a pre-paid cell phone, the kind you can get at stores and right away use without a plan."

"Yes," Mark said. "And you think it's mine?"

"At first I thought it was my brother Stefan's," Petrak said. "It had his picture on it, and pictures of other people. The other people looked like they could be his friends. But I have talked to Stefan, and it is not his phone."

"All right," Mark said. This was going to take forever.

"I looked at the phone and I found things," Petrak said. "I found the video. The video of Father Tibor with the gavel. The one that was on the Internet."

It took everything Mark had not to react to that one. There had to be dozens of city cops looking for the source of that video. If this boy had brought that video into the office—but then, what else could he have done? And what was Mark supposed to do now?

"You think this was my cell phone?" Mark asked. "You think I took the video of the priest killing—?"

But Petrak Maldovanian was shaking his head vigorously. "No, no," he said. "It would not be your phone. It had your name and number on the contacts list. You do not put your name and number on your own contacts list. I think this was the phone of Judge Martha Handling. I think it was not her regular phone but a special phone she had. I saw her regular phone. It was on the desk in the room where she was. Where her body was."

"Was it?" Mark said.

"It was a nice phone, her regular phone," Petrak said. "I envied it."

There wasn't a single thing Mark could think of to say to that.

The boy twisted in the single visitor's chair. It was an uncomfortable chair. Mark wasn't expected to have visitors.

Mark thought he was going to go crazy. The kid just wouldn't get on with it. He was looking around the room again.

"All right," Mark said finally. "You found this phone, and you found my name on it. And it's got the video on it. Maybe somebody just downloaded the video from the Internet. Everybody else on the planet did."

"No," Petrak said. "It's a video made on this phone. You can see it. You can tell when a video is made on the phone. It's different when it's been downloaded."

Mark didn't know if that was true. He did know where to go next. "Fine," he said. "Show it to me."

This time, the boy shot him a look of complete and utter contempt. "I do not have the phone with me," he said. "I would not bring the phone with me. I have it in a safe place. I will give it to you—I will give it to you after."

"After I give you money," Mark said. "So far, you haven't given me any reason to think it might be worth any money. To me, at least."

"I don't want money," Petrak said.

"You don't? What the hell else could you want?"

Petrak seemed to come to some great decision. "I have looked at the phone over and over again," he said. "I have come to the conclusion that it is a phone belonging to Judge Handling—"

"You've *said* all that," Mark interrupted.

"—I have listened to the messages on the voice mail. Three of these voice mail messages are from you."

"So?"

"One of these messages talks about my brother, Stefan. You say you are sending her the picture. You talk about what my brother, Stefan, has done and that he should be locked away for long because he is a—" Petrak searched the ceiling. "—a psychotic."

"Psychopath," Mark said dryly. "And you still want to tell me you don't want any money?"

"When Mr. Donahue told us that it would be Judge Handling who would be the judge for Stefan's hearing, he said that there were many rumors that Judge Handling was taking bribes to send people to the juvenile prison for long times. I didn't understand that exactly, but Mr. Donahue explained that your company, you and your company, you run the prisons as a capitalist company and the government pays you money for every prisoner you have in your jails. You gave Judge Handling money to put people in your prisons and that is a crime and you could go to jail for doing it."

"Go on," Mark said.

"In this I think I am entirely correct," Petrak said. "Also I think that if I gave this phone to the authorities, they would look through it and they would find these things, and they would arrest you and send you to jail. I think you would not want this to happen."

"Nobody wants to go to jail," Mark agreed.

"I think that if you pay one judge to send people to jail, you must pay other judges to send people to jail," Petrak said. "I think it is never just one. I think also if you can pay a judge to put somebody in jail, you can pay a judge not to put somebody in jail."

"Why would I pay a judge not to put somebody in jail?"

"I think you could do that if you wanted to," Petrak said. "I think I will give you back the phone if you will do that for my brother, Stefan."

"From what I hear, your brother, Stefan, is on track to be deported."

"*Tcha,*" Petrak said. "You are not about the deported. You are about the jail. You will pay a judge, the new judge for Stefan, so that he does not go to jail. After that, I will give you the phone."

"After that, you'll use the phone to get me to give you money."

"No," Petrak said.

Just that. No. As if that were all that needed to be said.

And maybe it was.

Of course, Mark didn't actually have another juvenile judge in his pocket. Martha Handling was the only one he had found. Juvenile judges seemed to be a lot stickier than adult court kind. But he could see that Petrak Maldovanian didn't know that, and Petrak Maldovanian had that damned phone.

"All right," Mark said. "But first, you're going to do something for me. You're going to strip, and then we're going to go through your clothes and that backpack. We're going to look in the pockets and the seams and the book spines and everywhere. Because if you're wired, I want to know it now."

3

It was after six o'clock when Russ Donahue looked up from the papers on his desk and realized that time had passed. It was already dark outside, in spite of the everlasting daylight saving time that was going to go on until November.

He ran that through his head a couple of times. Mikel Dekanian was supposed to have come by for an appointment about the papers Russ was working on now. The girls in the office should have noticed that. He should have had some notification from somebody that Mikel had not come in.

Russ looked at the enormous pile of paperwork on his desk, which was only about a third of what he'd been trying to look through on the computer. Computers were great, but sometimes he found it easier to concentrate if he could just lay things out on paper.

Today, that had not been the case. Today, no matter how he'd moved things around, or set them up as charts, or put them in columns, nothing made any sense. He could see no way out of the tangle. He had managed to get one thing done, at the very beginning of the day, which would keep the bank from foreclosing for the foreseeable future, but the rest of the day had been a wash.

He got up from behind his desk and went out into the reception area. The offices around the perimeter were all dark. The receptionist had gone home. Most of the secretaries had gone, too.

Russ heard a sound and turned to see Mary Langdon just heading out from the back of the offices, her enormous shoulder bag slapping at the side of her body like a wrecking ball. That had to hurt.

"Mary?"

Mary was Max's personal secretary. She was the one he went to when he got crazy about money, not enough money coming in, too much money going out, the entire small firm project ending in a heap of debts. Mary was a very calm person.

"Russ," she said, "I thought I saw a light under your door. Are you all right?"

"Yes, of course, I'm fine," Russ said. "But I had an appointment. With Mikel Dekanian, you know—"

"The mortgage case," Mary said. "I do know. Isn't that awful, though? The poor man hasn't ever had anything to do with J.P. CitiWells, and they still manage to screw him up. He was supposed to come in today?"

"A few hours ago," Russ said. "You didn't see him?"

"Well, no, I didn't, but I'm not the best one to ask about that. I'm not usually out front here. But if he'd come in, I'm sure somebody would have told you about it. Unless you were out, of course."

"I went out for lunch, but that was at around noon. He was supposed to come in at three thirty."

"Maybe he got hung up somehow and forgot to phone," Mary said. "Or maybe he didn't forget to phone but somebody forgot to give you the message. That's happened a couple of more times than I like to think about. Would you like me to call him for you so you can find out what's going on?"

"What?" Russ said. "No, that's all right. I'll look into it in the morning. I probably ought to be going home myself."

"You probably should," Mary said. "Donna's probably frantic. See you tomorrow, then."

"See you tomorrow."

Russ watched her leave.

Then he went back into his office and packed up as much of the paper as he could get into his briefcase.

He didn't see what good it was going to do, but he had to try.

FIVE

1

By the time Gregor had finished visiting offices, he had a stack of paper on him heavy enough to break his back, and enough new files on his computer to last him for days. It was not well sorted and organized paper. The police had their suspect, even if one or two of them wasn't completely happy with who and what they had. The prosecutor *was* happy with who and what he had. And he had every reason to be. If the man now in custody for the murder of Martha Handling had been anybody at all but Father Tibor Kasparian, Gregor himself would have been happy with who and what they had.

In ways that Gregor barely wanted to think about, that bothered him. He didn't expect himself to pay attention to every crime committed everywhere, or even every murder. There were a lot of them, and most of them were not even minorly interesting. Gregor had always counted himself lucky that he had not spent his childhood immersed in detective fiction. He hadn't read any detective fiction at all until he was in middle age and Father Tibor had given him some. Then he'd spent a few months reading through the writers Tibor called the Great Masters: Christie, Sayers, Stout, Chandler, Hammett. He'd found something to like in most of them, and found Christie far more perceptive than he'd thought he would. But the only one of the lot that he'd felt was really *real* was a writer named Ed McBain.

Real as the McBain stories were, though, they were nothing at all like real police work, or real murders. Real murders were, almost invariably, mind-numbingly stupid. All the studies said that less intelligent people were more likely to commit violent crimes than more intelligent people. Gregor thought that might be hiding something more sinister. Maybe more intelligent people were less likely to get caught committing violent crimes than less intelligent people. Maybe there were, out there somewhere, dozens of bodies buried on the assumption that they'd died of natural causes, or accidents, or simple old age, when they'd actually been cleverly done in by family and friends.

Maybe, but Gregor didn't think so. The kinds of crimes that made for interesting books and television shows were probably in reality very rare. Most intelligent criminals turned out not to be as intelligent as they thought they were. Most murders consisted of sudden and irrevocable losses of control: two guys who got liquored up and infuriated in a bar when one or both of them had a weapon; the nineteen-year-old boyfriend who promised to babysit and found out he couldn't stand the sound of the baby crying; the mental defectives who thought a gun meant nobody could say no to them and ended up being resisted by the owner of the convenience store they'd set out to rob.

There was a reality show out there called *World's Dumbest*

Criminals. Gregor did not like reality shows as a rule, but he thought that one had a point. Stupid, he'd once heard somebody say, is an unlimited resource. He liked the line from Isaac Asimov better: "Violence is the last refuge of the incompetent."

In this thing with Tibor, it was less the violence he was concerned about than the events that followed the violence. There were all those people in the corridor. There was the picture sent out by the woman who had eventually found the body. There was Tibor's behavior, which was not only strange but strange in a particular way.

He walked the street for a while until it got dark. He found himself getting annoyed over the fact that it was still daylight saving time. Not that any daylight was being saved at the moment. It was late, and it was September.

He was very tired and very hungry. He found a streetlight bright enough to read his watch by and saw that it was close to eight. He'd have missed dinner at the Ararat while everybody else was there. Bennis would make him something if he asked, but Gregor had learned that it was better not to ask. Bennis seemed to approach cooking as an adversary competition. She was competing with the food, which wanted to be edible, but would not win.

He got his phone out and called her. She sounded enormously relieved when she heard his voice. That surprised him.

"How am I supposed to know what's going on out there?" she asked. "You could be walking around the streets of Philadelphia in a fog. And some parts of Philadelphia, you shouldn't do that in."

"I'm getting a cab. You've probably had dinner. Could you meet me at the Ararat anyway? Maybe you could call ahead in case the place is busy tonight? Linda will find a place for us if she knows we're coming."

"Yes, of course I can," Bennis said. "You haven't eaten? That means you really were wandering around the streets of Philadelphia thinking."

"I shouldn't be long," Gregor said.

He closed up and stepped out into the street to hail a cab. This was not something worth arguing about, because Bennis was right.

The cab was just turning into Cavanaugh Street when Gregor realized what it was that had been bothering him, and then he wasn't sure it made any difference. He made the driver stop just outside the Ararat's front door, gave him a decent-enough tip, and got out onto the sidewalk. Bennis was right where he could see her, sitting in the booth that bordered the big plate glass window. Gregor wasn't sure how he felt about that. That was the same booth where he and Tibor had had breakfast together for years.

He dragged the briefcase with the papers and the laptop in it into the Ararat. He should have stopped at home and dropped it off. He waved to Debbie Melajian when she waved to him. Her sister Linda opened the restaurant in the morning and worked through lunch. Debbie came on just after lunch and closed up after dinner.

Gregor went over to the booth and slipped in across from Bennis.

"What do you have in that thing?" Bennis asked. "It looks like you're carrying rocks."

"It feels like I'm carrying rocks," Gregor said. "It's my laptop plus enough paperwork to denude the forests, and none of it is going to make any difference that I can see. I have, however, had what you and Donna like to call an Aha Moment."

"Really?" Bennis said. "About what?"

Debbie Melajian came over with her pad. "Bennis, are you going to stick to coffee or do you want something serious to drink? My mother was betting on something serious to drink."

"I'll have a Drambuie on ice," Bennis said.

"I'll have a double Scotch on the rocks except not much on the rocks. And make it Johnnie Walker Blue if you still have a bottle somewhere."

"We've got it in the back for you," Debbie said, "not that you drink it often. Do you want me to bring dinner after? Bennis has already had—"

"Imam bayildi," Gregor said. "But give me about twenty minutes to finish the Scotch."

"Absolutely," Debbie said, and whisked away with her pad.

Bennis was giving him One of Those Looks. "I take it that whatever this Aha Moment was, it wasn't good news," she said.

Gregor shrugged. "It's not good news and it's not bad news. It's just one of those things we all should have thought about before, but we didn't."

"And what's that?"

"There's a video out there that looks as if it shows Tibor pounding that gavel into Martha Handling's head," Gregor said.

Bennis snorted in exasperation. "Of course there is," she said. "What do you think we've all been worried about from when this started—?"

"Yes, yes," Gregor said, "but think about it. This was a juvenile court. They don't go bonkers over cell phone cameras in adult courts anymore, but they still do in juvenile courts. You can't take a cell phone into a juvenile court if the cell phone has a camera in it."

Debbie brought over the drinks and put them down on little square napkins. Gregor picked his up and took a long gulp of it. You shouldn't gulp Johnnie Walker Blue, but he didn't care.

"Bennis," he said. "The police are convinced that that video was made by a cell phone. But if it was made by a cell phone camera, it couldn't have been made by anybody who came in through the front door of that courthouse except judges and security personnel, because they're the only ones who aren't walked through a metal detector and don't have their pocketbooks and briefcases and backpacks X-rayed."

"I still don't see—"

"Bennis, think," Gregor said. "And this is the problem with cases like this, where everybody thinks they already know what's going on. None of the people we know were in that corridor leading to the corridor to the chambers could have had a cell phone on him. But if that video was made with a cell phone, somebody must have. The police are going to check all the cell phones of all the people who were there, but it isn't going to make any difference, because all those phones will have been lying on the check-in table in little manila envelopes. None of those people could have brought a cell phone into Martha Handling's chambers and taken that video. And no security personnel or other judges did that either, because none of those people were there until *after* the murder."

Gregor felt a certain amount of satisfaction that Bennis was looking confused.

"Well," she said, "maybe somebody had a digital camera, a cheap one, or something—"

"That would have been caught at the desk, too."

"Somebody had to have taken that video. We all saw it. I still have the wretched thing on *my* phone."

"I agree," Gregor said. "But the video has to have been taken by a phone brought in by somebody who didn't come through the front."

"And that would be?"

"The most obvious person," Gregor said, "would be Martha Handling herself. She would have come in from the parking lot in the back, since she drove to work. She would have had her phone on her, obviously. There are only two things wrong with that."

"What are those?"

"First," Gregor said, "there's the fact that the video was not taken on her phone. The police found her phone. They checked it out. The video was not taken with that. But there's also the fact that the only way that video makes sense, or the only way I can see at the moment, is if somebody had the phone on him, walked in on the crime being committed, and started filming almost by remote control. But the way things are, that cannot be the way it happened. The secretaries and the assistants were all out at a funeral. The judges who were in were in their courts. Nobody unauthorized could have come through that back door either, because although the camera right at the door was blocked by paint, the other cameras in that parking lot weren't."

"So—what then?" Bennis asked. "Somebody didn't walk in on Tibor? I don't understand—"

"I think," Gregor said, "that that video was staged, and it was staged with a readily available instrument. The police found Martha Handling's phone. There must have been another phone, somewhere available."

"What other phone?" Bennis asked. "Whose phone?"

"What if the rumors are true," Gregor said, "and Martha Handling was taking bribes to put juveniles in jail for longer sentences than they would usually get for the kinds of crimes they committed. Let's say she was doing that—would she take calls relating to that on her regular cell phone?"

"Oh, I see," Bennis said. "You think she had another phone. Maybe one of those throwaway ones. And it was—what? Lying somewhere in plain sight?"

"Right," Gregor said. "Someone walked into the room, saw Tibor doing whatever he was doing—"

"I'd like to know what that was," Bennis said.

"Grabbed the phone and then did something with it," Gregor said. "Whoever it was had to have taken the phone away. It's entirely possible that Tibor didn't even realize that the person was there, if he was in fact the person who committed the murder. If he wasn't, and the scene was staged, then they staged it together. But whoever it was took the phone away, and the phone wasn't found on him or her during the investigation. Which means that either the person ditched it, or he wasn't one of the people found on the scene and interviewed immediately. And we've got a candidate for that. The guy who runs local operations for Administrative Solutions, the company that runs the prisons, was in the courthouse that day. And we've got security tape to prove it. And he'd want to take that phone away with him. And nobody would have checked him going out."

Gregor saw Bennis's face fall.

"It's progress," he said gently. "It's not much, yet, but it's progress. And that the man from Administrative Solutions killed Martha Handling over the bribes he was paying her makes more sense as a motive than that Tibor did it for no reason we've been able to find out yet."

"But don't you see?" Bennis said. "It doesn't even start to prove that. If it was the way you just worked out, then this Adminstrative Solutions man still has to have come in to find Tibor pounding away with that gavel, and if that's the case, then Tibor could still have committed the murder, and I just don't—"

"Ahem," somebody said, right next to Gregor's ear.

Gregor would have jumped out of his seat, except that the way the booth was constructed wouldn't allow it. He did bang his knee against the table's wood.

Bennis looked frigid.

Standing next to their table was a squat, frazzled-looking woman in ballet flats and Native folk art jewelry. Gregor recognized her, but only vaguely. He thought of her as the lady that screamed.

"Excuse me," the woman said. "I'm very sorry to bother you, but I've been waiting and waiting. For hours. Because you always come in. Then I thought you weren't coming tonight and I thought I'd go to your house and try there. It's very important. My name is Janice Loftus, and I know all about Martha Handling."

2

Bennis Hannaford Demarkian was the sanest woman Gregor knew, but every once in a while she took an instant dislike to somebody, and once she had done that, all bets were off. She took an instant dislike to the squat woman standing next to their table, and the reaction was so strongly visceral, Gregor had expected her to explode. The reality was that Bennis did not explode. When she was mortally, irrevocably offended, she got so polite, she could make your teeth bleed.

If Janice Loftus had noticed Bennis's deep freeze, she gave no sign of it. Gregor guessed that she hadn't noticed it. Janice Loftus was the kind of woman who wouldn't notice much of anything, and especially wouldn't notice other people's reactions to her or anything else. She talked a mile a minute. Her eyes darted all around the room. Her hands fluttered and waved.

Then she pushed herself onto the bench beside Bennis and stared across the table at him.

Bennis moved because she had to. She was wearing the face of her own great-grandmother, who had been the most austere and unforgiving hostess on the Main Line. She had had to be, because she was married to a real live robber baron.

Debbie Melajian came over to the booth, looking just a little puzzled. "Can I get you something?" she asked Janice Loftus.

Janice Loftus looked back. "They've got something," she said. "I don't have to compromise myself any more than I already have. You should order in fair trade coffee, that's what you should do. You'd get a lot more business from socially responsible diners."

"I'll get you some water," Debbie said.

"The bottled water industry—"

"It's just water from the tap," Debbie said. Then she sped off toward the back.

Bennis looked like she was about to breathe fire.

"People are much smarter about these things than they used to be," Janice Loftus said, "but not enough of them are, and too many people don't care. Bottled water—corporations are taking over our water supply. What are we going to do when it's gone? And what they call soft drinks—"

"Excuse me?" Gregor said. He said it because he didn't want Bennis to say anything. And Bennis was about to say something.

"Oh," Janice Loftus said. "Yes. Well, I'll save that for another time. But it's important, especially for prominent people. Americans are obsessed with celebrity, of course, that's why nothing can ever get done. The plutocrats make sure there are lots of circuses, even if there isn't a lot of bread. But we can use their tactics against them if we're smart. The more celebrities who come out for fair trade and for—"

Debbie was back with Janice Loftus's water and Gregor's imam bayildi. Janice stared at the imam bayildi as if it were a space alien. Debbie got out of the way fast.

"Well," Janice said. "That's . . . that's very . . . you don't see that much anymore. Real food from real cultural cuisines. Everything's franchised and frozen and packaged these days."

Back in the days when Bennis smoked cigarettes, this was when she would have lit up.

Janice Loftus stared at the imam bayildi a little longer, as if it could tell her something she needed to know. Then she dragged her eyes back to Gregor and said, "I'm sorry to bother you in the middle of the night"—the apology was mechanical—"but I tried to talk to the police and nobody would listen to me. Except they kept trying to imply that I must have killed Martha because she used to be my roommate, which is the silliest thing I've ever heard. If I was going to kill Martha because she was my roommate, I'd have done it when she actually was my roommate. And I thought about it. Let me tell you. I thought about it a lot."

"Have you thought about it since?" Bennis asked.

Janice Loftus ignored her. "The thing is, she did it twice that I know of, and one more time that I don't know of because of course I don't belong to those kinds of clubs. But even twice is a pattern, isn't it? And patterns are what matter. But the police are just being the police, and they won't listen. I thought maybe you'd listen."

"I'll listen," Gregor said. "To tell the truth, you were on my list to talk to eventually anyway."

"Well, I hope it wasn't about that nonsense about how I must have wanted to kill her because she used to be my roommate and I hated her," Janice said. "I don't hate people. It uses up too much energy and we need the energy, all we can get. There's so much work to be done."

"Martha Handling used to be your roommate," Gregor said.

"At Bryn Mawr College," Janice said. "You know what kind of place that is. One of the original Seven Sisters. All those rich girls with Porsches and cashmere sweaters and parents working on Wall Street. The teachers really tried to raise everybody's consciousness, but it was a losing battle for most of those girls. They just absolutely believed they deserved every one of their privileges."

"And Martha Handling was one of the ones who believed that?" Gregor asked.

"Well, yes," Janice Loftus said. "Of course she believed that. Even I believed that in the beginning. It's very hard to separate yourself from your background. And in those days, I just idolized my father. I thought he walked on water. I didn't realize what he was doing to me. I didn't realize that abuse didn't have to be physical to be abuse."

"Wait," Bennis said. "Loftus. *Patrick* Loftus? You're Patrick Loftus's daughter?"

This time, Janice Loftus did look at Bennis. "Don't sound so impressed. There's nothing to be impressed with. It's not like my father ever did any real work. He didn't dig ditches or grow food. He wasn't even a change agent. He was just a greedy man who knew where to get money."

"Patrick Loftus," Bennis said. "The man who founded Pacific Microsystems. The man who invented—"

"The very tool that lets the government spy on its citizens and get away with it," Janice Loftus said. "If you think that's an achievement, I think you live a very impoverished life."

It was time to head this off at the pass.

"Let's get back to Martha Handling," Gregor said. "She was your roommate in your freshman year?"

"That's right," Janice Loftus said. "You could pick your own roommate if you already knew someone, and I did know someone, a girl in my house at Miss Porter's, but, well, we didn't get along, and I don't think she wanted to room with me any more than I wanted to room with her. So I told the college to pick for me and I got Martha Handling."

"And that was bad, too?" Gregor asked. "Right from the beginning?"

"Oh, no, it wasn't too bad at the beginning," Janice said. "I mean, the woman was a complete fascist, but I didn't know about fascism then. And she was just like everybody else, really. Except the whole thing was her idea."

"What was her idea?" Gregor asked.

"Patrick Loftus," Bennis said. "Miss Porter's. For God's sake."

Janice had gone back to ignoring her. "It was her idea that we should work together to cheat," Janice said. "We all had this absolutely terrible teacher for history. He wanted everybody to know dates and all that kind of thing, and he went on about battles and things and he was really old and he had tenure. Bryn Mawr is a very progressive place. There are wonderful teachers there, teachers who understand gender and race and class and know how to put you right into history. And make you understand what things mean. But he wasn't one of them, and he had tenure, of course, so we were stuck with him."

"Why didn't you drop the course?" Bennis asked.

"It got too late to do that," Janice said, "and then it was a requirement if you wanted to take other history courses, and almost all of us wanted to do that because you have to if you want to major in Women's Studies or political science or sociology. We had a test every third week, and when he handed back the first one, a lot of us knew we were going to fail. We just knew it. There wasn't going to be any way to avoid it. And that's when Martha said she had the idea."

"An idea to cheat," Gregor said.

"Martha said that the reason people got caught cheating is that they went about it by themselves," Janice said. "She said people who cheated were always ashamed of it, so they tried to hide it, not just from the authorities but even from themselves. So they did all the stupid stuff that everybody knew about already, and they got caught, because it wasn't hard to catch them. She said what we ought to do was work as a team. She said if we worked as a team, it would be almost impossible to catch us, because no one of us would be doing any of the things they were expecting. Oh, I don't know. It sounded good at the time, and I didn't want to fail."

"What could you have done that was so different?" Gregor asked.

"Martha said she'd seen it in a movie," Janice said. "I don't remember the name of the movie. It isn't anything you'd recognize.

The course was this big lecture thing twice a week, and then the class was broken up into seminar sessions that met at different times, with only ten people in each of them. And there were about ten of us, and only one of us in the first one. So, what we'd do, the one of us in the first session would take two copies of the test when it was handed out and also two blue books. Then that person would hand in her blue book very early and bring the extra copy of the test and the extra blue book back to the dorm and we'd make copies of it. And while we were doing that some of the others of us would be filling in the answers in the blue books. And then when that was done, when the seminar sessions were over, some other couple of us would find a way to get the blue book out of the pile and the fixed one into it. We'd go to his office right when the seminar was letting out and one of us would distract him and the other would do the things with the books. The rest of us would have the test answers going in and we wouldn't have to do all that."

"And that worked?" Bennis asked. "Really?"

"It worked for months," Janice said. "I don't think it would have, except that he always used test days to meet students, so he was pretty much distracted or he'd be out of the room in the hall talking to somebody. It was a two-semester course and it worked for everything except the big midterm at the end of the first se-mester, and that was a scramble, but I think it would have worked all the way through if Martha hadn't turned us all in."

"She turned you in," Gregor said. "That means she turned her-self in."

"We didn't think we had to worry about it," Janice said. "What kind of an idiot turns herself in in a situation like that. But she did. One day when the year was finally over, she went to the dean of students and spilled the whole thing. We all got F's in the course, and we all got excluded from the college for a semester. That meant we had to leave campus and stay away for the whole next fall semester before we could come back. But Martha didn't get excluded. She got put on probation and she just went on attending classes and living in the dorm as if nothing had ever happened. And if you ask me, she knew that was going to happen. She knew that if she blew the whole thing, she wouldn't get punished much at all."

"All right," Gregor said slowly. "I would think that would be a natural reaction on the part of the administration, though."

"Was it a natural reaction that they almost treated her like a hero?" Janice asked, sounding frustrated. "Everywhere you looked, you saw little notes in the alumnae magazine and the college newsletter, saying how awful we all were and what a wonderful person she was for coming forward and doing the honorable thing. It was worse than infuriating, it really was. And then, two years after all that, she did it again. She got this job as a camp counselor for the summer and the counselors pulled these pranks, like crop circles, and she was one of them and then she turned herself and all of them in. One of the girls in the year below us was one of the counselors. She told us all about it. And it was the same thing. It was almost as if she hadn't done anything wrong."

"Oh, my God," Bennis said. "I know what she's talking about. The thing about the black balls at the Athenaeum Club."

"Exactly," Janice said.

"Does somebody want to explain it to me?" Gregor asked.

"It doesn't matter," Janice Loftus said. "It's a pattern, can't you see that? She gets herself into these things. She even started the first one. Maybe she started all of them. She gets into them and then she blows the whole thing up and she not only doesn't get punished, people tell her how wonderful and principled she is. It's like a thing."

"And you think she was doing that here?" Gregor asked.

"There were all those rumors about her taking bribes," Janice said. "And they were more than rumors. A lot of people just knew, even if they couldn't prove it. You can't tell me you think she was the only judge taking bribes from these people, and there have to be other people in the system taking them, too, not just judges. There have to be. And she'd done it at least twice before, and now look at it."

"Three times," Bennis said. "It was just that way with the Athenaeum thing. She was the only one who wasn't forced to resign."

"If she was taking bribes, I'll bet you anything she was going to blow up the whole thing," Janice Loftus said. "And if somebody was going to murder her, I'll bet it's one of the people who was taking bribes, too, or the person who was giving them."

"And if that's what happened," Bennis said, "then whoever killed the woman wasn't Father Tibor."

3

Gregor Demarkian would have liked to tell Bennis that he never believed Father Tibor had killed Martha Handling, but after they saw Janice Loftus off in a cab, he couldn't get a word in edgeways.

"None of the motives the police came up with made any sense at all," Bennis insisted as they walked down the street to home. "And don't tell me the prosecution doesn't have to prove motive. You know as well as I do that juries want motive, and besides, you need motive for making sense of it. And there was never any motive for Tibor that made any sense."

"Just try to consider this one thing," Gregor managed when they came in through their front door. "Taking bribes as a judge isn't like cheating on a history test. Or even ten. You go to jail for taking bribes as a judge."

"Bet she thought she wouldn't," Bennis said. "Bet she thought she'd get probation."

"She'd be disbarred."

"You can be rehabilitated by the bar," Bennis said. "My brother Bobby's done it twice."

"Your brother Bobby wasn't a judge," Gregor said.

"Nobody in his right mind would hire Bobby as a lawyer, never mind make him a judge," Bennis said, "and that is, again, beside the point. If you can prove this woman was taking bribes, then—"

"Then what?"

"Then we'll be able to get Tibor out of this," Bennis said. "And yes, I know how he's been behaving, but forget it. There's got to be some explanation of it. And we'll find it out, and everything will be all right. My God, I feel sleepy for the first time in days."

Gregor did not feel sleepy, but he went upstairs and did the ritual bedroom thing anyway. Bennis threw on a nightgown and was alseep, on top of the covers, on her side of the bed, before Gregor had finished brushing his teeth.

Gregor watched her for a while, in that way when he was surprised to find he'd ended up here. She was a beautiful woman awake and a beautiful woman asleep. Gregor often found her not quite real.

He was exhausted, but he knew he wasn't going to sleep. He went downstairs in his pajamas and his robe and took his brief-case to the kitchen table. There he opened up his laptop and brought up the files he'd been given on the case. Then he took out the wads and wads of paper and spread them out.

He was still bent over the piles and piles of them at three o'clock in the morning, when the doorbell started ringing and somebody started pounding on the front door.

PART THREE

ONE

1

Gregor Demarkian had always thought of himself as the sensible one on Cavanaugh Street, the one who didn't accidentally leave his doors open all night, the one who didn't open up to strangers on the doorstep. There was something about the frantic ringing and pounding that went right through him. His first thought was that somebody must have been hurt on the street. He'd never known Cavanaugh Street to have a mugging, but that didn't mean it was impossible. His second thought was that one of the people he knew was in the middle of an emergency and just too frantic to think of the phone.

He pulled the door open without thinking twice about what he might find there, and ended up face-to-face with Asha Dekanian. It had started raining sometime in the night. The rain was coming down hard. Asha was wearing a thick overcoat over what looked like it might be a nightgown. Her hair was wet through and plastered to the sides of her face.

Gregor stepped back away from the door to let her in, and immediately heard movement above him on the stairs. Bennis was awake.

"Asha, come in," Gregor said, "get out of the rain. Are you all right? Are the children all right? What are you doing here?"

Asha scooted in rather than walked, and stood in the hallway while Gregor shut the door behind her. She was shaking so hard, her teeth were rattling. "I didn't know where else to go," she said. "I left the house, I was going to go to Mr. Donahue's, but then I thought, there are very small children there, practically a baby, I would ring on the doorbell and I would wake the baby. But I was already out in the street and I had to go somewhere. I came here. I came here because I thought you could know."

"Know what?" Gregor asked.

"Know where Mikel is," Asha said. "He didn't come home. He had an appointment but he went a little early to see about something and then he called me and then he didn't come home. It is three o'clock in the morning and he didn't come home."

Bennis had come the rest of the way down the stairs. "I'm going to put on some coffee. Or would you prefer tea, Asha? Are the children all right? Are they at home? Is there anybody with them?"

"The children are sleeping," Asha said. "I left them in their beds. They were sleeping. I had to come. You know Mikel. He would not go out and not come back all night. Mikel does not miss his dinner. I waited and I waited. I thought if I waited long enough he would have to come home. He always comes home. And now it is three o'clock in the morning, and I do not know where he is."

"I'll make the coffee and then I'll run over to Asha's house," Bennis said. "Kids have a remarkable tendency to wake up in the middle of these things."

She went to the back of the house, and Gregor started to urge Asha in that same direction.

"I did not know what to do," Asha said, crying. "I knew something had to be wrong when he was not home for dinner. He never misses his dinner, my Mikel. Sometimes in Armenia we would be missing dinner because there was no dinner to be had, but here he never misses his dinner."

It was one of those conversations that was going nowhere, but Gregor let the woman babble. He took her into the kitchen and found Bennis standing at one of the counters, putting out coffee cups.

Gregor herded Asha into a chair and got a cup to put in front of her. "Now," he said while Bennis watched the coffeemaker. "Start from the beginning. Mikel was supposed to have an appointment."

"This afternoon," Asha said. "He was supposed to go to Mr. Donahue's office about the mortgage. It is a terrible thing, what is happening with the mortgage. People call all hours of the day and night. Men come to the door and give me papers that I don't understand. They put big signs up in front of the house. They say they are going to put me into the street and with the children. There was a sign there yesterday and only this morning it was taken off. Mikel was very upset."

"Of course he was very upset," Gregor said.

Bennis brought the coffee over along another cup and poured out for both of them. "Give me your keys," she said to Asha. "I'll go over and babysit."

Asha looked at Bennis blankly.

"Oh, Lord," Bennis said. "You didn't bring your keys. Did you lock your door?"

Asha was trying very hard to think. "The door locks by itself," she said finally. "You pull the door and it locks by itself."

"Why did I know that was going to be the answer?" Bennis said. "Okay, let me get dressed and I'll wake up Steve Tekemanian."

"Why Steve Tekemanian?" Gregor asked.

"He's the only one I know with burglar's tools," Bennis said.

Gregor wanted to ask why Steve Tekemanian had burglar's tools, but Bennis was gone and Asha had gone back to crying.

"All right," he said. "So Mikel went out for an appointment this afternoon—"

"They came and took the sign down from the door," Asha said, "and Mikel had an appointment with Mr. Donahue. He took time off for the appointment. But maybe it was too much time off, because he got nervous. He paced up and down. He got very . . . agitated?" She let out with a string of Armenian, none of which Gregor understood.

Gregor tried again. "So," he said, "Mikel was home for that, and he was upset, and then you said he left early for his appointment."

Asha drank half her coffee in one gulp. Gregor thought it must have scalded her throat. She showed no signs of noticing.

"He thought of something," she said. "He thought that everybody was trying to show that there was no mortgage on our house from this big bank, but he thought maybe that was the wrong way to look at it. We did have a mortgage on our house, from our bank, from the American Amity Savings Bank. He thought we should go to see the mortgage at the Amity Savings Bank and then—" She stopped suddenly. "This is wrong. I don't understand it and I am getting it wrong."

"That's all right," Gregor said. "It's probably not something we need to know. He thought of an idea, a way to approach the problem with the big bank. Then what did he do?"

"He called Mr. Donahue," Asha said. "At his office. At Mr. Donahue's office. Mikel called him but he was not in. And the people at the office didn't know when he would be back. And Mikel was still very nervous. And he said he would go and look himself, to find this thing he'd thought of. And then he left."

"And that was when?"

"It was just after lunch," Asha said. "It was just about noon. Mikel always eats his lunch at eleven o'clock. He gets up very early in the morning."

"Did he say where he was going to check this thing?"

Asha nodded. "The Hall of Records. I remember the name. It was like a name from a textbook in Armenia. The buildings all had names like that."

"All right," Gregor said. "That makes sense. I saw him after lunch, maybe at two o'clock or so—"

"You saw him?" Asha said. "And he was all right? He was alive?"

"He was certainly alive," Gregor said. "He was in a big hurry. He didn't stop to talk. But it makes sense because I was at Homicide, and there are a lot of government buildings in that area. I think he could have been coming from the Hall of Records. I'll have to check a map. He was in a hurry and he said he had an appointment."

"Yes, yes," Asha said. "He had an appointment. He had an appointment with Mr. Donahue."

"And did you call Russ's office?"

"I thought that the appointment was going on for a long time. I thought that might be good news. And then when I did begin to worry, it was too late. When I called the office, I got only the answering machine. And then I really began to worry."

"Does Mikel have a cell phone?"

"Yes, of course. Everybody has a cell phone. Bums in the street have cell phones."

"Have you tried calling his cell phone?"

Asha nodded. "The first time it rang and rang and rang. The other times it only gave me voice mail."

"All right," Gregor said.

Bennis popped her head through the door. "I'm on my way. Steve is going to meet me there. He doesn't want to get started until I get there, though, because he says if he's going to get picked up by the cops, he wants Mrs. Gregor Demarkian along to get him out of jail."

"I should go back to get the children," Asha said.

"You don't have any keys either," Bennis said. "And your children know me. They even know Steve."

"We're going to call Russ Donahue and see if Mikel ever made his appointment," Gregor said. "Maybe we'll go over there and have a talk."

"I've got *my* keys," Bennis said. "And besides, I know how to get in without them."

She disappeared from the kitchen door, and Gregor noticed he was not spending his time reassuring Asha Dekanian.

2

Gregor called Russ, at home, but on his cell phone, so that he didn't wake up the entire house. He did wake up Donna. Gregor could hear her fussing in the background, asking about making coffee and putting out something for everybody to eat. Russ got her calmed down as best he could and agreed to go down the street to Gregor's to talk. Almost as soon as Russ rang off, Bennis called to tell them she was in the house, with Steve, and nobody had been arrested.

"Can you imagine us getting away with this on Cavanaugh Street?" she asked. "I think Hannah and Sheila stay up all night with binoculars."

Gregor didn't believe that it was exactly that bad, but he took her point. This little episode was going to be all over the Ararat in the morning, and it was already nearly morning. There was nothing to be done about it.

He kept hovering back and forth in the hall so that he would hear the doorbell as soon as it rang. He didn't want Russ pounding the way Asha had.

Russ's ring was barely any ring at all. The only reason he didn't walk right through the front door was that he probably thought Gregor had locked it. He had thrown on jeans and a cotton sweater and a raincoat so wrinkled, it must have been balled up in a drawer for months. He looked exhausted.

"I hope we didn't wake everybody up," Gregor said. "Asha came here because she didn't want to pound on your door and get the children out of bed. I didn't call on the landline for the same reason. I've got no idea if any of that did any good at all."

"You didn't wake up the children," Russ said. "Most of the time, I'd have said you couldn't have no matter what you did. They sleep like rocks. But the past few days, Tommy's been a little . . . rocky."

"Does he know what's going on?"

"Probably," Russ said. "Not that we've told him anything directly. Donna thinks it's better if he doesn't know. He's been destabilized already. But for God's sake, Gregor, what are the odds? He's a very bright kid. He sees the newspaper. He sees the news. He must have a fairly good idea."

"He hasn't asked about it?"

"No," Russ said. "Donna says he hasn't even asked her. With me—well, I'm a little rocky myself these days. I think he's gotten the impression that he should stay away from it where I'm concerned."

"He is a bright kid," Gregor said.

By then they'd reached the kitchen. Asha Dekanian was sitting at the kitchen table where Gregor had left her, crying into a handkerchief that was no longer much use.

"Oh," she said when they walked in. "Mr. Donahue!"

Russ went to the coffeemaker and set it up again. Nobody trusted Gregor to make coffee. Nobody trusted Tibor to make coffee either, but nobody was going to mention that now.

"Mikel is missing," Asha said. "He is not at home. He has not come home since he went out to see you."

"He also didn't see me," Russ said.

Asha Dekanian blanched. "He did not come to your appointment?"

"Not that I know of," Russ said. "I got back from a hearing and that was before he was due, so I got to working on the case and the next thing I knew, it was after six. And I'd assume that if he came in, somebody would have told me. He was in my appointment book."

"I suppose your secretaries would have six kinds of fits if we checked with them about it," Gregor said.

"Probably," Russ said. "But we could. Everybody's walking on eggshells anyway. The explosion is likely to be muted. But I don't think we can wake them up at this hour of the morning to do it."

"Mikel said you had told him you had good news," Asha said. "He was very happy about it. And that big sign came down off the front of the house. I was very happy about it."

"I do have good news," Russ said. "I actually got the court to grant an injunction. Why they should do it now when they wouldn't for the last six months is beyond me, but they did it. That means that nobody can go forward with the foreclosure until we've been able to bring our entire case into court on the countersuit. And that means that you're safe in your house for the foreseeable future. Safe from J.P. CitiWells, anyway. If you've got a problem with American Amity, that's something else."

"There is no problem with our real bank," Asha said stiffly. "Mikel is always on time with all his payments. Also his payments for electricity and everything else."

"I think the problem now is to find out what's happened to him," Gregor said. "I told Asha here that I'd seen him this afternoon. He was rushing off to an appointment. That could have been his appointment with you. Except I think it was just after lunch, and if his appointment with you was—"

"After three o'clock," Russ said.

"It seems a little early," Gregor said. "It seems a lot early. But he was very excited. He didn't stop to talk. And he looked frantic."

"He was going to the Hall of Records," Asha said. "He was going to look there for something to help our case."

Russ looked puzzled. "The Hall of Records? But why? There wouldn't be anything there. The only crux of this case is the fact that J.P. CitiWells didn't use the Hall of Records. They used that online database. If they'd used the Hall of Records, we could have had this whole thing cleared up in a day."

"There wasn't anything he could have found there at all?" Gregor said.

"I don't see what," Russ said. "The real mortgage is filed there, the one from American Amity Savings. But there's nothing wrong with that mortgage. And there's nothing there about J.P. CitiWells."

"I think maybe there is something he could find," Asha said. "And then these people, these people from the big bank with the ridiculous name, maybe they wanted to stop him from telling you about it."

Russ shook his head. "There really isn't anywhere to go with that. There isn't anything anybody could have found out that would make J.P. CitiWells want to . . . uh . . ."

"Liquidate him," Asha said firmly.

"Right," Russ said. "Liquidate him. There really isn't any reason why somebody from J.P. CitiWells would want to liquidate him. Or anybody else. No matter what they found out."

"They could go to jail for what they are doing," Asha said. "They don't want to go to jail."

"Nobody at J.P. CitiWells is going to jail for anything they're doing," Russ said. "No matter what it is. I can't even think of a scenario where that would be the case. Hell, they nearly wrecked the entire country and none of them went to jail. And this is, what? Yet another case of a mortgage mess the same as dozens they've had before."

"It's the dozens part I can't get over," Gregor said. "But I agree with Russ here. I don't think it's plausible to believe that somebody from J.P. CitiWells sent a hit man after Mikel, even if the timing wasn't so tight. Even if he found something out, how would the bank had known he'd found it? We're talking about the space of a few hours here."

"You said he was running," Asha said. "He was running for his life."

"He said he was late for an appointment," Gregor said. "It sounds to me as if that was too early to be his appointment with Russ here. Did he say anything about another appointment?"

"No," Asha said. "He said he was going to the Hall of Records, and then he was going to see Mr. Donahue."

"Maybe he made another appointment while he was out," Gregor said. "We should try to think of whom he'd make an appointment with. That might help."

"I hate to say it," Russ said, "but I think the most plausible explanation is that Mikel ran into trouble somewhere. You know what Philadelphia is like. There are neighborhoods and then there are other neighborhoods and they change in a flash. If he ended up somewhere that wasn't safe—"

"You are saying my Mikel is dead," Asha Dekanian said. Her voice was edging up into the frantic range. "You are saying somebody killed him and left his body in the street."

"I'm not saying anything of the kind," Russ said firmly. "I'm saying that the first thing we ought to do is to check the hospitals, because if he did run into trouble and got knocked out, he could be in one of those. He wouldn't necessarily still have his wallet with him. They would take the wallet. Did he have anything else on him that would identify him? You didn't by any chance sew a tag into his clothes."

"A tag? What is a tag?" Asha asked.

"It's a little printed label that you sew into clothes when you're going to go to camp or to a boarding school," Gregor said. "It's usually done for children."

"Mikel is not a child," Asha said.

"Of course not," Russ said. "But sometimes—" He looked at Asha's face and gave it up. "Let's get started calling hospitals," he said. "There aren't that many of them. If we don't find him, we'll think of something else."

The first thing Gregor thought of was the morgue, and he knew better than to say anything about that.

3

Three quarters of an hour later, they had found no trace of anybody who might be Mikel Dekanian at any of the hospitals, and they had also not found any trace of him at the morgue. Gregor had taken care of the morgue himself, going into a room where Asha couldn't hear him and getting a deputy coroner out of bed. The deputy coroner got two other people out of bed, and one of those finally found the woman who had access to the records they needed. No body brought into the morgue for the last twenty-four hours fit the description of Mikel Dekanian, even vaguely.

By then it was after five o'clock in the morning and the first traces of sun were coming up on the horizon. Gregor felt jet-lagged, and Russ looked it. Asha Dekanian was shaking in her chair.

"He has disappeared into thin air," she said. "He is lying dead somewhere and we will never find him."

"Don't go on like that," Gregor said. "There are still a lot of things that might have happened, and all of them are more likely than that he's lying dead somewhere. I think the next thing we need to do is to notify the authorities and get them to issue a silver alert—"

Russ shook his head. "You're not going to get them to do that today, no matter what you do," he said. "It hasn't even been twenty-four hours. As far as the police are concerned, he isn't even a missing person yet."

"I thought the point of the alerts was to start looking for missing people earlier," Gregor said.

"It is," Russ said, "but you've got to look at it from their point of view. He's a grown man, in good health, and in his right mind as far as anybody can tell. He's got an absolute right to go where he wants to go and to inform people of that or not as he wants. If they put out a silver alert for him right away and bring in the resources to go looking for him and it turns out he's just gone off to visit a friend in Sheboygan—"

"What is this Sheboygan?" Asha demanded.

"If it turns out he's gone off for some reason of his own," Russ went on, "they've not only wasted a lot of time and resources, but they're also stuck with the bill."

"Are you telling me Mikel would have gone away without telling me?" Asha demanded. "For what purpose? To see a woman? You think Mikel has run away with a woman?"

There was a sudden stream of vigorous and infuriated Armenian. Neither Gregor nor Russ knew what it meant, but they both winced.

"I don't think that's the likely explanation either," Gregor said, although there was a part of him that could see why it might be very likely indeed. "And I don't see why it would hurt to ask the authorities to put out an alert. If they say no, they say no. If he wanders in on his own, there's been no harm done even if they've said yes—"

"Except to the finances of the City of Philadelphia," Russ said.

"And let's face it," Gregor said, "we'll all feel a lot better. So let's get that done, and let's get Asha here back to her children, and then I'm going to go to the Ararat and have breakfast. I think sleeping is not very likely on this particular morning."

"All right," Russ said. "I'll go call in the alert."

Asha Dekanian hesitated. "I will return to my house," she said. "I will send Mrs. Demarkian back home. But Mikel is not somewhere with a woman. Mikel would not ever go away with a woman."

Gregor didn't think Mikel Dekanian had gone off with a woman either, but he wasn't sure why he didn't. He ushered Russ into the living room to make the call and bundled Asha Dekanian up to send her home and wished he didn't feel as tired as he did.

He'd just got Asha out into the morning when Russ came out of the living room, looking like hell.

"I take it you can't go back to sleep any more than I can," Gregor said.

Russ shrugged. "It's not like I'm sleeping all that well anyway," he said. "This is a hell of a mess. It really is."

"I take it you're not talking about Mikel Dekanian."

"I think the odds are that Mikel Dekanian met some friend of his somewhere and they tied one on but good, and he'll show up in a couple of hours with egg on his face."

"Is Mikel prone to that kind of thing?"

"No," Russ said, "but you don't have to be prone to that kind of thing to do it. And that is the way these things usually turn out. I've seen maybe six of them in my career, and that's the way all of those turned out. No, it's not Mikel. It's not even the mortgage thing. I've made some progress in the mortgage thing."

"If it helps any, Tibor isn't talking to me any more than he's talking to you," Gregor said.

"You know who he is talking to?" Russ asked. "Hannah Krekorian. Hannah went over to the jail to see him yesterday, and he saw her. Agreed to talk to her through those telephone hookups."

"All right," Gregor said. "That could be a good sign. Did you talk to her? Did she tell you anything Tibor said?"

"I didn't talk to her, Donna did," Russ said. "And from what I gather, he said practically nothing, and she spent the entire visiting time crying and accusing him of things. You know Hannah. And what does that mean, that he'd talk to Hannah and not to either of us?"

"It could mean he's ashamed of himself," Gregor said.

"Do you believe that?"

"No," Gregor said. "At least, not in the way it sounds. I don't think he killed that woman and now he's afraid to face us. I think maybe he's afraid to talk to us because he knows that if he did talk to us, he might not be able to keep his silence about what actually happened. I just wish I could think of what that might be."

"Right," Russ said. "I wish I could think of anything. I'd better go home, Gregor. Donna's probably frantic. And Bennis will be home in a minute. I've actually got work to do today."

"I know," Gregor said. "So do I."

"It's just so strange," Russ said. "I always knew Tibor was the bedrock of this neighborhood, but I think I always thought of that as an abstraction. It's just so strange for him not to be here. As if the whole place has emptied out."

"I know exactly what you mean," Gregor said.

And he did.

TWO

1

When Father Tibor Kasparian was honest with himself, he had to admit that he was going a little crazy. He was almost certain that he would be allowed to have books if he asked for them. He'd seen that on television once or twice. Even prisoners on death row were allowed to have books. What he wasn't so clear on was the way it worked. Was there a prison library somewhere, where he could borrow books? He hadn't seen a prison library or heard of one, but he spent all but an hour a day in this small cell. Anything could be going on out there, and he wouldn't know about it.

Maybe the problem was that he was not in prison. He was in jail. He had been vaguely aware, before all this happened, that there was a difference, but he'd never paid much attention to it. Jail was where you waited for your trial. Prison was where you served your sentence. He was pretty sure he had that right. He wondered if prison was like this, with small cells with solid doors and almost no way to look out. He wondered if prisoners were like this, not just cooped up but also so bored, it was hard to remember how to breathe. If they were, then Tibor Kasparian was no longer the least surprised that there were prison riots.

Somewhere along the line, Tibor had passed through a barrier, and he knew it. He was bored and lonely and desperately isolated. Things were going on in the world, and he knew about none of them. Things were going on with the case, yes, but they were also going on in the real world. There were elections coming up in a couple of months. There would be political ads and debates and television opinion shows where everybody was lying. There were episodes of *Downton Abbey* he hadn't gotten around to watching on Netflix. He had not been in jail for a full calendar week, so the church was all right for the moment. It wouldn't be all right in the long run. There would be no service Sunday, unless somebody did something drastic. Tibor didn't see who would or what that would be. Sometime along the line, they would have to get another priest.

He wanted to think that the jails where they kept juveniles were not like this, but he was sure they were. He imagined Stefan Maldovanian locked up in a small room with nothing to do. He imagined Petrak Maldovanian, too, although Petrak would probably be sent to an adult prison. Closed up and bored. Losing their minds. Never making anything of themselves, because there was less and less of themselves to make every single day.

When they came and told him he had visitors, he didn't hesitate. He really *had* crossed a line. He needed to see people. He needed to talk to them. He didn't think he would agree to talk to Gregor. Talking to Gregor would be far too dangerous. But he would talk to anybody else. He would even talk to Bennis and Donna, if they came.

It was not Bennis and Donna who came. The guard who brought the message garbled the names, but Tibor had no problem at all knowing what they were.

"I haven't seen them yet myself," the young woman guard said when she got him out and all trussed up to move. "But I'll tell you, Chris downstairs couldn't stop laughing."

Tibor would have bet his life that Chris downstairs wasn't laughing where the Very Old Ladies could hear him. Nobody laughed at the Very Old Ladies unless he was suicidal.

Tibor wondered absently what they were doing about the setup downstairs, which allowed only one person to sit down in the cubicle and talk through the phone.

He also wondered what time it was. It was after breakfast and the long rigamarole that was getting teeth brushed and generally cleaned up. After that, there had been A Lot of Time, but that could mean anything.

When he got to the booth where they wanted him to sit, Tibor saw that Mrs. Vespasian was in the seat in front of the glass panel, and her two minions were standing right behind her. All three of the women were exceedingly frail. All three of them had to be well into their nineties. Not one of them was headed for a nursing home anytime soon.

Mrs. Vespasian had her walking stick with her, the ebony one with the ivory handle that one of her great-grandchildren had bought for her on a trip to London. She looked grim, but she always looked grim. The other two only looked worried.

"This is ridiculous," she said when she picked up the phone.

"What do they expect me to do with a walking stick? If it's not on the ground as my fifth leg, I cannot stand up."

She could always use it to whack people when she was sitting down, Tibor thought. He didn't say it.

"And this thing," Mrs. Vespasian said, gesturing to the cubicle and the glass and the phone. "What is this thing? What do they expect three old women are going to do? What do they expect you are going to do? You never hurt anyone in your life."

This wasn't true. Tibor let it go. "I am very glad to see you," he said. "It becomes very boring in here. And I do not hear news."

"It wouldn't be so boring if you got out of here," Mrs. Vespasian said, "and I am sure you can get out of here if you tell me what is going on." Suddenly she switched to Armenian. It had been seventy years since she last saw Armenia, but she had not forgotten the language. "This is a ridiculous thing you are doing. Nobody believes in it. Even you do not believe in it. I can see it in your face."

"But I do believe in it," Tibor said, also in Armenian. "That is the one thing I am sure of."

"I am sure that Krekor Demarkian says you are a fool," Mrs. Vespasian said, "and I think he knows fools. You are a priest. You should act with morality. If you have committed this murder, you should say so. If you have not committed this murder, you should say what really happened. I do not think you have committed this murder. Do you want to know why?"

"Yes," Tibor said.

"If you think I am going to say that I know you and I know you would not commit a murder, this is false," Mrs. Vespasian said. "I know what people are. I know what they will do if they are pushed into the wrong place. No, I do not know for certain that you would not commit a murder. But I know that that video film everyone is showing everybody else on their phones is a fake."

Tibor suddenly felt as if he *really* couldn't breathe. He felt as he did when he'd fallen off a slide as a child and had all the wind knocked out of him.

"Fake," he said.

"I am hard of hearing, Father, and you know it," Mrs. Vespasian said. "So I have a phone my great-granddaughter got for me, it has special powers to help my hearing. And I can turn it up until it is very loud. So I watched that silly video, and then I turned the sound all the way up and I listened. And do you know what I heard?"

"No," Tibor said.

"Your hand would go up and then it would come down and there would be a thud, a hard thud, the hammer was coming down on a hard place. On wood. You can hear the sound of wood. If the hammer had been coming down on the body of that woman, the sound would not be hard or sharp. It would be . . . squish."

Tibor winced. He had heard that squish, and he never wanted to hear it again. He never wanted to think about it. He could barely believe that old Mrs. Vespasian had thought about it.

"Don't treat me like an idiot," Mrs. Vespasian said. "I am not a delicate flower. I was in Yerevan at least once when the Turks came. And I was very small."

"This is not the Turks," Tibor said.

"This is not a movie of a murder," Mrs. Vespasian said. "This is a fake. And I have come to find out what it is you think you're doing."

"*Tcha,*" Tibor said.

"If you do not tell me," Mrs. Vespasian said, "I will go to Gregor Demarkian and make sure he knows that this movie is a fake."

"*Tcha,*" Tibor said again.

"At least it will stop him worrying about this fool man who has run away from his wife," Mrs. Vespasian said. "I have never heard so much fuss and nonsense in my life. I will go now, Father, and I will show this to Gregor Demarkian, and he will know what to do with the information."

2

Mark Granby was standing at the window of his office, trying to work out his options, when he saw Gregor Demarkian get out of a cab in front of the building. There was no mistaking what that was going to be about. If everybody else had heard the rumors about Martha Handling's corruption, Gregor Demarkian must have, too. And Gregor Demarkian was supposed to still have friends in the FBI. It was possible he knew a lot more than anybody else. Rumors sparked investigations. Mark hadn't seen any sign of these investigations, but ever since Martha Handling died, he'd been thinking about them.

And then there was the other thing. Mark had been thinking about the other thing since it first showed up on his doorstep. He still didn't know what to make of it.

He heard the wheeze of the elevator in the hallway, even though the door of the office suite was closed. He heard the door of the office suite creak open. Everything was cheap, and everything was just a little bit dangerous. But he'd known that when he first came in.

He'd also known that what he was doing was against the law. It would be really nice to say there was some confusion, but he knew he couldn't try it without cracking up. They had a lot of euphemisms for bribery at Administrative Solutions, but all of them were transparent.

The girl in the outer office came in and announced that Gregor Demarkian was waiting to see him. She allowed as how Gregor Demarkian didn't have an appointment. She admitted that she should have told him Mark wasn't there. She had not done any such thing. Gregor Demarkian was somebody she'd heard of. She was impressed by people she thought of as "celebrities" and thought Mark ought to be impressed by "celebrities," too.

Did the New York office work this cheap? Did they scrimp on the salaries of secretaries so that they got only half-brained reality TV–addled incompetents with no sense at all? If they did, Mark was in much worse trouble than he'd thought he was in.

The girl came back in with Demarkian in tow. He was a massive man, not fat but ridiculously tall and broad across the shoulders. It was like looking at a superhero on a television show, only older.

The girl went back out and did not close the door behind her. Mark got up and did it himself. Then he gestured Gregor to the single visitor's chair and sat down behind his desk.

"So," he said. "I was expecting you."

Gregor Demarkian cocked his head, looking puzzled. "I came up here thinking you were going to stonewall me," he said. "But you're not going to do that. Why not?"

"I've got my sources of information just like you have," Mark said. "Some of my sources may even be better than yours."

"I doubt it," Demarkian said.

"Faster, then," Mark said. "I take it there are investigations into Martha Handling and all her works. And she was a piece of work, let me tell you."

"You didn't like her." It wasn't a question.

"It was hard to like Martha," Mark said. "There was good reason her secretaries left her practically as soon as they started. Excuse me, personal assistants. We don't call them secretaries any longer."

"She was an unpleasant person," Demarkian said.

"Not really," Mark told him. "She could be very pleasant and charming on the right occasion, and she didn't throw full-throttle tantrums. There's some kind of bizarre connection between judges who are willing to take bribes and full-throttle tantrums. That wasn't Martha's problem. Martha's problem was that she was a fundamentally dishonest person. She was dishonest about things she didn't need to be dishonest about. It creeped out everybody who had to spend time with her. She'd even push her assistants to do things, steal office supplies and bring them to her house, all kinds of stupid little things."

"And yet she had a very distinguished career," Gregor said. "Somebody had to make her a judge."

"Maybe that just tells you something about the state of things up in Harrisburg," Mark said. "There are a lot of things that ought to be investigated up in Harrisburg."

"Did you know Martha Handling spray-painted the lenses of the security cameras in the places she went in the courthouse?"

"Oh, sure," Mark said. "She told me about that one herself. My God, paranoid? You wouldn't have believed the woman. She was convinced they were bugging her house and her chambers and just about everything else, everywhere. I thought it was kind

236

of weird. Somebody that dishonest, you'd figure she wouldn't be that insane about getting caught. But she was."

"Did you know that she didn't actually get all the cameras?" Demarkian asked. "Did you know that the cameras in front, right after you came in from the street, and all the way down the corridor on the right to where the restrooms were, were functioning?"

"And they showed me coming in and going down the hall?" Mark asked. "That figures. Did they show anything important, like my going down the hall to her chambers?"

"No."

"One point for my side."

"But you must have gone all the way down the corridor to her chambers," Demarkian said, "because that was the only reason you could have been there. You have no actual business in the courthouse. And you wouldn't go there to talk to Martha Handling about bribes, or to give her bribe money. It was insane for you to go anywhere near the place. So why were you there?"

Mark considered that. "I was kidding myself," he said.

"I don't know what that means," Demarkian said.

"When I first started with this, when I was first hired by Administrative Solutions and found out what we were doing behind the scenes, I told myself that I'd let it go so far and no farther, so I didn't end up in jail. I don't think I ever believed it, not all the way. I think I knew in the back of my mind that when the shit hit the fan, I was going to be over. But I did a pretty good job of kidding myself."

"And it didn't bother you that you were paying Martha Handling to give jail sentences to kids for things they'd normally only get probation for? That these kids, some of them as young as eight or nine, that you were incarcerating these kids, taking them away from their families and their schools and their friends and everything they'd ever known and probably ending any chance they would ever have for a real future?"

"It wasn't only kids," Mark said. "Though between mandatory minimums and the whole 'law and order,' 'throw away the key' mentality, there was no need to pay judges in the adult courts. There's one guy in Pittsburgh they call Ninety-nine Klein because he doesn't like to give sentences less than ninety-nine years. And then he piles on anything extra he can get away with and has them all run consecutively. We've got one guy in the state prison doing two hundred twenty-five. It'll be ninety-nine years before he's eligible for parole. And all he did was have a gun on him while he was smoking crack."

"I still think that's a far cry from locking up children," Demarkian said.

"Yeah, well," Mark said. "If you want to lie to yourself about that, you tell yourself there are predatory children. And there are. Predatory children. Born psychopaths."

"So you went to the courthouse on the day Martha Handling was murdered to talk to her about predatory children?"

"No, of course not. I went there to retrieve a cell phone. Martha being the paranoid nutcase that she was, she wouldn't talk to me on a regular phone. She brought prepaid cell phones, new ones every few weeks, always entirely different numbers. It was enough to want to make you shoot her on principle."

"I don't think it's entirely implausible that her phone might be tapped," Demarkian said. "There are investigations ongoing. Somebody could have gotten a warrant."

"True," Mark said, "but it's like I said: She was a paranoid nutcase. We never talked about anything in plain English. If somebody had listened in on our conversations, all they would have heard was gibberish."

"Then why try to retrieve the cell phone?" Demarkian asked. "That was a big risk to take."

"Because cell phones store information," Mark said. "And that wouldn't be enough by itself, but Martha was making noises about going to the authorities. She seemed to think that if she turned herself in and gave them everything they needed to prosecute—well, everybody—that she'd be in a better position herself."

"Prosecutors do make deals of that kind."

"I know they do," Mark said, "but only if they haven't got the information any other way. And you don't get a really good deal unless you go to the authorities before they actually know that anything is happening. And I'm pretty sure they all knew that something was happening, even if they hadn't got around to nailing it yet."

"Martha Handling wanting to go to the authorities is more of a motive for murder than for retrieving the cell phone," Demarkian said.

"Sure it was," Mark agreed. "But it wasn't just a motive for me. There were dozens of people involved in these things, and I don't even know most of them. There were the judges, I know them, but the judges couldn't do what they were doing without at least some collaboration from at least some of the lawyers, and then there were the guards and the social workers and the psychologists. We paid Martha Handling a set scale of fees for each juvenile she incarcerated for a year or longer, but sometimes to get the back up to do that, she'd have to pay somebody to give her the kind of report she wanted or play the defense just the right way. And we told her—right from the beginning—that whatever was going on with that, we didn't want to know about it. As far as we were concerned, she could do whatever she wanted with whoever she wanted, but we didn't want to know about it. And we didn't. As far as I know, she was flying blind. But that's the thing. Those people, whoever they were, had to have more of a reason to kill her than I did. As far as I know, those people were completely clean as long as Martha didn't open her mouth. I was going to be in for it no matter what."

"Then why try to retrieve the cell phone?" Demarkian asked.

"Because without the cell phone, I thought it would be all 'he said, she said.' The cell phone was hard evidence."

"And did you retrieve it?"

"No," Mark said. "The day after the murder, I nearly killed myself going in there and trying to find it. I thought the police might have missed it. And before you start—yes, I know that was a crazy idea. But Martha was so paranoid, I thought that if she had it on her, she would have put it somewhere safe. So I went out there a couple of times and went looking around. There was police tape up, but there weren't all that many people there, and they weren't really watching. But I couldn't find it. I thought the police must have it, at first."

"At first?"

"Well," Mark said, "I think maybe I ought to tell you about the kid."

3

Petrak Maldovanian was not a happy person. When he had first started doing what he was doing, he had had only one object in mind. He wanted his brother, Stefan, out of jail, and if he could manage it, he wanted Stefan still in the United States. That second thing was not as important as the first, because if Stefan was deported, it would not be to Armenia. He would be sent back to Canada and their other aunt. Canada was a pretty good place, and safe. It just wasn't right in Petrak's lap.

And Petrak had been thinking about it. So far, the experiment with the United States had not been working out for Stefan as he'd hoped it would. The United States was fine, but Stefan himself was behaving like an idiot. Only an idiot ran around shoplifting things in order to join a club. Even if Stefan was being completely accurate and the club was not a gang—and Petrak hadn't conceded that point yet—even so, it was a stupid thing to do, and a club like that was not a good influence. If they were able to keep Stefan in the United States, then they would have to find him another school. He had to be away from the club and the other boys in it.

Stefan would be away from the other boys if he was in Canada. Petrak now thought it might be a better idea if Stefan went back to Canada.

Stefan could not go back to Canada if he was in jail. Jail was the important thing now. And Petrak hated to see Stefan the way he was in jail, with the jumpsuit and the locks and the way people acted as if he were a wild animal that would turn and savage them without warning and at any moment. Petrak was very sure that this was not a good way to treat people. People would not be better for it. A boy like Stefan would not be better for it. It would change the way he thought of himself, and that would change everything else he did.

This was, really, more than Petrak felt capable of thinking through. His impressions were vague. His feelings were confused. He didn't know anything about jails or how they worked, or even about Stefan and how he worked. He just had impressions, and the impressions were very strong.

His instinct was to sit back and wait for Mark Granby to do what he had asked him to do. This might take a long time, which made him edgy. He went to see Stefan every chance he got, and he paid attention to what was happening with the case. Nothing was happening with the case. The judge was dead, and everybody was milling around, talking but doing nothing. Stefan was supposed to have another hearing. He couldn't have another hearing until a hearing was scheduled. As of this morning, no hearing had been scheduled. Not until a hearing was scheduled could they know which judge would preside, and until they knew that, they couldn't do anything.

"It's very important," Mark Granby had said. "We don't do these things right out in the open. And I can't go. You have to go."

Mark Granby's voice sounded odd. It reminded Petrak of the noise people made in their throats when they were being strangled in the movies. He was also whispering, as if he were close to other people and afraid of being overheard. It made Petrak uneasy.

"You have to go," Mark Granby insisted.

All Petrak could think of was that the man was setting him up for a mob hit.

The impression of an impending mob hit was so strong, Petrak nearly ignored the whole thing. It occurred to him that Mark Granby now knew something he hadn't known before. He knew that Petrak had been lying. Petrak did carry the phone on him. He carried it on him at all times. There was no place safe to put it. Aunt Sophie cleaned religiously and often. She'd find it no matter where he put it in his room. She'd look at it, too.

And that would be the end of everything.

Petrak thought about the phone. He thought about the mob hit. He thought about the place where he was supposed to be meeting a woman named Lydia Bird. It was a ridiculous name, Lydia Bird. He couldn't find her name on the list of city employees. But maybe judges were not city employees, and maybe Lydia Bird was not a judge. It was impossibly difficult to know what to do.

In the end, he went, all the way down to the center of the city, in a part of town he knew nothing about. He had a vague impression that he should know where he was, that he didn't know only because he had come the wrong way around. Since he could not connect that thought to any solid information, he let it go and concentrated on the three-by-five card where he had written down the information.

There were big official-looking buildings all around him, but when he made the next turn, there were mostly small stores and filling stations and pawnshops. Petrak didn't like pawnshops. They made him depressed.

Petrak made one more turn and found himself in an alley. The alley was lined with big garbage bins, but at the very end of it was a door into the back of one of the brick buildings that backed on the alley. That would be their garbage cans he was passing.

That would be the door he was supposed to go through.

It looked . . . wrong.

Petrak swallowed his fear and walked all the way down to the door, all the way past the garbage cans. Of course it felt wrong. It was wrong. All the things they were doing here—it was all wrong. It had to be wrong to take a kid like Stefan and lock him up for years for shoplifting a couple of video games.

The last instruction was the easiest to follow: "Don't knock. Walk right in."

Petrak did not knock.

He stood in front of the door. He took deep breaths to calm the shaking in his arms.

He grabbed the door and pulled it open.

There was no mob hit waiting for him. There were no thick men with machine guns. There was no hired assassin in black spandex with a silencer on his rifle.

There was only the dead body of a man Petrak Maldovanian knew, but took a few minutes to recognize.

THREE

1

It took Gregor Demarkian three calls to George Edelson—and George Edelson seven calls to people as far away as Harrisburg—to get Gregor into the juvenile detention center to see Stefan Maldovanian. It took that long, and yet Gregor still wasn't sure why he wanted the interview.

Mark Granby told Gregor about "the kid," and the kid had turned out to be Petrak Maldovanian. That gave Gregor not one, but two possible motives for the murder of Martha Handling, both of them more plausible than the motive now on the table. More than that, it gave him a possible explanation for Tibor's behavior. That was more than anybody had had up to this point, and it was also the weak spot in the prosecutor's case. What was even better, that explanation did not require Tibor to have killed anyone.

Still, there were pieces, pieces that didn't fit, pieces that bothered him. The most logical explanation would be that Mark

Granby, or somebody like him, somebody involved in the corruption, had killed Martha Handling before she had had a chance to rat them all out. But even Mark Granby had seen the flaw in that.

"Your priest has been running around like an idiot, doing God knows what," Mark said. "Do you honestly think he'd do that to protect somebody who was involved in bribery? It makes more sense to go with what the police think and assume he killed the woman because he wanted that kid out of her court. Out of it and not likely to go to juvenile detention for two years. Or more."

This was, unfortunately, true. If Tibor was not guilty of murder, then he had to be protecting someone, he had to be diverting the blame. Gregor had had a vague inkling of that from the beginning, but it had come up against a wall of logic. The wall said that it was not likely that Tibor would shield a murderer. Tibor was not an idiot. He knew why that would not be a good idea.

But if the murderer were a child, or close to a child, if he was just a "kid" starting out . . . there might be a possibility there.

"And if you think the kid didn't have it in him," Mark Granby said, "let me disabuse you of the notion. He's as cold as ice. And he means what he says. And he'd thought it all through. He's got that cell phone hidden away somewhere, and he's going to hold on to it until I deliver. I didn't tell him I almost certainly couldn't deliver, because I didn't want him giving that damn thing to the police, but he knows what he wants and he knows what to threaten. And then there's the other thing."

"What's that?" Gregor asked.

"He's got that cell phone," Mark Granby said. "He says he picked it up on the floor where somebody dropped it, but does that make any sense to you? It was Martha Handling's cell phone. The only people who would have taken it out of the murder room were people who knew what was on it and wanted to get it away before the police found it. And virtually all of those people are people involved in the bribes, or the actual killer, looking for some kind of edge."

Gregor thought that Mark Granby didn't know that cell phone was probably the one on which the video had been made. If it was the one on which the video had been made, then—then what? Then the video was staged. He'd already considered that. And it was just possible that Tibor would stage something like that to protect a kid. *Just* possible.

But was Petrak Maldovanian a kid? He was over eighteen.

"All I can tell you," Mark Granby said, "is that he was in this office, and he had Martha Granby's throwaway cell phone. You can take it from there."

Gregor had no idea where to take it. He wanted to talk to Petrak Maldovanian, but after making a few tries at finding him, he realized it wasn't going to happen. Sophie Maldovanian had no patience with the entire project.

"He *should* be at school," she told Gregor, "and if he's not there, he should be at work. The Ohanians have him lifting boxes and that kind of thing while Mary Ohanian's ankle heals up. But don't ask me if he's gone either place, because I just don't know. He's like the Flying Dutchman, that kid is. You never know where he is or what he's doing, and he doesn't know it himself."

Sophie gave Gregor Petrak's cell phone number, but when Gregor had called it, he was sent directly to voice mail. Maybe Petrak was at school or work and had turned the phone off so he would not be interrupted.

It was after that that Gregor thought about Stefan, and started the round of phone calls that ended with his standing in the foyer of JDF. The place was barren and old, just slightly dirty around the edges, and it had the most depressing aura Gregor had ever experienced. Did they really bring kids to a place like this? Kids as young as seven ended up in juvenile hall. Kids who had done . . . what?

Gregor had never thought very much about juvenile crime. He was vaguely aware that juveniles could go to jail for actual crimes, but could also go to jail for things that were not crimes for adults, like skipping too much school or being too obviously and consistently sexually active at too young an age. There was something arbitrary about the whole thing. Some kids who were sexually active, even kids who gave birth at twelve or thirteen, got help from the state to set up homes for themselves and their children and accommodations from the schools so that they could stay to graduate from high school. Others got sent to jail. Gregor didn't know why the decisions were made, or even by whom.

The policewoman at the entry desk apologized when she ran him up and down with one of those metal detecting wands and then made him empty his pockets and walk through a metal detector as well. "We really aren't being melodramatic about all this," she said. "We have constant problems—you really wouldn't believe them. The threat of violence is the worst, of course, but it isn't the most common thing. It's contraband that's the most common thing. Marijuana. Pills. Anything they can use to commit suicide."

"Suicide?"

"It stands to reason," the policewoman said. "It's frightening, coming into a place like this. They don't think it through. They don't consider the ways in which the system can help them. They just think they're looking at the end of the world."

Gregor thought that if he had ever ended up in a place like this, he would have considered it the end of the world. This was not a system that seemed to offer any help. It wasn't one in the foyer, and it didn't become one when he passed through the locked solid metal fire door into the hallways beyond. This was a system meant to cage in people who were dangerous and unpredictable.

Another policewoman met him in the corridor. She had a nightstick at her hip and a huge ring of keys on her belt. "Mr. Demarkian?" she asked. "We have instructions from the office of the governor. It's usually contrary to regulations to allow visits by anyone but the family and the attorney, and except for the attorneys, we don't usually allow visits outside of scheduled visiting hours. We do understand that this visit is important and may have long-term implications for Stefan's case, but we do ask you to keep this as brief as you can. It disrupts the routine."

"I'll be as quick as I can," Gregor said.

"Not that there's all that much of a routine," the woman said. "Dispositions in these cases are supposed to be fairly rapid. We need them to be rapid, because we really can't handle a full-scale education program here. Clients are supposed to come here for a day or two and then go home, or to a full-service facility. And education is important. Education is the key to making sure that these kids don't end up in the system forever."

"And does that work?" Gregor asked. "Does education stop most of these kids from ending up in the system forever?"

The policewoman gave Gregor a dry and sardonic look. "No," she said, "but you'd better understand something else: This one seems to be harmless enough, but there are a fair number of children here who are not. It may shock you to realize it, but there are children in the system who have committed very serious crimes. Crimes of violence. Even murders. If they're fifteen, the Commonwealth tries them as adults. If they're younger, you have to find something to do with them."

"I'm sure you do," Gregor said, but he couldn't force himself to say anything more encouraging.

They had come to yet another solid metal door. The policewoman opened it to reveal a tall, cadaverous teenager in a jumpsuit sitting at a laminated table. His hands were not cuffed, but Gregor caught a look at his feet, and saw that his legs were in irons.

"This is Mr. Demarkian, Stefan," the policewoman said. "He wants to talk to you."

She went out of the room as quickly as she could, and both Gregor and Stefan heard the door click locked behind her.

Stefan seemed to be in a trance. He stared at the door. He stared at Gregor Demarkian. He didn't blink. Then, suddenly, he let out a stream of words Gregor mostly didn't understand.

"Sorry," Gregor said. "I was born and raised right here in Philadelphia. I know almost no Armenian at all. I can swear a little. I can say hello and good-bye. I can order food. That's about it."

Stefan looked around the small, cramped room. "They listen to you," he said. "If you speak in English or even in Spanish, they hear everything you say. I think they do that even when the lawyers are here. They say they don't, but they do."

"If they really do listen in when the lawyers are here," Gregor said, "you'd have a very good case for a rights violation. That's not just against the law, it's against the Constitution."

Stefan shrugged. "I don't think they care about anything," he said. "They are always smiling at you, except when they're not smiling, and then that is . . . more honest. When I first came here, they said I would only have to be here one week, but it is now very much longer. And nobody will tell me anything. Even Mr. Donahue won't tell me anything. He only says the hearing will have to be rescheduled."

"I think that may be all he knows," Gregor said. "Things are a little disorganized now, and it's only the third day after. Under the circumstances—"

"She was an evil woman," Stefan said. "Everything you heard about her said she was an evil woman."

"Had you ever seen her before the day she died?"

"I never saw her," Stefan said. "She was out of the courtroom before they brought me in. There was a hearing before mine, and she went away somewhere."

"So you'd only heard she was a bad person?"

"Petrak saw her," Stefan said. "He didn't see her in the courtroom that day, but when he heard she was the judge I would have to see, he went to the courthouse and hung around until he saw her. They won't let anyone into the hearings who are not part of the hearings, so he said he had to wait around a very long time and he only saw her by accident. He said he had to walk around in the corridors and then it was just an accident and he only knew who she was because another woman said her name. He said she was like that woman in Harry Potter."

"Woman in Harry Potter?"

Stefan considered this. "Umbridge," he said. "Dolores Umbridge. She is an evil woman in the Harry Potter movies. I know there are Harry Potter books, but my English is not good enough for them. And I don't like to read, even in Armenian."

If Tibor were here, he would have staged a fit at that one, but Gregor didn't bother.

"So you've never seen her," he said, "and on the day in the courtroom, you were seated at the desk for the defense?"

"I was seated at a table," Stefan said. "It was probably the table for the defense, yes. And Mr. Donahue was there. And there were chairs behind us, there was a railing right behind us and there were chairs behind that, and Petrak and our aunt Sophie were sitting in the chairs. We were waiting for the judge and we were waiting for Father Kasparian, because he had promised to come, and to speak for me. But Mr. Donahue was not happy. He did not think there was much hope. He said that this judge sent everybody to jail and sent them to jail for a very long time. I think—"

"Yes?"

"I know it is wrong, what I did," Stefan said. "I am not trying to say it was not wrong. They say that to you here over and over again. You cannot go home from here if you say what you did was not wrong. I am trying only to say that it was a stupid thing, not an evil thing. It was wrong but it was only stupid."

"All right," Gregor said. "From what I've heard, it was pretty damned stupid."

"There is a boy here who has murdered his mother," Stefan said. His eyes got that blinkless stare again, the one he'd worn when the policewoman was still here. "He is eight years old and he took a kitchen knife and stabbed her seven times in the throat. He knocked her over and he stabbed her. He talks about it all the time. He talks about the blood and he talks about how awful she was and all the things she did to him, but I do not know what is the truth and what is not the truth. When I first got here, there was a boy who screamed all the time, screamed and said bad words, but they took him away. They said they took him to a hospital."

252

"You do need to get out of here," Gregor said. "I'm sure they're doing the best they can. I'll go ask questions of the people in charge, if you want me to."

"I want to go home," Stefan said. He was over six feet tall, but he suddenly looked as small as a toddler, and as scared. "I want to go to Aunt Sophie's or to Canada or even to Armenia. I want to go home. I did a stupid thing and it was wrong, but it was not evil. It was not evil."

"Yes," Gregor said. "I know that. I think most of the people involved in this know that."

"It was not evil," Stefan said again.

"Try to think of something else for just a minute," Gregor said. "It may make a lot of difference to figuring out what happened that day. And if we can figure out what happened that day, maybe we can get all this straightened out."

"Petrak said that Father Kasparian killed that judge for me," Stefan said. "He said that Father Kasparian killed that judge because she gave long sentences and the next judge would not and it would be better for me."

"Did you see him leave the courtroom the day the judge died?"

"Everybody left the courtroom the day the judge died," Stefan said. "Not everybody. Everybody with me. Mr. Donahue went to see if Father Kasparian was outside, and Petrak went out to find them, and Aunt Sophie went out because they were gone so long, and then she was gone long and when she came back she said something had happened but she didn't know what. And it was all very crazy and it took a very long time, but I couldn't go anywhere because the police guards were always there. So I just sat at the table and waited. I stared straight ahead so nobody could say I was thinking of something."

"And you're sure you didn't see anything," Gregor said. "You didn't see the judge, you didn't see anything unusual on any of the people when they came back to the courtroom."

"They didn't come back to the courtroom," Stefan said. "They went away and it was a long time and then the guards came and took me back here. And I heard people talking about it in the hallways, but nobody told me right away. But Petrak told me later. He said that Father Kasparian was in the room near the body of the judge and he had blood on him everywhere, but everybody else had blood on them, too; there were a lot of people. Even Petrak had blood on him, and his teacher who had given him the ride to the court, she had it all over her. He said there was blood everywhere."

"Did he tell you anything about a cell phone? Not his cell phone, but another one?"

Gregor saw it happen right before his eyes. The blank stare went. The head turned away.

And suddenly, Stefan Maldovanian could speak nothing but Armenian.

2

The call came just as Gregor was getting into a cab outside JDF, and since it was from George Edelson, he took it.

"I've just gotten word of something very peculiar," Edelson said. "Tony Monteverdi and Ray Berle have just caught another murder case."

"And that's peculiar? Murder isn't all that peculiar in Philadelphia."

"The guy the uniforms detained turns out to be somebody

you know," Edelson said. "Kid by the name of Petrak Maldovanian. On the suspect list for the murder of Martha Handling, if there was a suspect list when the DA's office thinks the case has been solved. Brother of the kid whose hearing was supposed to happen the day Martha Handling was killed."

Gregor considered this. "Who was killed?"

"I don't know," Edelson said. "Ray called and he told me about the Maldovanian kid, but he didn't give me a full report. We should both be glad he called. He said if you wanted to come down and talk to the kid, he and Tony'd wear it. I thought you might want to go."

"Did Mr. Berle say if they were interested in arresting Petrak Maldovanian? Do they think he committed the murder?"

"I don't know that either," Edelson said. "Let me give you the address. Go check it out yourself. I'll bet anything John didn't think it was going to go this far when he decided to call you in and give you some rope."

"John doesn't think Tibor killed Martha Handling any more than I do." Gregor fumbled around in his coat pocket and came up with a stub of a pencil and a crumpled envelope. DON'T THROW THIS OUT! the envelope said. YOU CAN SAVE BIG!

"Go ahead," Gregor said.

Instead of an address, Edelson gave a city block and directions to follow the police cars to an alley.

"I know that sounds crazy," Edelson said. "But there's a full-bore police investigation going on. You won't be able to miss it."

"I'll be one of a hundred rubberneckers."

"Nope on that, too," Edelson said. "Ray's left word with the guys at the tape to let you through. I don't suppose there's a possibility we have a baby serial killer on our hands."

"There's always a possibility," Gregor said.

Gregor gave the driver the instructions, and the driver looked visibly annoyed. "You could've *walked* there," he said. Then he took off, and Gregor tried to get himself oriented.

It turned out the driver was right. Gregor probably could have walked there. The ride was so short, it was almost embarrassing.

The destination was unmistakable. The block was packed solid with police cars, mobile crime unit vans, ambulance, medical examiner's office cars, and God only knew what. There was crime scene tape up at their end of the block, and Gregor was sure there would be crime scene tape up at the other end. There was a uniform directing traffic.

"I don't think you're getting through this," the driver said as the uniform came up to warn them off.

The uniform was another policewoman. Gregor cranked down his window and gave her his name. "I was told—"

"Detective Berle," the woman said. "We were warned. You can come on through, but we can't let the vehicle in. There isn't any room."

Gregor got out his wallet and dumped a twenty-dollar bill on the front seat next to the driver. It was twice what the meter read.

"Is the Homicide Division building somewhere around here?" he asked.

"Right around the corner," the policewoman said. "Right on our doorstep, so to speak. Why?"

"I'm just trying to figure out where I am," Gregor said.

Gregor made his way through the vehicles, a little surprised that none of them was a news van. He found the alley by heading for the real logjam, and just as he came up to the opening, four men came out, carrying something in an evidence bag. It was not the body. It was too small.

A moment later, Ray Berle emerged from the melee. He looked tense as hell. "Come on back," he said. "The kid says you can identify the body. He says he can identify the body. We want a second opinion."

"It's somebody I know?"

"Well, that's the question, isn't it?" Ray said. "Maybe it's somebody you know, and maybe what we've got here is a psychopath. And don't ask what this has to do with the thing with the priest, because we don't know it has anything to do with it. It's just that we took one look at this guy's name, and it's not a hard name to remember. Also, what's the odds the kid stumbles on two bodies in one week?"

The alley was narrow and there were too many people in it. Gregor followed Ray Berle as best he could until they came to a short line of doors and even more people, bunched up together and looking like they were doing nothing. A stretcher and a body bag lay on the ground a little to the side of the center door.

Just then, Gregor saw Petrak Maldovanian. He was sitting off to the side, just outside the door. He looked as dejected, and as oddly small, as his brother had looked in juvenile detention.

It was astonishing how small trouble could make someone look, when it really got hold of him. Petrak, like his brother, had to be taller than six-three.

Petrak stood up as soon as he saw Gregor. "Mr. Demarkian," he said. "Mr. Demarkian. I didn't do anything. I just found him, he was in the door, and it was where I was told to go, and then I called them. I called the police. I wouldn't have called the police if I'd killed him, and why would I kill him? What did he have to do with me?"

Tony Monteverdi emerged from the building. "Don't ask me what's going on here," he said. "Right now, I just don't know. The kid here says the body belongs to a man named Mikel Dekanian."

"What?" Gregor said.

"He says he knows him from church," Tony said. "He says you know him from church. Am I hearing this right?"

"Holy Trinity Armenian Christian Church," Gregor said. "Yes, that would be right. If the body is Mikel Dekanian, that would be right. There aren't that many Armenian churches in the city. A lot of us go there." Gregor paused for a moment. "It's Father Tibor Kasparian's church. He's the priest there."

"Jesus Christ," Tony said. "Yes, of course, why wouldn't it be? Will you come in here and see if you can confirm identification of the body?"

Gregor went into the cramped dark space that must be used as a service area. There were mops and brooms leaning against the wall. There were buckets in a stack near a utilitarian back staircase. Mikel Dekanian's head had been bashed in at the back, so that there was a crater the size of a boulder just at the curve coming down from the crown. Tony touched the corpse's shoulder and moved it just a bit, so that the head fell back and the face was clearly visible. It was Mikel Dekanian's face.

Gregor nodded.

"Well, that's one less mystery we've got to solve," Tony said. "Do you have any idea at all what this guy was doing in this neighborhood? The kid says he lives, the guy lives, over near Cavanaugh Street, and that isn't anywhere near here. Does he work near here? Does he have relatives?"

Gregor shook his head. "He works for a guy named Howard Kashinian. I don't know what he does. Kashinian is a wheeler-dealer sort of person. He's got interests in some city construction. It might be that."

"Would any of that be in this neighborhood?"

"I don't think so," Gregor said. "I don't know, really. I don't pay that much attention to Howard."

"The kid's got quite a story," Tony said. "Sounds like James Bond."

"Do you think he killed Dekanian?"

"We don't know," Tony said. "But if he did, he did it yesterday and then came back to call us. The body's been cold for at least eighteen hours."

"Eighteen hours," Gregor said.

"Is that significant to you?" Tony asked.

"Remember our meeting yesterday?" Gregor said. "I saw him when I was coming out of that. He was in a big hurry. He said he had an appointment. He said he'd been to the Hall of Records."

"Was he headed this way?" Tony asked.

Gregor nodded. "I think he was."

"You'd better go talk to the kid. He said he wanted to talk to you. He said we could listen in. We're going to."

3

Petrak Maldovanian was sitting just where he had been when Gregor first saw him. He still looked very dejected and very small. When he noticed Gregor standing over him, he said, "Everything Stefan has said is true. They tell you they want you to tell the truth. Then when you tell the truth, they don't believe you."

"Let's start from the beginning," Gregor said. "What the hell are you doing down here? Why are you in this alley?"

"Because," Petrak said. "He told me to come here. He called me on this phone—" He took a small black phone out of his pocket and waved it. "—and he told me to come right away, that I had to meet a man and talk to him, and if I met this man and talked to him, then we would be able, Stefan would be able—it's a whole pile of crap and I should have known it was a whole pile of crap."

Gregor took the phone out of Petrak's hand and turned it over and over. It was made of cheap black plastic. He opened it up. It took him less than half a minute to find the video. He closed it up again.

"Where did you get it?" he asked.

Petrak shrugged. "It was in the hallway," he said, "in the back, where the evil judge was. I went to look for Father Tibor and also for Mr. Donahue and I looked in the bathroom, and then I heard noise, so I went on back. And I went into the room where the noise was coming from, and there was Father Tibor and Mr. Donahue and Dr. Loftus and I think there might have been other people. And there was blood everywhere, and I sort of stumbled in some of it and then I got scared and backed out, and then I don't know, the police were there, and then . . . it was just lying in the hallway. The phone was."

"And you picked it up."

Petrak nodded. "I didn't think about it. It was just there and I picked it up, and I went back out into the foyer and more police came and I forgot I had it. And then later I found it in my pocket when I was home. And I looked at it."

"And?"

Petrak gestured to the phone in Gregor's hand. "And then I looked at it. And there were things on it. There were calls and voice mails from the man from Administrative Solutions. That was the name. Administrative Solutions. This is the private company that runs the prisons. You know about that?"

"I know about that."

"There were rumors that this judge, she was taking money from the prison company to put people in jail for long times," Petrak said. "And I looked at the phone and I thought I could see how there were things there that would prove that to be true. So I used the phone and I called the man."

"Which man?"

"You can see in the address book," Petrak said. "Mark Granby. He works for the company that runs the prisons. I called him and then, later, I went to see him. And I told him, I told him that if he could pay a judge to put people in prison, he could pay one not to put people in prison, and I wanted Stefan sent home and I would give him back the phone if he would, if he would make sure that Stefan came home and did not go to jail."

"Marvelous," Gregor said. "Have you told any of this to the police?"

"No. I was waiting for you."

"You should have been waiting for Russ Donahue," Gregor said. "You're going to need a lawyer."

"I do not think Mr. Donahue is a very good lawyer," Petrak said. "I think he should not have allowed the evil judge to hear Stefan's case."

"I don't think that's usually in the power of the defense attorney," Gregor said. "How did you get here today? How did you just happen to find the body?"

"It did not just happen," Petrak said. "I got a call on the phone. I have the phone on me all the time because I can't leave it at home, because Aunt Sophie looks through everything. I was at school and the phone rang and I thought it was my own phone, maybe, but the ring tone was wrong. And I saw it was this phone and I answered it and it was him, and he told me I was supposed to come here, I was supposed to meet a woman about Stefan and it had to be very secret. So I came."

"Do you remember the name of this person?"

"Yes," Petrak said. "I do. It was a silly name, so I remembered it. Lydia Bird."

"Do you know who this person was supposed to be?"

"I think she was a judge, or somebody who worked for a judge. Mr. Granby didn't say that. Only that I was to come and meet here because we had to talk if Stefan was going to come home. He said it was hard to do because Stefan had committed a very serious job and every judge would want to put him in jail, but now there was this one but she had to talk to me. So I thought she was a judge."

"And this conversation," Gregor said. "It took place when?"

"This morning at ten o'clock."

Gregor looked at him in astonishment. "You had a phone call this morning at ten o'clock from Mark Granby."

"Yes."

"At ten o'clock *this* morning."

"Yes."

"Petrak, I don't know what you're trying to pull here, but you can't, you *can't* lie to the police in a case like this. You could be prosecuted just for lying to them, never mind for everything else that's going on. And it doesn't make any sense for you to lie to me, either."

"I am not lying to you," Petrak said.

"Petrak, for God's sake," Gregor said. "At ten o'clock this morning, I was in Mark Granby's office myself. I was there from quarter to ten till quarter after. And he made no phone calls. He didn't leave the office even once. He didn't call anybody. I was *there*."

"He called *me*," Petrak said. "I recognized his voice."

"You recognized Mark Granby's voice," Gregor said.

"It was familiar as soon as it started to speak," Petrak said. "He whispered, but it was familiar. And he told me who he was."

"You said the name was in the address book," Gregor said. "That's how you found him in the first place. Did the name come up in the caller ID when you answered the phone?"

"No," Petrak said. "It was just a number. I didn't think about it."

"Petrak, for God's sake," Gregor said. "The only way Mark Granby could have called you at ten o'clock this morning is if he's figured out a way to be two places at once, and—"

"And that's impossible," Petrak finished for him.

Gregor was thinking that it wasn't necessarily impossible at all.

FOUR

1

Father Tibor Kasparian had been waiting for Krekor Demarkian all day. He had been waiting from the moment old Mrs. Vespasian slammed the communicator phone down into its receiver, stood up, and stomped off with her two aged minions behind her. The minions had not said anything, but they never said anything, except to Mrs. Vespasian herself, and then almost always in Armenian. Mrs. Vespasian was, indeed, very, very old. It didn't matter. She was in remarkable shape, and she knew her own mind and followed it.

Tibor assumed the Very Old Ladies had gone straight to the nearest phone they knew how to use and called Krekor and told him all about the video. That would be bad enough, but Tibor suspected that Gregor had known all along that the video was faked. The real problem would be what else Krekor would have figured out. In most things, Tibor would have trusted Krekor with his life, but this was not most things. In this case, Krekor would be unreliable.

When the guard came to tell him he had visitors, he did think about refusing to see them. The guard said his visitor was "your lawyer, Mr. Edelson, and some people." As soon as Tibor heard that "your lawyer," he knew there was no point in arguing. They called George Edelson "your lawyer" only when Edelson and the mayor, and Krekor himself, were pulling something.

Tibor thought of half a dozen legal protests to being forced to see visitors he didn't want to see, but he knew they wouldn't matter. It wouldn't matter if he threatened to file a lawsuit for the violation of his civil rights. They wanted to talk to him now. They were going to talk to him now.

Or talk at him.

Tibor submitted to the handcuffs and the leg irons and all the rest of it. The trussing up had ceased to depress him, and now only made him feel foolish. He allowed the guard to follow him down the hall. She kept just behind him, with a hand on his elbow, until the very end, when she went just ahead and guided him down a hallway he hadn't expected. Unexpected or not, Tibor knew what the hallway was. They weren't taking him to the booths with the phones and the bulletproof glass. They were taking him to the big conference room where he had met George Edelson for the first, and he'd hoped the last, time.

When they got to the door of the conference room, the guard opened it and stood back to let him go inside. Tibor saw George Edelson standing near the window with his hands behind his back. The guard ushered Tibor in and then took the handcuffs off. By then, Tibor was trying his best not to look at the other end of the conference table.

Krekor Demarkian was sitting at the other end of the conference table, breathing fire.

If Tibor didn't know it was impossible, he would have said that Krekor Demarkian was *actually* breathing fire.

Tibor sat down, as far away from Krekor as he could get.

Krekor stood up.

"I'd invite you to stretch your legs," Krekor said acidly, "but you can't do that, because you're in leg irons."

George Edelson cleared his throat. "I think shouting is not necessarily the way we want to proceed with this."

"I think shouting is exactly the way we want to proceed with this," Krekor said, marching up from his end of the table until he was standing over Tibor like a large tree entirely filled with the wrath of God. "'I have the right to remain silent.' For the love of God. 'I have the right to remain silent.' What the hell did you think you were doing?"

"But he does have the right to remain silent," George Edelson said. "The right to refuse to incriminate himself is one of the most fundamental—"

"He's not refusing to incriminate himself," Krekor said. "I'll bet you anything that if you look back at all the statements he's made since this thing started, you won't find a single case where he says he refuses to incriminate himself. He didn't even say that in court. He's not refusing to incriminate himself, because he *can't* incriminate himself, except maybe as an accessory after the fact, and—" Krekor turned to hover directly over Tibor's face. "—you will *not* try to tell me that it's just your way of trying to put it when your first language isn't English. Not only is your English better than mine, but you've got an apartment full of detective novels and courtroom dramas and police procedurals and I don't know what else, and you know the proper formula better

266

than the lawyers do. You know it better than the judges do. And do you know how I know that's true? Because you said it over and over and over again and nobody caught it, not even the judge at the arraignment, and all I did was think about how odd it sounded and not know why."

"It made sense, Krekor," Tibor said. "You do not understand the circumstances. It made sense."

"Wait," George Edelson said. "He's okay with being an accessory after the fact to murder, but he won't lie?"

"There isn't a single thing in this mess you've caused that makes sense," Krekor said. "And don't think I'm not telling the truth here. This is a mess that you caused, all on your own, even though you didn't murder Martha Handling."

"Krekor, please," Tibor said. "It's wrong of you to do this. I am an old man. Yes, I know, I am not so old as you, but I am old and he is young. He is very young. And it doesn't matter what happens to me. It doesn't—"

"I could say you wouldn't last a month in state prison," Krekor said, "because you wouldn't, but it's not the point. The point is that it's wrong. It's wrong on every level. And you ought to know it's wrong."

"Krekor, please," Tibor said. "This is, this was an act of madness, a temporary insanity. This woman was evil. Not just misguided, but evil. And she did not listen to reason. She would never listen to reason. And the boy Stefan, very young and now he would be put away in a prison, just as awful as any prison, and she would not listen to reason and so he just snapped. Do you want to ruin a life because he just snapped? Because for one moment he did not know what he was doing?

Think about the rest of his life. Think about the lives of the people who love him."

"Were you in the judge's chambers when he just snapped?" Krekor asked.

"I came in just after," Tibor said. "But I could see the way he was. He was exploding and the gavel was going up and down and up and down and then when he saw me, he stopped and I could see he was coming back from far away and then I knew I had to do something. I knew what would happen if the police were involved and I did not want it to happen to him. I do not want it to happen to him."

"I think that you know better than this," Krekor said. "You've always known better than this."

"If you continue with this, Krekor, I will lie. I will confess to the murder."

"If you do, you'll have to explain the video," Krekor said. "Mrs. Vespasian called me."

"I will explain the video," Tibor said.

"I'll explain it better," Gregor said. "But it doesn't matter, because you won't go through with it."

"I do lie, Krekor. Sometimes."

"You won't want to lie."

"I have told you—"

"Mikel Dekanian is dead," Krekor said.

It took a long moment. For most of that time, Tibor couldn't make the words make sense.

"What?"

"Finally," Krekor said. "I got your attention. Mikel Dekanian is dead, found in the back of a house at the end of an alley with his skull smashed in and Petrak Maldovanian standing right over him."

"Tcha," Tibor said.

It was an all-purpose word. It meant whatever you wanted it to mean. Tibor's brain felt like soup.

Krekor pulled out a chair right next to Tibor's and sat down again. "We're making arrangements right now. John Jackman has his people on it, and we've got people at the governor's office, so don't bother trying to pull anything more. George here has become your attorney of record. He's filed a writ of habeus corpus. We've pulled three judges out of their lunches and their golf games. In about another forty-five minutes, you're going to be out on bail, and when you are, you're coming with George and me and we're going to see Petrak Maldovanian and *his* lawyer, and then it's really going to hit the fan. Because I'm not going to stop until you come to your senses."

"Tcha," Tibor said again. He was desperately buying time. He needed time.

"When this is over," Krekor said, "and it's going to be over—and it's going to be over my way, and not yours—when this is over, you are never going to hear the end of it again. Ever. For the rest of your life, I will remind you of this. I'll remind you over and over and over again. And if I die before you do, I'll come back as a ghost and remind you of it some more. Of all the stupid, asinine, dangerous things anybody could ever do, this has got to be the prize."

"Tcha," Tibor said yet again, as if he couldn't force any other sound out of his throat. And maybe he couldn't.

Before he walked into this room, he'd been absolutely sure of what he was doing and why. He'd been resolved to carry it through.

And now, all of a sudden, he wasn't sure.

2

The news reports began just after noon, and from the first, Janice Loftus found them confusing. At first she thought Petrak Maldovanian had been arrested, but that turned out to be untrue. What was true was that there had been a murder, and that Petrak had been found at the murder, near the body, doing something. There were a lot of deep, dark hints, the way there always were when nobody actually knew what was happening.

At least two of the local news Web sites contained long articles that were careful to point out that Petrak had been found in the corridors around the chambers where Martha Handling was murdered, and even that he had had blood on him. That was completely typical. Of course Petrak Maldovanian had had blood on him. Everybody had blood on them by the time it was over. People kept coming into the room and wandering around in it, walking over to the body, walking back out into the corridor again. She herself had done it. Martha Handling was lying there so still and so awful looking and she hadn't been able to help herself.

That was something she hadn't known until that day. Blood smelled like copper. The whole room smelled like copper. And blood squished. When you stepped on it, it didn't feel like other things did under your feet. It squished and it slid, and all you wanted was to be away from it.

Janice made her mind blank it out as best she could. That was not the important point now. The important point was that they were going to arrest Petrak eventually. You could tell that much in the news reports. They might have let him go for now, but it wouldn't be long, and then they would not only arrest him for this murder but for the murder of Martha Handling, too. But that wasn't right. She had been there at the murder of Martha Handling. She'd walked into the room only moments after it must have occurred. She'd not seen anything, and nothing of what she'd seen had been Petrak Maldovanian.

It was anti-immigrant sentiment—that's what it was. Janice saw it all the time. She saw it at school, where half her fellow teachers spent their time deriding all the "morons" who couldn't get their verb tenses right or didn't know anything about what had happened at Appomattox Court House. Of course, it wasn't only immigrants who didn't know those things, but nobody was going to come out and call Americans "morons" in a collegiate setting. They especially weren't going to call them morons if they were people of color. If there was one sure way to make your career end, that was it.

Unfortunately, the fear and the abhorence of the Other weren't restricted to the campuses of community colleges. They were every-where. They were in the news media that put out these stories. In the nice minds of all the nice people who owned little shops in the city, worked for corporations, or drove cars to shop or any-thing else. The bigotry was even in the minds of the people who worked for organizations like Pennsylvania Justice.

"It's not accidental," Janice had tried to tell Kasey Holbrook as soon as she heard the news about Petrak. That was the first time Janice had called. "I know you don't like to talk about conspiracies, Kasey, but sometimes there are conspiracies. There's a conspiracy here. It's the friends of that priest—it's Gregor Demarkian and those people. They'll do anything to get him off."

"And you know that how?" Kasey demanded. "Janice, you've got to see reason. We have real work to do here. The lives of dozens of people depend on us and our work. If we get the reputation for being a pack of moonbeam nutcases, nobody will ever listen to us again."

"That's a tactic of the patriarchy, too," Janice said. "Get all the good guys fighting with each other and being scared to do anything because somebody will call them names. I was there, Kasey, I was right there when it happened, and I'm telling you. Petrak Maldovanian isn't the one who killed Martha Handling. He couldn't have been. They're getting together right now to frame him for this murder, and the way you're acting, you're going to help."

"I don't see how you can blame this on the patriarchy," Kasey said. "Everybody involved in it seems to be men."

"Martha Handling wasn't a man," Janice said. "She was a male-identified woman, but she wasn't a man. And it wouldn't matter if she were a man. The patriarchy isn't just afraid of women. It's afraid of everybody. It's marginalized the whole world, and now it has to watch those marginalized people in case they get ideas. The patriarchy is just as afraid of immigrants as it is of women."

"I thought that priest you've been going on about was an immigrant," Kasey said.

"He's a friend of Gregor Demarkian's," Janice said. "Don't you see? It's the way these things work. He's one of the most powerful men in the entire city. And this priest is his friend. And he won't let anything put his friend away. Even though you know the priest has to have done it. He's got to be like all priests—he can't stand women, he can't stand equality, he wants to do his mumbo jumbo and keep everybody in thrall."

"If you're trying to tell me it was Gregor Demarkian who killed Martha Handling, I'm pretty sure that was impossible."

"I just told you it wasn't Gregor Demarkian," Janice said. "He wasn't even there. It was that priest. I walked in and I saw him. He had the gavel in his hand and he was covered with blood. If he were anybody except a friend of Gregor Demarkian's, they would have—"

"They would have what, Janice? They've already arrested him. They've already charged him with the murder of Martha Handling. I don't know what else it is you think they ought to do."

"It's all a sham," Janice said desperately. "Don't you see that? They arrested the priest, but they're letting Gregor Demarkian do anything he wants. That's because this is what he does. He gets people off when there are murder charges—"

"Last time I checked, we were generally in favor of getting people off on murder charges."

"Only when the charges aren't true," Janice said. "That's what makes the charges so sinister. They'll maneuver it around so that the priest gets off and it looks like this poor immigrant kid did the whole thing and then they'll be safe, probably forever. Then even Pennsylvania Justice won't be able to straighten it out."

"If they do arrest this kid and there's reason to think there was a frame, we'll step in then," Kasey said. "Be reasonable, Janice. That's what we do."

"You'll let a kid who hasn't done anything be arrested and convicted and go to jail and then when that's all over, you'll step in and help out. After the injustice has been done. When the kid doesn't have a chance anymore. When his life has been ruined. And you call yourself a social justice organization!"

"It's getting late, Janice. I've got actual work I have to do." Kasey Holbrook hung up.

Janice couldn't believe it. You didn't hang up on one of your best volunteers. You didn't hang up on one of your most significant contributors, either. Janice knew that she was both those things. And she was not indulging in conspiracy theories, either. She'd been *there*. She'd seen the priest with the blood all over him and the other people coming in and out of the room, and she knew Petrak Maldovanian had not murdered Martha Handling.

She made herself do the whole thing. She closed her eyes and took deep breaths. She repeated her soothing words over and over again: *peace, justice, equality, fairness, love.* It did not work so well as she wanted it to. It had never worked so well as she wanted it to. Sometimes nothing worked. She got so angry and so upset that she couldn't help herself. She got so angry and upset, she just had to explode.

Sometimes exploding was even the right thing to do.

She did not think it was the right thing to do this time.

She worked at it some more, and eventually she came to a place where her breathing was no longer heavy and she didn't think she would explode at the first signs of frustration.

She called Kasey Holbrook back and got her assistant instead. She waited for what seemed like forever. When the assistant came back on the line, the message was that Kasey had gone uptown for a meeting, and wasn't expected to come back to the office until tomorrow. This was so transparently a lie, even the assistant who delivered it didn't bother to try to make it sound true.

The control slipped, just for a moment. But it was enough.

"Tell Kasey I've gone out to do her job for her," Janice said. Then she hung up the phone herself.

After that, she had to think. She didn't know if anybody would take her word for anything. This was a deep enough conspiracy that she was sure people were being paid off. If people were being paid off, they wouldn't want to hear what she had to say. They might even think they had to get rid of her.

She needed something solid to use, something she could show to reporters, something that would corroborate what she had to say.

And she was pretty sure she knew where to get it.

3

When Gregor Demarkian called, Russ Donahue was knee-deep in Petrak Maldovanian's story, which was not the same thing as his alibi. He was also knee-deep in Petrak Maldovanian's aunt, who was sort of a global source code for life on Cavanaugh Street. She was very small, but she made Tasmanian devils look composed.

"I'm not an idiot," Sophie Maldovanian was saying. "I don't think they're lily-white little angels, the two of them. I know Stefan stole those things. I knew it before the police ever knew it, and if they'd come to me, I'd have told them. I should have marched him right down to the precinct the first time I found that stuff in his room and turned him in. That would have put an end to it. That would have put an end to it right there."

"I don't think it would have been a good idea," Russ said. He was trying to be careful. He was not Armenian. He didn't know how to negotiate these things as well as Gregor Demarkian did. Or as well as Father Tibor did.

"I think that, under the circumstances, you might have exacerbated the problem," he said carefully. "If you'd wanted to do something like that, and you'd asked me about it, I would have suggested that Stefan talk directly to the store. You could have gone with him to the store and he could have made a confession to the people there and given back the items. The store might still have prosecuted, you understand, but it would have looked very good at Stefan's hearing. I don't think it would have made much of a difference to Martha Handling, but it would have given us something to work with to stage an appeal. And if we'd caught a judge like Sarah Shore or Margaret Heiss-Landum, Stefan would have walked away with probation. An ankle bracelet at the very worst."

"Instead I did nothing," Sophie said, "and look where it landed us. Stefan has been in jail for over a week. And we still don't know what's going to happen. I've been to visit him every chance I have, and he's in very bad shape. He's in *very* bad shape. Yes, for God's sake. The kid behaved like an idiot and worse, but this is ridiculous. And I don't want to make the same mistake again."

"No, of course not," Russ said.

Sophie Maldovanian saw his confusion. "I don't want to do nothing," she said. "With this thing with Petrak. I don't want to do nothing."

"But Miss Maldovanian, I'm not sure what we can do. Petrak hasn't been charged with anything. And I'm not sure what you're saying. Are you saying that Petrak killed Mikel Dekanian?"

Petrak was sitting in a chair a little behind his aunt. He scowled.

Sophie Maldovanian blew a raspberry. "Of course I'm not saying that Petrak killed Mikel Dekanian. Even if I didn't know the boy couldn't commit a murder if his life depended on it, what would be the point of killing Mikel Dekanian? I can't see anyone wanting to kill Mikel Dekanian, except maybe some of those banks you're suing for him, and banks don't do things like that. I think it would be more likely Mikel would want to kill somebody at the banks. And that idiot police officer. Did you hear that idiot police officer? Implying that Petrak killed that judge and Mikel knew something about it, so he killed Mikel. Is that the most asinine thing you've ever heard, or what? Even if Petrak killed that judge—and he didn't do that either, let me tell you, but even if he did—what would Mikel Dekanian know about it?"

"Yes," Russ said. "Yes, I do see that. But Petrak wasn't charged, so no matter what the police may have said when you talked to them, they probably aren't taking that theory all that seriously. I think that they were just trying to come up with a suggestion—"

"They could have said Petrak was the Easter bunny, and it would have been more plausible," Sophie said.

"I am not the Easter bunny," Petrak said.

There were times when dealing with Cavanaugh Street that Russ Donahue thought he needed antipsychotic drugs.

"Yes," he said finally. "But the theory isn't all that odd. Petrak and Mikel knew each other. Petrak may have said something in Mikel's hearing or to Mikel himself, or Mikel may have seen something Petrak carried on him—"

"Where?" Sophie demanded. "At church? Because that's the only time Petrak saw the Dekanians, at church. We don't live in the neighborhood. It's not like he's around there all the time."

"I know that," Russ said. "I was just trying to show you how the police were thinking about it when—"

"And Petrak called them," Sophie said. "He found the body and then he called them. Would he have done that if he had just murdered the man?"

"Actually," Russ said, "people do do things like that, some-times—"

"Are you now saying you think Petrak killed Mikel Dekanian? And—what?—that he killed that judge, too?"

"I don't think Petrak killed anyone," Russ said. "It's not that. I'm just trying to explain how things stand and what we ought to prepare for—"

"That's what I want to do," Sophie said. "I want to prepare. I want to be way out ahead of this before they do arrest him."

"Then the most important thing to do," Russ said, "is to try to figure out what happened with that phone call. Gregor says he was with Mark Granby when Petrak says he got the phone call, and those two things can't be true at once. If we could just figure out who made the phone call, we'd almost certainly have the murderer, because whoever it was must have known the body was there."

"It was Mark Granby who made the phone call," Petrak in-sisted. "He killed the judge. He was paying her bribes. He didn't want it to get out. He killed Mikel Dekanian. He set me up to find the body and be accused."

"It makes as much sense as anything they're trying to pin on Petrak," Sophie said.

Russ Donahue had never had a migraine headache in his life, but he thought he was about to get one. There was so much pres-sure inside his head, it felt as if his skull were going to pop any second.

"No," he said, speaking slowly and clearly. Why you always thought people would understand you better if you spoke slowly and clearly, he didn't know. "No, it doesn't make as much sense. Mark Granby didn't know Mikel Dekanian. Okay, I should say Mikel Dekanian didn't know Mark Granby. On any level. There's no reason to assume the two of them ever met. But Petrak and Mikel have met. They met at church if they didn't meet anywhere else. Therefore, there is an established connection—"

"And you *do* think Petrak murdered Mikel Dekanian," Sophie said. "His own lawyer. Isn't *that* nice."

"Miss Maldovanian," Russ started.

And then the miracle happened. The phone rang.

Russ excused himself and picked up, and his assistant announced, "Gregor Demarkian is calling for you. He says it's urgent."

Russ had never been so happy to hear from anyone in his life.

FIVE

1

It took longer than Gregor had expected it to, and it required so much cooperation from so many people at so many levels of city and state government, Gregor began to think he was running for office.

"The only reason you're getting away with this," John Jackman said, "is that I know you're good for it. If you say you know who, what, when, where, and why, then you know who, what, when, where, and why. And if Barack Obama hadn't already become the first black President of the United States, I still might not let you get away with it."

"Technically," Gregor said, "Barack Obama is the first mixed-race President of the United States, so you could still—"

"Get out of here," John said. "Get out of here before I kill you myself. That'd be an interesting news cycle."

Gregor was not feeling flippant, even though he sounded that way some of the time. He hated these situations where, in order to get anything done, he had to sit around passively while other people helped him. He hated situations where he had to sit passively for any reason. There was, in his mind, something essentially wrong with passivity itself.

They kept Tibor in the conference room while they made the rest of the arrangements. He was still in leg irons, and he would be in handcuffs when they took him to the courthouse once they found a judge ready to squeeze him in on an emergency basis. Gregor was glad to see that he looked despondent instead of blank. Despondent meant he had at least half a clue as to what was going on here.

Gregor was still stunned almost beyond belief that this situation had gone so far, that Tibor made the decisions he had, that—well, there was no way to make it make sense. Before all this started, Gregor would have said that Tibor was incapable of making this kind of mistake. Tibor had grown up in a Communist dictatorship and taken Holy Orders when religion was effectively prohibitive. He'd had enough trouble in his life, and seen enough in his capacity as a priest, to be thoroughly disenchanted with human nature. He understood, better than Gregor himself, that there was never a time or place when you could trust a criminal.

Gregor didn't believe that criminals were born that way, but he did believe that once a person made the choice, the choice was largely irrevocable.

George Edelson came in at last with the news Gregor had been waiting for.

"Oldham will take it," he said. "We've got half an hour to get over there. And he's still royally pissed off, so there better not be any screwups."

Edelson looked meaningfully at Tibor. Tibor shrugged.

After that there came the most frustrating part of all, because they had to give Tibor back to the jail staff. Gregor would have liked to tie Tibor up in a knot and haul him out to the courthouse himself, but he knew he was asking too many people for too many favors not to get with the program, no matter how annoying it was. If they got lucky with all this, there would come a time when he could sit with Tibor in Tibor's own living room and have a complete and utter blowout fit.

They took Tibor out, and Gregor and George Edelson went to find a cab. When they got into one, Gregor called Bennis.

"I know where that is. That's where we went yesterday. I can be there in time," she said.

"Not a bad idea," Gregor said. "You can lend him moral support. In other words, you can make him feel guilty."

"I'll see who else I can round up," Bennis said. "Donna's at some school thing and Lida's babysitting Tommy and the baby, but I'll bet I can get someone. A deputation from Cavanaugh Street. All wanting to beat his brains in."

"If you take too long, you'll miss it," Gregor said. "This is really going to take no time at all. We've set the whole damned thing up ahead of time. After we've got him safely out on bail, we're going over to Martha Handling's chambers. I don't know if they'll let you back there. Never mind you and the Very Old Ladies."

"Why are you going to Martha Handling's chambers?"

"Because if I'm going to have the reputation of an Armenian American Hercule Poirot, I ought to earn it," Gregor said. "And also because I need to force a confrontation. Mainly because I need to force a confrontation. It's going to be hard, getting this untangled."

"I thought you hated being called the Armenian American Hercule Poirot."

"I do," Gregor said, "but it's coming in useful at the moment, and I'm going to use it."

"All right," Bennis said. "I guess that makes sense. On some level."

"I really know what I'm doing, Bennis."

"You usually do," Bennis said.

Gregor put his phone back in his pocket.

"Was that your wife?" George Edelson said. "I've seen pictures of her. She's a very beautiful woman."

"She's also a force of nature," Gregor said, "and when this is all over with, she's going to have my hide."

"Really? Just because you solved a murder? Don't you solve murders all the time? Or is it just because Father Kasparian is somebody she knows?"

"It's not solving the murder," Gregor said. "It's not telling her everything I was thinking about when I was solving the murder. And yes, that's because Tibor is somebody she knows. That's because she knows too many people involved in this to begin with."

They got caught in a traffic jam. There were cars stopped everywhere. There was gridlock at an intersection. There were police officers who were taking their own sweet time. Gregor kept going over and over it all in his head. He had a wish list a mile long of things he hoped would not go wrong. Tibor should get there on time. They should get there on time. Ray Berle and Tony Monteverdi should get there on time. Petrak Maldovanian and Russ Donahue should be there together and also on time.

The problem with setting up one of these things was that there were so many moving parts, it was hard to get them all into place at once. That was something Agatha Christie and Rex Stout never thought of.

When they got to the courtroom, Tibor was already sitting at the defense table, and Russ and Petrak and Sophie were sitting in the spectators' seats. Russ looked better than he had since Tibor had been arrested, as if he were finally interested in something again. Petrak Maldovanian looked sullen and resentful. Sophie Maldovanian just looked confused.

"I've got to go sit up with Father Kasparian," Edelson said. "I'm the attorney of record. I hope I'm not stepping on toes, Mr. Donahue. If it makes you feel any better, he didn't want me any more than he didn't want you."

"No," Russ said. "No, no. I'm just glad we're finally getting him out of this."

George Edelson went to the front. The doors opened at the back, and Bennis came in, toting Hannah Krekorian, two of the Ohanian girls, Sheila Kashinian, and the Very Old Ladies. She pulled in behind Gregor, Russ, Petrak, and Sophie and said, "Just made it. Everybody wanted to come. I had to talk Lida out of bringing Tommy. Mrs. Vespasian is offering to help with the walking stick, but I thought that might be pushing it. She gets away with hitting people with that thing, but I bet I wouldn't. Are you sure you have this straightened out? And Tibor won't go to jail?"

"There's the 'accessory after the fact' business," Gregor said, "but we'll deal with it when we get there."

"All rise," the bailiff said from the front of the court.

Gregor turned toward the front of the court and stood up.

Roger Maris Oldham looked one step away from sentencing everybody in front of him to at least forty years, and Tibor Kasparian to 176. Gregor was very happy that they had set this up in advance, because if they hadn't, he wasn't sure Oldham would have been willing to set bail.

Everybody else sat down. The bailiff read off a series of letters and numbers and case file names and whatever else had to go first before they could get to the serious part. Gregor didn't listen.

When the bailiff was done, Judge Oldham leaned across his desk and looked at Tibor. "Father Kasparian," he said, "before we get started, I want to make a few things absolutely clear."

"Excuse me, Your Honor," George Edelson said, standing up again. "I am appearing for Father Kasparian."

"So I've heard," Oldham said. "Am I to understand that you have Father Kasparian's permission to appear for him?"

"Yes, Your Honor," George Edelson said.

"Father Kasparian?" Judge Oldham said.

"Yes, Your Honor," Tibor said. Tibor seemed to be contemplating standing up. He didn't.

"Very good," Judge Oldham said. "But now let me get these things very clear. I have been told that this is an emergency, and that everything needs to be done in haste in order to prevent an injustice and possible harm to innocent persons. I am willing to bend the usual formality of the procedure under those conditions. I am aware that under certain conditions such things are necessary. I am told that bail has been arranged and will be made available at the end of this hearing so that there may be no delay. And all of this, as I said, is acceptable to me. What is not acceptable to me is another performance like the one you put on the last time I saw you, Father Kasparian. I expect you to plead to these charges, Father Kasparian. A real plea. Not nonsense. Is Father Kasparian ready to plead?"

"Yes, Your Honor," George Edelson said.

"And how does Father Kasparian plead?"

"Not guilty, Your Honor," George Edelson said.

Judge Oldham turned to look at Tibor again. "Is that acceptable to you, Father Kasparian? Do you in fact want to plead not guilty? I'm not going to wake up tomorrow morning and read in the paper that you were coerced into pleading and you don't want to plead anything and you're back to standing on your right to remain silent?"

"No," Tibor said, looking thoroughly miserable.

The judge sat back. "Good," he said. "Because if your answers had been different in any respect, Father Kasparian, I would have taken a great deal of pleasure in locking you up for contempt of court. I have never—and I mean never—had to deal with such idiocy in all my life, and I have presided at the trials of some truly magnificent idiots. Bail is set at fifty thousand dollars. Go get that straightened out and get out of here. This is a gift, and as far as I'm concerned, you don't deserve it."

"Well," Bennis said.

"Let's just hope this one isn't the judge when the accessory thing comes up," Gregor said.

There was a lot of shuffling around, and Bennis went up to the defense table. "I'm glad you're not asserting your right to remain silent anymore," she said. "It had us all worried."

Tibor sighed. "There is no point in asserting my right to remain silent," he said. "Krekor is here, and he will not shut up."

2

After that, everything was done with what people kept saying was "extreme dispatch," but what felt to Gregor Demarkian like "forever." Tibor and George Edelson disappeared for a while, and when they were gone, Ray Berle and Tony Monteverdi showed up, looking harassed.

"You know the only reason you're doing this is because you've got the reputation of getting everything right," Tony Monteverdi said. "You'd better get everything right."

"I don't understand why I have to be here," Petrak Maldovanian said. "This is some kind of parlor trick. I haven't done anything wrong."

"For God's sake," Russ Donahue said. "Just for once, help yourself out. Just for once."

"We've still got a dead guy we need to ask you some questions about," Ray Berle said. "We could go do that instead of this."

"Ah," Tony Monteverdi said. "We checked. You were right. Mark Granby left his office for lunch and never came back. We've got a watch on the airport."

"I told you," Gregor said. "You've got to get the feds to cooperate and put a watch on all the airports. If I were in his place, I'd go by car somewhere well away from Philadelphia and catch a plane there. And I'd go by myself. He's got family, but I don't think he'll try to take them with him at this point. The trick is to actually get out."

"They don't usually get out," Ray Berle said.

Tibor and George Edelson came back into the courtroom, and Gregor felt as if something could finally get done. Gregor was also gratified to see that Tibor was wearing neither handcuffs nor leg irons. He did look perfectly miserable.

"We got nailed by a guy from the prosecutor's office," George Edelson said. "He did not look pleased. My guess is that the blowback from all this is not going to be fun."

"We'll worry about the blowback when we get there," Gregor

said. "Let's just make sure. We're all ready? We should be there within half an hour, just to keep the security people from losing it. They're probably losing it already. Everybody set? Russ? You've got your car?"

"I've got my car."

"Good. Then we don't have to wait around for you to get a taxi. Let's go."

"Can we go?" Bennis asked.

"I take it you're going to need a taxi," Gregor said. "Get there if you can get there. As far as I can tell, anyone can come in who wants to come in, so why not."

"Excellent," Bennis said.

"I don't understand what's going on," Hannah Krekorian said.

"I'll explain it on the way over," Bennis promised her.

Mrs. Vespasian let out with a stream of Armenian, and the other Very Old Ladies started chattering too. Gregor was glad they were going to be following Bennis and not him.

Gregor watched Tibor watch them all go.

Then the priest turned to Gregor and said, "You're wrong, Krekor. You are very wrong. About all of this."

"No," Gregor said. "I'm not. And I'm going to prove it to you."

3

They could have gone into the juvenile court in a lot of different ways, but Gregor wanted to go in through the front door, and that was what George Edelson did. They were stopped at the security checkpoint and wanded and sent through the metal detector. Gregor opened his briefcase and let the guard look through it for contraband or weapons. Then they all waited while Ray Berle and Tony Monteverdi came in from the back.

The courthouse was not busy. It was close to the end of the day. Hearings were winding down. Judges were going home. Even so, there were more than a few people milling around, and if a hearing was going on in Martha Handling's old courtroom, there would soon be more.

"All right," Gregor said, moving to the head of the corridor that led to the restrooms and, from there, to the rest of the building. "This corridor leads to the restrooms, as you can see. Then it continues to the corridors we're interested in. There are two things you need to remember. The first one is the security checkpoint we just came through. Nobody is getting into the building through that door without being checked over. Which means that nobody is getting in through that door without a weapon."

"I stand corrected," Gregor said. "Police officers can get through that door with weapons. What about cell phones?"

"We keep all our communications devices, yeah," Tony Monteverdi said. "It's a safety precaution. In case something happens."

"Also, I'm not sure it matters about the weapons," Ray said. "She wasn't killed by a weapon brought in from the outside. She was killed with one of her own gavels."

"I agree," Gregor said. "But maybe not in the way you think I should. Just note. First, you can't get a weapon or a cell phone in through this door if you're coming in, but there would be no problem with getting either through this door if you were going out. This may seem like a minor issue, but it isn't."

"It explains how somebody took away that other cell phone," Tony said. "But we know that."

"The other issue are the security cameras," Gregor said. "Did they get fixed, by the way? Did somebody come in here and clean them off."

"The city is getting around to it," Tony Monteverdi said dryly.

"Wonderful," Gregor said. "Then I can stay in the present tense. The security cameras along this corridor were all working properly, right down to the one just in front of the restrooms. But the one after that, and all the security cameras leading down to Martha Handling's chambers, and all the ones in the two corridors leading from Martha Handling's chambers to the back door where the judge's parking lot is, and the one at the back door that is supposed to catch whoever's coming in or going out of the building that way, all those have had their lenses spray-painted with black paint. That means that anybody could walk past the restrooms into the corridors beyond without being spotted, and anyone could walk in through the back door and to the judges' chambers without being spotted. So far, so good?"

"You gave us this speech before," Ray Berle said.

"I gave it to you, I didn't give it to everybody," Gregor said. "I didn't give it to Father Tibor here, for instance. I just want to make sure we're all clear."

"For God's sake, Krekor," Tibor said. "We're all clear."

"I wish we were," Gregor said, "but we're not. Not yet. I'm getting there. Next thing: we have security camera tapes for movement in this corridor for the relevant times. There are a lot of people on those tapes, but we'll stick to the ones we know were later in Martha Handling's chambers. They included Father Tibor here, Russ Donahue, Petrak Maldovanian, and that woman, Janice Loftus—"

"But I'm here," a thin little voice came from the back of the little crowd that had begun to gather around Gregor's lecture.

There was a rustling and a string of apologies and the squat little woman came to the front, panting. "I wanted to talk to somebody, and nobody would talk to me at the police station and nobody would talk to me at Pennsylvania Justice and nobody understands, nobody does, but it's very important. And I thought there would be police here and I could talk to them because they wouldn't be able to go anywhere if they were guarding it, and then—"

"You can stay here and follow along if you keep quiet until I'm done," Gregor said. "In fact, you might even be a help."

"But I have something to say!" Janice Loftus said. "And it's important!"

"You can say it later," Gregor said. "Now, where was I? Ah, people in the corridor who were also, certainly, in Martha Handling's chambers later. There's another person of interest in the corridor, but we can't place him in Martha Handling's chambers. That doesn't mean he wasn't there. That person was Mark Granby, the local executive in charge of operations for Administrative Solutions of America. Administrative Solutions of America is the company that runs prisons in the Commonwealth of Pennsylvania. They get paid by the 'inmate day,' as they put it. For each inmate, they get paid a set sum for each day the inmate is incarcerated. That means the more inmates, and the longer their sentences, the more money Administrative Solutions makes."

"I don't understand what this has to do with Petrak," Sophie Maldovanian said. Gregor looked up to see her way in the back, with Russ and Petrak himself. He hadn't noticed her come in.

"I know you say Petrak was in the corridor and I understand he was in the chambers, but he was just looking for Mr. Donahue, and Mr. Donahue was in the chambers and so was everybody

291

else. There's no reason to think Petrak did anything he shouldn't have done except go wandering back there."

"I'll say the same thing to you that I said to Dr. Loftus," Gregor said. "For the moment, keep quiet. All right? Okay. Mark Granby was a very interesting person to find on that security tape, because as part of its attempt to make as much money as possible, he was systematically bribing judges, corrections officers, state evaluating psychologists, and a fair number of other people involved in the process. He was doing this here, and with Martha Handling. Martha Handling was taking money for incarcerating the juveniles that came before her, as often as she possibly could and for as long as she possibly could. And she had been taking it for at least the last few years. And that meant that there were rumors, and there were suspicions—and rumors and suspicions often led to investigations."

"Was there an investigation?" Russ Donahue asked. "I heard all those rumors, too, but I could never figure out if anything official was happening."

"Nothing official was happening yet," Gregor said, "but it was on its way and it was inevitable. I heard the same rumors, some of them from people in the Bureau, and once it gets there, something's going to follow. So Martha Handling was getting a little squiffy. Dr. Loftus here told me that she had a tendency, when she was involved in something she could get into trouble for, to rat out early and thus get the benefit of being the person with the most to trade for favorable treatment."

"It wasn't just favorable treatment," Janice Loftus said. "She got off scot free of everything and hailed as a hero half the time."

"Possibly," Gregor said, "but that doesn't really matter, in a way, because for whatever reason she was thinking of turning herself in, she was thinking of turning herself in. Mark Granby told me that himself when I talked to him. And if Martha Handling turned herself in, and if she talked her head off when she turned herself in, then Mark Granby was going to go to jail for a long time. And that makes him, as you can see, our prime suspect when it comes to motive."

"It doesn't explain what the motive for Petrak was supposed to be," Sophie said. "What was the motive for Petrak supposed to be?"

"In the beginning," Gregor said, "the idea was that Petrak, knowing that Judge Handling was the one most likely to give Stefan a long sentence, was looking to get Martha Handling out of the way so that Stefan's case would be moved to another judge."

"That's ridiculous," Sophie said.

"Maybe," Gregor said, "but that was the thinking. Ever since the death of Mikel Dekanian, the thinking has been that Petrak may be something of a sociopath."

"That's just persecution of immigrants," Janice Loftus said furiously. "That's exactly the kind of thing you people would think up to say."

"And that's possibly true, too," Gregor said, "but it's largely beside the point. We don't know that Mark Granby came down the corridor toward Martha Handling's chambers, but we do know he could have, and since he could have, we're going to put him on the list. Dr. Loftus here is also on the list, because Dr. Loftus knew Martha Handling for many years, and there's always the possibility that there is something in their past that hasn't come to light yet."

"Ridiculous," Janice said.

"I told you to be quiet," Gregor said. "If you'll all follow me, we'll get on to the next part."

Gregor went off down the hall, and the crowd followed him. It was almost all of the crowd, and not just the people whom he had brought along himself.

He stopped near the bathrooms and pointed back at the security camera on the ceiling. "That's the last functioning camera," he said. "It points in the other direction, so it can see people going toward the bathrooms, but it can't tell us who went into the bathrooms, or who went past them and into the farther corridors. Or, for that matter, who went into the bathrooms and who then came out and went down the other corridors toward Martha Handling's chambers. But there are some things that must have happened by necessity. The murderer must have been the first person to go down the corridors to Martha Handling's chambers."

"The first person to go down to Martha Handling's chambers was Father Kasparian here," Ray Berle said.

Gregor shook his head. "No. Father Tibor was the first one to come down the corridor to the bathrooms, but he did enter the bathrooms. All the other people came afterwards, but we don't know who went into the bathrooms and for how long. So Father Tibor goes into the bathroom, and when he comes out, he sees one of our suspects going off down the corridor in the other direction from the court, and he follows. You should follow."

They followed. The crowd thinned out a lot, but it did not thin absolutely. Gregor was half surprised that Ray Berle and Tony Monteverdi didn't shoo them all off.

He walked first down one corridor and then the other and stopped when he got to Martha Handling's chambers.

"All right," he said. "Two things. One is that although Father Tibor isn't particularly old, he is not in the best shape, courtesy of many years of abuse in a dictatorship. When he saw the murderer going down the hall, the murderer was probably already nearly to the next corridor. Tibor walks slowly. The murderer, on the other hand, is young. He was fast. Very fast. He walked through this door and found Martha Handling occupying it. He closed the door behind him. The gavel was on the desk, probably in the stand that was there and empty when the body and Father Tibor were later discovered. The murderer picked up the gavel and smashed the woman's head into the mess you all saw. He did it quickly. He did it viciously. And just as he was finished, Tibor—who had been following him and saw him go through the door to Martha Handling's chambers—came in and found him finishing up."

"And you think you can prove that," Ray Berle said.

Gregor opened the door to Martha Handling's chambers and shooed them all in.

"You've got only one other alternative," Gregor said. "It was either that, or somebody else walked in on Tibor, and Tibor went on pounding the woman's head in for nearly a minute and a half before he noticed anybody was there."

"You're the one with only one more alternative," Tony Monteverdi said. "You're trying to tell us that Father Kasparian here walked in to find somebody bashing in the head of a woman and responded to that by—what? Arranging to fake a video of the murder? Are you serious?"

"I'm very serious," Gregor said. "And it's not as strange as you think it is. It's exactly the kind of thing Tibor would do, if the circumstances were right. The murderer is young, as Tibor told me himself. He has his entire life ahead of him. He has people who love him and would be hurt if his life were ruined. And, what's more, Tibor is sure he knows this person, that what he's seen must be an act of temporary insanity, a blowup that got out of control. And he wants to save this person's life. Martha Handling's cell phone is on her desk. So is the cell phone she uses to make the calls to Administrative Solutions and to other people she knows who are part of the bribery scheme. The murderer picks up this phone, and they stage the murder video—which wasn't all that good once you started to really pay attention to it. It doesn't show the body on purpose, of course, because Tibor wasn't hitting the body. But that video has sound, and if you turn it up, you can hear the gavel hitting the floor, a hard wooden crack, not the squish the body would have made. But Tibor had promised to help him. And the murderer thought it would be more than just the video and the cover-up. He thought Tibor would plead guilty. And when somebody pleads guilty, all investigation stops. It didn't occur to him that in Tibor's addled brain, covering up a murder would be acceptable, but lying would not."

"That one—" Tony Monteverdi pointed at Tibor. "—must be a world-class loon."

"I have not admitted to this," Tibor said. "I go back to my right to remain silent."

"They made the movie. The murderer left the room and went into one of the corridors to send the movie to Facebook. And then the murderer came back, supposedly following an odd noise, which was part of the cover-up, too, because it was the only way the murderer could explain all the blood he had on him. I don't think either he or Tibor expected that anybody else would come in, but of course there were a ton of them, and Janice Loftus got there first. As it turned out, that was actually good news. It made the cover-up story all the more plausible. From then on out, the murderer told his story absolutely truthfully, except he started it the second time he came into this room."

"And you think my Petrak did this," Sophie said. "You think he's a psychopath. You think I wouldn't know that he was a psychopath. He lives in my house. I would have noticed if he was a psychopath. I'd have picked up something."

"You'd be amazed at how often nobody does," Tony Monteverdi said.

"You honestly think my Petrak did this," Sophie said. "You're an idiot. You're a complete fool."

"Oh, for God's sake," Russ Donahue said. "Of course he doesn't think Petrak did this. He thinks I did."

Gregor could hear the stillness of the room around him as if somebody had died. He looked around to find Bennis and Hannah and Sheila and the Very Old Ladies. Hannah looked confused. Bennis looked too shocked to move.

Then a shiver went through her as if she'd had an electric shock. "But, Gregor," she said. "That's not possible. It isn't—"

"He's the only one Tibor would have done it for," Gregor said. "He's the only one who might possibly have known where Judge Handling's chambers were. And he's the only one who had any reason to kill Mikel Dekanian. Because Tibor is wrong, Bennis. This wasn't a sudden loss of temper—a righteous fury because of the way Martha Handling operated—that got out of hand before he knew it. This was part of a pattern. He was taking bribes from Administrative Solutions. And if we look into the Dekanian mortgage mess, if we go to the Hall of Records and look, just as Mikel Dekanian did, we'll find out that it was Russ who took out that mortgage with J.P. CitiWells. Because that's the only thing that makes any sense."

"But, *Gregor,*" Bennis said.

It was then that Gregor saw the gun. It was a surprisingly big gun, and he was a little upset with himself because it hadn't occurred to him that Russ would have one.

"You came in the back," Gregor said. "That's another nail in the coffin, Russ. You knew how to get into that back door, which means you must have a code, and you could only have gotten it if somebody authorized to use it gave it to you. And then there's the fact that Petrak recognized the voice on the phone. He did recognize it. He was just so sure it had to be Mark Granby calling him, he took the fact that it was familiar to mean it was Granby's. That was your good luck. But good luck doesn't last forever, and you don't have much in the way of skill. You're not very good at this. And I've got two police officers here with guns of their own. Do you really think you're going to get out of here? What would be the point of even trying?"

"I'm not expecting to get out of here," Russ said. "I don't even want to."

Gregor was just thinking that that would have to be just as true as everything else, when the gun went off in his face.

EPILOGUE

October 23

1

Going up the drive, Bennis Hannaford Demarkian had been feeling dull and futile, a woman carrying out a mission that could not mean anything to anybody. When she got closer to the front door of Glenwydd House and saw Sheree Coleman standing at the large front window, obviously looking out for her, she went completely cold.

It wasn't that she hadn't considered that Gregor might die. She'd considered it every single day since Russ Donahue shot him in the face. She'd been convinced he was gone when the event itself happened. She woke up in the middle of the night, hearing that gun go off and seeing Gregor's face explode in blood. Then she'd sat up in bed and had no one to turn to. She couldn't talk to Gregor, because he was in a coma. She couldn't talk to Donna because . . . well, nobody could talk to Donna these days.

Sometimes she thought it was all wrong, the way she was taking this thing. It was as if she had turned into one of those adolescent jerks she had known so well growing up. It was as if she could not get off herself. It was Gregor who was lying there helpless, scheduled to be dead. Thinking about that only made her more and more aware of how isolated she was, without him. It also made her more and more aware of how isolated he was. People came from Cavanaugh Street to see him. They sat in his room and talked about nothing that made any sense to her, but they talked.

She brought audiobooks that he probably couldn't hear, or absorb. She brought them because she'd read too many stories about coma victims who woke up after years and remembered everything that had ever gone on around them. She thought the stories were probably not true.

It was Tibor who came to see him most often, coming out to Bryn Mawr in a hired car that must have cost him a fortune because he wouldn't let anyone else drive him. It was Tibor's visits that made Bennis hope that Gregor's coma was a complete blank. The only person who blamed Tibor Kasparian for what had happened was Tibor Kasparian, but it didn't help to know that. It didn't even help Tibor to know that. The guilt was so deep and had become such a part of him that he was like the walking dead. Bennis was sure that the only reason he hadn't committed suicide was that he thought he deserved to go through this trial for being an accessory after the fact and then to go to jail for it.

She knew from what he'd said to her that the only reason he didn't plead guilty was that she'd told him Gregor wouldn't like it, and he knew that that was true.

If Gregor were dead now, there would be nothing to stop him.

Bennis was finding it hard to make it the rest of the way up the walk. Her body felt heavy. Her shoes felt filled with lead. Sheree was up there, in the window, bouncing up and down and waving. Then she disappeared.

Bennis hesitated. That did not make a lot of sense. Sheree was a bouncy person, but surely she knew enough not to bounce when someone had died. And why would it be Sheree waiting for her to give her the news? It would be Dr. Albright, or even Tibor, because Tibor would have been there since early this morning.

The lead feeling lifted just a little and her heart began to pound. Sheree had not returned to the window. Nobody else was visible in the window. There was just that ridiculous potted tree and one of those unbelievably silly modern sculpted armchairs. The big window had not been a part of the house when the Cadwalladers and the Finchleys lived in it. She'd never wondered before whose idea it had been to put it in.

The important thing was not to jump to conclusions. She should not have jumped to the conclusion Gregor was dead, and she should not be jumping to the conclusion now that something good must have happened, that there was about to be news she would want to hear.

She turned into the last bit of walk, the one aimed directly at the front door, and saw that the door was open.

Sheree Coleman was standing in it, bouncing away. "Oh, Mrs. Demarkian!" Sheree started squealing as soon as she saw Bennis on the pavement. It was still quite a walk. Sheree had to screech to be heard. "Mrs. Demarkian, where have you been? We've been calling and calling for hours. And we called everybody we thought might know where you were, and they've been piling in here for hours, and now the room is full of people and

301

Dr. Albright is about to pitch a fit. And we called and called, and nobody could find you, and we didn't know what to do."

Bennis had reached the door now. She thought she might have stopped breathing. "He isn't dead," she said.

"No, he isn't dead," Sheree said. "He's just the opposite. It happened right after breakfast this morning. Father Tibor was there, talking to him, and of course he wasn't eating, he had a tube, and I went in to check it, and all of a sudden he opened his eyes and tried to say something, but nothing came out. So I went running to tell everybody and I got some water on crushed ice and brought it back and he was still wide awake and trying to say something, so I gave him something to drink. And he took a sip and then he took another sip—"

"Can he speak?" Bennis asked, beginning to feel desperate.

"He could after he took a few sips of water," Sheree said. The bouncing had become so exaggerated, it was surreal. "Then he looked at Father Tibor and said, 'Don't you dare.' Just like that. 'Don't you dare.' Does that make any sense to you?"

"Yes," Bennis said.

"Well, anyway, we tried to call you and tell you, but you weren't answering your phone and we didn't know what to do, so like I said, we called everybody we could think of and we called Dr. Albright to come on out and we're all just *so* glad you're finally here—"

Bennis stepped across the threshhold into the old foyer with its twenty-foot-high ceilings. There was a buzzing in her ears.

"I turn the phone off when I'm driving," she said.

She was about to say that she had been driving that morning, that she'd had errands, that she'd needed to do a hundred things before coming out here.

She never got the chance.

First her mind went absolutely blank.

Then she hit the floor.

2

When she came to, she was sitting in an armchair with her legs stretched out across an ottoman, and she had the vague impression that she was at a cocktail party. It even seemed to make sense that there were doctors and nurses at this party, and that they were all in uniform. Then she made her eyes focus and saw that Gregor was across the room in bed, sitting up, with a large glass of something on ice in front of him. It looked like urine. His face was still a mess, the entire right side of it bandaged and the right eye bloodshot and raw. Even after all these weeks, it was raw.

"What's that?" she asked, pointing to the glass of yellow liquid.

"Asinine," Gregor said, looking right at her.

"It's ginger ale," Sheree Coleman said, patting her on the arm. "We'll get you some yourself if you want."

"I want a pint and a half of Johnnie Walker Blue," Bennis said. "And I mean it."

"You may mean it," Dr. Albright said, stepping into her line of vision, "but we don't carry it. We did try to warn you in advance. We tried repeatedly."

"Yes," Bennis said. "Sheree told me. Is he all right? Is he just all right? What in the name of hell is going on here?"

"I'm sitting right in front of you," Gregor said. "You can ask me."

"His throat is very sore," Dr. Albright said. "I'll tell you. He woke up. It happens. There's no way to tell, with coma victims, how that will happen or even if that will happen. I told you that before. They come out of it. They don't come out of it. He wasn't brain-dead or even close. There was always a chance."

"And he's been listening to everything?" Bennis said. "He knows what's been going on? He knows what people have been telling him?"

"He seems to know a lot of it," Dr. Albright said.

"I'm over *here*," Gregor said. His voice was clear. There was no slur. And he was getting angry.

Bennis looked around the room. Father Tibor was there, but that was to be expected. The Very Old Ladies were there. They came out every once in a while. The rest of the crowd was bewildering. George Edelson was there. Ray Berle and Tony Monteverdi were there. Petrak, Sophie, and Stefan Maldovanian were there. Asha Dekanian was there. Lydia Arkmanian and Hannah Krekorian were there. And Janice Loftus was there. Bennis didn't know what to make of it. That woman got in everywhere. How did she get in everywhere? There was a guard at the gate of this place, for God's sake.

"Wait," Bennis said. "You called this person because you thought she would know where I was?"

"Nobody had to call me," Janice Loftus said. "I come at least twice a week. I knew he'd wake up eventually. I wanted to be here. I have something important to say."

"I have something important to hear," Gregor said. "And I'm going to hear it. Right away. And don't give me any crap about how I shouldn't do too much too soon. There are laws in this country about keeping a person incarcerated against his will, and I'll use them. I'm either going to hear what I need to hear, or I'm going to walk right out the door."

"Not without help, you're not," Dr. Albright said. "And I won't supply the help."

"He will." Gregor pointed at Father Tibor. "And you won't be able to talk him out of it. I need to know what's been going on."

Father Tibor took a deep breath. "The first thing," he said, "is to know that Russ Donahue is not dead."

3

After that, Bennis just sat back and listened to them, keeping one eye on Gregor and one on Janice Loftus at all times. The existence of Janice Loftus in this place still did not make sense. Bennis had the horrible feeling that it never would.

It was George Edelson who took charge. "In the first place, Father Tibor is right. Russ Donahue is not dead. Ray and Tony might have shot at him if they'd gotten the chance."

"It's not usually a good idea to fire into crowd of people in a not-all-that-large room," Tony Monteverdi said.

"In the end, he didn't need to, because this lady over here—" Edelson pointed to Mrs. Vespasian, sitting in a chair and tapping her walking stick on the floor. "—this lady took that stick and hit him sqaure in the stomach, then she put the point of the stick down on his foot. I saw it all, but I didn't see it, if you know what I mean. She was standing right next to Donahue, Tony and Ray were standing on the other side of the room—"

"We didn't think it was Donahue we had to worry about," Ray said. "You could have said something. It would probably have resulted in your not getting shot."

"Anyway, she whacked him and sort of stabbed him and he doubled over and Tony and Ray came running to jump on

305

him, and that was that. Donahue was hurt but not fatally," George Edelson said, "and after we got working on the things you'd said, we found pretty much all of it. There was the bribery. Administrative Solutions was paying him to skew his cases so that they'd be more easily resolved by incarceration. Not all the judges were on the take, so they needed some help from other people. We're rounding up the people. But you were right about the Dekanian mortgage, too. Once we knew where to look, we found the trail. He'd just taken the mortgage and sold it, and it was illegal six ways to Sunday, too. He'd represented it to J.P. CitiWells as unencumbered, which nobody bothered to check, which tells you something about the way those banks were operating."

Gregor made a confirmatory grunt.

George Edelson said, "Yeah, I know," and went on. "Once we started looking, we found stuff going back just about four years. Mortgages. Trusts. The bribe thing."

"When they opened the office," Bennis said. "When he went out on his own."

"Was it?" Edelson said. "He was smart about it. You have to give him that. He wasn't buying fancy cars and he wasn't gambling or doing any of that other stuff. No mistresses. Just steady streams of money. If they were all like this, we wouldn't catch half of them."

"He went out on his own," Bennis said. "He left a big firm to do it. And Donna was always worried that they wouldn't have enough money to get by, because she was staying home with the children and she wasn't working. But they never did run short that she could tell. And maybe we should have known, because his partner, that Mac Cafton, he was short all the time."

"Whatever it was," Edelson said. "Martha Handling was going to turn herself in and blow the whistle on everybody, and he went to talk to her that day to see if he couldn't get her to see what he thought of as reason. Martha Handling never saw reason, and she was infuriating on a regular basis, and Donahue just picked up the gavel and smashed her. And, as you said, Father Tibor found them, and the rest was you talking in chambers the day you got shot. What's more interesting is the phone."

"I kept trying to tell you about the phone," Sophie Maldovanian said.

"The phone," Edelson said, "was the key to the end of it. Donahue and Tibor here made the video, then Donahue was supposed to send it to YouTube and ditch the phone. But the corridor was already full of people, and when he got out there, he couldn't do anything without somebody noticing. He tried going toward the back, to the back door, and out that way, but he still wasn't unobserved. Then Dr. Loftus here started screaming, and Russ went back to the chambers, because part of the plan was that Donahue was going to find Tibor in the act. He had the phone in his pocket, and he started hurrying, and it dropped out. It took him a couple of seconds to realize it, but when he turned back to retrieve it, Petrak here was picking it up."

"It was just lying there on the floor," Petrak said. "I didn't even think about it."

"When Petrak didn't turn the phone in, and nobody else did, and there wasn't any sign of it, I think Donahue thought he'd gotten lucky with that one," Edelson said. "When Mikel Dekanian called up and told him what he'd found at the Hall of Records, the record of the sale, the documents with his forged signature on them, Russ told him to meet up at that alley, and as soon as Mikel got there, he killed him. I don't think it occurred to Dekanian that Russ was responsible for what he'd found."

"It didn't occur to him," Asha said. "He called me and said to me he knew what the banks had done to hurt us. Then he said he had an appointment with Mr. Donahue, but he did have an appointment with Mr. Donahue. That's why he went downtown in the first place."

"He did have an appointment with Donahue," Edelson said. "It was just later in the afternoon and in Donahue's office. Anyway, that's about all you don't know. Except that Russ Donahue has decided to plead not guilty. And that Tibor has been charged as an accessory after the fact."

"Idiot," Gregor said.

"Yes, Krekor," Tibor said. "I am an idiot. We have established that."

"Mark Granby," Gregor said.

"Ah," Edelson said. "That one's good. He managed to get out of the country. He turned up in Guatemala and was spotted almost immediately. Then he tried to claim political asylum. Nobody could figure out what he thought he was doing. The Guatemalan government kicked him out in a week."

"Good," Gregor said.

"Finished," Dr. Albright said. "And I do mean finished. Now. This is a mob scene. You're going to put him back in that coma. I want you all out of here, now. Except for Mrs. Demarkian. You can stay if you behave yourself."

"I'll behave myself," Bennis said. She meant it, but she wasn't entirely sure she wouldn't faint.

Sheree Coleman began shooing everybody out of the room, making little clucking noises. She sounded like a chicken.

Tibor and Ray and Tony and George and the rest of them

went more or less quietly, saying good-bye to Gregor and telling them how happy they were.

Only Janice Loftus was recalcitrant. "But you don't understand!" she insisted. "I have important information. You're getting the whole case all wrong—"

Sheree Coleman gave her a sharp little shove in the small of her back, and Janice Loftus disappeared, still screeching.

4

Father Tibor came back for just a moment after all the others had left. "I wanted to say that I am glad to see you again," he said. "And to say that you were right, about Russ."

"I'm right about you, too," Gregor said. "The right course of action here is not to fall on your sword. We'll work this out. There will be a way. Maybe we'll even get a judge who hasn't been bribed by Administrative Solutions."

"*Tcha,*" Tibor said.

Then he went back out the door.

Bennis got up and went all the way over to Gregor in bed, something she hadn't done yet. She sat down on the mattress and stroked his forehead. He didn't like things like that. At the moment, she didn't care. She wanted to touch him.

"You should find out when they're going to let me out of this place," he said. "It must be costing you a fortune."

"I've got money."

"Which isn't the point," Gregor said.

"What is the point?"

Gregor looked away. Bennis knew that body language. It was the way Gregor was when he had to say something that hurt.

"Donna," he said finally. "I really was aware of a lot of what was going on. I remember your being here. I remember Tibor being here. I even remember John Jackman once, if I wasn't dreaming it."

"You weren't dreaming it," Bennis said. "He came out three times that I know of, and every time he was swearing at you. You got a lot of people annoyed."

"I don't remember Donna coming out."

"Ah," Bennis said.

"I didn't really expect her to come out," Gregor said. "Under the circumstances. But I'm worried about how she is. And how Tommy is. I've been worried about that since I realized what was going on."

"Tommy isn't Russ's biological son."

"I know. But he's the only father Tommy has ever known."

"It's not as bad as you think," Bennis said. "I don't think she's angry at you. She certainly isn't angry at me. She's just numb, mostly. And she's not here."

"Where is she?"

"Her parents took her to Corfu for a month, with the children, of course," Bennis said. "I think they're going to take her back again when the case finally goes to trial. I think she just wants to be away from it."

"Has she seen Russ?"

"Once," Bennis said. "Before she left. And no, I don't know how the interview went, and neither does anybody else. She went in alone and in tears. She came out alone and in tears. She didn't want to talk about it."

"All right," Gregor said.

"You're beginning to look exhausted," Bennis said. "Maybe Dr. Albright is right. Maybe we should stop all this before we put you back in a coma."

"I don't think comas work like that," Gregor said.

Bennis stroked Gregor's forehead again, and as she did, his eyes closed, and he was immediately deeply and calmly asleep. She didn't know if comas didn't work like that, but she knew he wasn't in a coma now, because the way he was sleeping was different from what she remembered from before.

In a world that was now infinitely dark and far away, Donna Moradanyan Donahue would have known what to say about this.